CW01668136

THE OFFICER'S WIFE

An utterly spellbinding uplifting historical saga

MERRYN ALLINGHAM

Daisy Driscoll Saga Book 1

Originally published as *The Girl from Cobb Street*

JOFFE BOOKS

Revised edition 2024
Joffe Books, London
www.joffebooks.com

First published in Great Britain by MIRA Books
in 2015 as *The Girl from Cobb Street*

This paperback edition was first published
in Great Britain in 2024

© Merryn Allingham 2015, 2024

This book is a work of fiction. Names, characters, businesses, organizations, places and events are either the product of the author's imagination or are used fictitiously. Any resemblance to actual persons, living or dead, events or locales is entirely coincidental. The spelling used is British English except where fidelity to the author's rendering of accent or dialect supersedes this. The right of Merryn Allingham to be identified as author of this work has been asserted in accordance with the Copyright, Designs and Patents Act 1988.

Cover art by Jarmila Takač

ISBN: 978-1-83526-338-9

Each betrayal begins with trust.
Unknown

CHAPTER ONE

Bombay, April 1938

Daisy Driscoll sat in a bubble of silence, a cardboard suitcase at her side. Her skin gleamed with sweat and her hair hung limp, the carefully pressed finger waves in a state of dissolution. Her make-up had slipped and the crimson lipstick was now an uneven gash.

Above her, the ceiling fan pushed against torpid air, the low growl of its rusty blades a counterpoint to the shrilling telephones and excited Hindi emerging in bursts from beyond the glass screen at the end of the room. From the quayside below, a rhythmic crunch of boots on stone sounded faintly through the open door, a steady train of soldiers chugging its way ashore.

Nervously, she fiddled with the ring, fourth finger, right hand, looking constantly from open door to glass partition, shifting from side to side in the shabby Windsor chair.

A shadow darkened the room. A military figure had appeared in the doorway and was walking towards her. She started to her feet, her smile feigning brightness, but a glance at the newcomer's face and she crumpled back onto the chair.

'Miss Driscoll?'

The young Indian's voice was soft and cultured, and his expression a mixture of dismay and compassion. She wasn't surprised. She hadn't dared to go in search of a mirror for fear of missing Gerald when he came. She'd donned her very best dress for the occasion but that was hours ago on board the *Viceroy of India*, and the heat and dust had already taken its toll on the silk print for which she had saved so hard.

'Yes,' she answered uncertainly, 'but Gerald . . .'

'He will be waiting at the church. My name is Anish. Anish Rana. I am a friend of Gerald's and I'm to take you to him.'

Her face fell at the news but he affected not to notice and continued in a smooth voice, 'He apologises for not coming himself but he had several important matters to attend to before the ceremony.'

She found herself wondering what could be more important than meeting the woman you were to marry after she had been three long weeks at sea, but she said nothing, grateful at least to have an escort. Getting to her feet once again, she bent to retrieve the bulging suitcase but Anish was quicker and scooped it up with ease, the knife-edged pleats of his uniform hardly wavering. Everything about him spoke ease, the kind that came with authority.

'Please, follow me.' His tall figure strode towards the open door. 'The port is very busy today and we must find our way through the crowds to the main road. I have a conveyance waiting.'

Dispirited by the unexpected turn of events, Daisy followed him obediently. At the door, he paused. 'Do you have some kind of head covering, Miss Driscoll? The April sun is very hot.'

'Only this,' and she took from her bag the fragile confection of feathers and net she had chosen for her wedding. His raised eyebrows made her horribly aware of how ill equipped she was for this strange country.

'Then we must make all haste,' he said, and flashed her an encouraging smile.

Together they walked from the waiting room and down a flight of steep stone steps onto the crowded quayside. The air was stifling and the sunlight so blinding that it hit her like a physical blow. For a moment she was overpowered by the heat, the noise, the smells. Spices and dust, she thought, jasmine and drains.

People swirled, pushing, begging, shouting in a hundred languages and dialects. There were men in white uniforms and women in saris almost as brilliant as the sun itself. Small children, their naked bodies bristling with flies, eyed the pair speculatively. Sellers of 'jolly decent fruit', of sticky sweets, of flower garlands, announced their wares at the top of their voices. Undeterred, Anish Rana strode ahead, scattering to one side vendors and children, and weaving his way expertly through family groups.

Ahead of her, Daisy saw the quay narrow and guessed they were nearing the road. She touched Anish lightly on the arm. 'Before we leave, Mr Rana, I'd like to visit a washroom. I think we may have just passed one.'

'You must be quick then. We should be at the church in a quarter of an hour.'

A few minutes before the cracked mirror and she had blotted the shine from flushed skin and corrected her lipstick, but a brush pulled through the drooping waves left them still sadly limp. Then out into the savage heat once more and into the seething city. She had thought the port crowded but here on the street, the smell and movement of a mass of humanity stopped her in her tracks. Everywhere, buses, horses, rickshaws jostled for space. To Daisy's eyes, there hardly seemed an inch of road unoccupied. Trucks with signs painted on their sides requesting everyone to 'Please Blow Horn' swerved between overloaded donkeys, stray dogs, and the occasional camel or bullock-drawn cart. Even the traffic island in the middle of the road was occupied, several cows lazily flicking long ears as they chewed on invisible grass.

Anish's voice broke her trance. 'We should go. See here, I have managed to acquire a *topi* for you.'

She reached out her hand for the khaki helmet. 'Where did you find it?'

'Better not to ask!'

He grinned and she thought how attractive he was with his white teeth and smooth brown skin. For the first time, her eyes smiled back. He hurried her forward to a four-wheeled carriage waiting by the kerbside. The horse between the shafts looked half-starved, and she felt guilty that the poor creature must carry her in this temperature. But Anish was bundling her into the Victoria and she could do nothing but settle herself as comfortably as she could within its musty leather.

As they swung out into the road, a man waved to her from the other side of the street. Grayson Harte. When he'd first introduced himself, she had thought it such an elegant name, the kind of name that would have invited instant punishment at Eden House. She had always been glad that hers was so down to earth. Not that she could be sure it was hers.

'Who is that?' Anish was looking surprised.

'His name is Grayson Harte. He was travelling on my ship and has a job with the Indian Civil Service. I believe that's what he called it.'

'One of the "heaven born" then!'

Grayson would be on his way to report for his new post and she wished him well. He had been kind to her, very kind, picking her up from that catastrophic fall and trying to persuade her to see a doctor. She'd accepted a cup of sweet tea and told him all was well. But it hadn't been. A stab of anger surprised her by its ferocity, though it was pointless to feel rage. The men who had sent her sprawling on deck in their bid to escape, could not know what they had done.

'Will Gerald be wearing a very smart uniform?' she asked after a while. 'I'm afraid I might let him down.'

'Gerald will be in plain service dress. Anything else would be far too hot at this time of the year. And you must not worry, you look splendid.'

She was grateful for the lie. Since she'd left the ship early that morning, her nerves had steadily grown more frayed, whispering loudly that she was travelling under false pretences and had no right to be in India. Should she even, at this late stage, ask Anish to stop the carriage and take her back to the port where she might beg a passage on the first liner leaving for Southampton?

But that was a fantasy. She had no money for a ticket and if, by some miracle, she could raise the funds to return, what would she be returning to? There was no home and her precious job was lost to her. It would be all right, she made herself believe, it must be all right. Gerald would understand. He would be at the church and she would confide everything to him before the ceremony. How much easier it would have been, though, if he had come to meet her.

'I'd hoped Gerald would be here,' she said. 'To help me, you know. Everything is so strange.'

'You will be with him very soon,' her escort said soothingly.

He talked on, pointing out places of interest, feeding her small glimpses of military life, slowly putting her at ease. He was a comfortable companion, interesting and amusing, and gradually she lost the tension that had been building. They were passing through a quieter neighbourhood now, one of wide, tree-lined roads, and in a short while drew up outside a large building of honeyed stone. Daisy craned her head upwards to follow the slender spire which emerged from the surrounding trees, so tall it almost touched the sky. A golden cross sat at its summit.

'This is the church we are to be married in?'

'It is. St John's Afghan Church. Built to commemorate the officers and soldiers who died in the Afghan campaigns. It has special memories for the military.'

It was unnerving to think of death on this day of all days but the church was exquisite, an oasis of calm, and far distant from any battlefield. She took a deep breath, trying to absorb some of its tranquillity, trying to stop her tired mind chasing down dark avenues. These would be the most important few minutes of her life and the thought was making her feel slightly sick. She loved Gerald and she believed he loved her in return. But it was months since she had last seen him and there had been — well, complications. But she must not allow herself to be deflected. The marriage would work, she thought fiercely; it had to, for she had nothing to go back to.

Anish offered her his arm and together they passed through a square, stone porch and plunged into the cool darkness of the church. A narrow ribbon of red carpet covered the floor's geometric tiles and made a pathway to the brass rails of the altar. They walked along the nave, between a procession of archways of intricately traced stone and, behind these, window after window of glorious stained glass.

Figures were moving in front of the altar and she picked out a white-frocked priest, half-hidden in the gloom, and two soldierly forms, one it seemed attempting to support the other. One of the figures turned as she made her way down the aisle. It was Gerald, but Gerald as she had never seen him: dishevelled, unsteadily clutching at his comrade, his face a blank mask. He was ill!

Daisy felt panic rise. This was why he'd not been at the port, why he'd sent Anish, who had not wanted to alarm her by telling her the truth. The confession she'd been rehearsing died on her lips and she quickened her step. She must get to him, take care of him. As she drew nearer to the group, the unmistakable smell of liquor assailed her. She might be young and naive, but she recognised the 'illness' immediately. He was drunk, drunk on his wedding day. She was seized with the impulse to turn tail and run. Except that she had nowhere to run to.

Drunk or not, her bridegroom managed his part in the brief ceremony with barely a hitch, needing only the occasional prompt from one or other of his friends, his responses slightly slurred but sufficient. In under ten minutes they were man and wife; a brief brush of lips on her cheek and Daisy was again outside in the molten day. The heat had grown even more intense and the air seemed to solidify around them. You could almost cut it with a sharp knife and step through the opening, she thought. The carriage was still waiting by the kerbside and with Gerald beside her, she took her seat once more, while their two witnesses waved them a relieved goodbye.

'Victoria Station, *jaldi*!'

Gerald gave the order, sitting stiffly beside her. She closed her eyes against the searing sun and against the unwelcome thoughts that came thick and fast. She couldn't bring herself to speak, for it was as though she shared the carriage with a stranger. The last time she had seen Gerald, their final goodbye in the London dawn, he had been warm and tender. She'd bought a platform ticket for the Southampton train and stood watching as his dear face slowly disappeared into the distance. He hadn't wanted to go, had promised that very soon they would be together again, together for life.

She glanced across at him. A bead of sweat had dripped from his brow to the end of his nose but he made no attempt to wipe it away. Perhaps after a while you grew not to notice the discomfort. His skin was sallow and his fair hair seemed unusually dull — and surely he should not be bareheaded — but the same wide hazel eyes and full mouth told her he was the man who'd waved her goodbye at Waterloo. It was her heart that told her he was not.

Coming to a halt outside a large building of red brick, Gerald half-stumbled from the carriage, leaving the driver to help her down, then strode impatiently ahead while she stood on the forecourt, still and bewildered. Seemingly every soul in the country was on the move. People streamed past, people of all shapes, sizes, genders, people walking or riding bicycles. A pushcart, laden with rolled rugs, bundles of washing and small children, narrowly missed colliding with her. She sidestepped quickly and followed Gerald towards the entrance of the Victoria Railway Terminus.

It was a monumental building, three tiers of arches, endless small domes and turrets and, above all, a much larger dome in the shape of a crown. The clock, she saw, showed half past one. She had been in India for six hours and she was consumed with loneliness. She wasn't sure why since she'd been alone all her life. It was easier that way, easier not to get too close, not to lay oneself open to inevitable hurt. The one friendship she'd braved had been unequal and was now broken.

Helena Maddox had been forced to close the London house to nurse a sick sister in Wales and her employer's news had shattered Daisy's world. Since then, she'd pasted together the pieces of her life but the experience had left its dents and cracks, and these were added to older scars. To the heedless gaze of those she met daily, though, they remained invisible. And that was how she wanted it.

But then Gerald had come into her life and stormed the barriers she had so carefully erected. When she'd first met him, she could hardly believe her good fortune; it had to be the most wonderful thing that had ever happened to her. He was kind and handsome and loving. He accepted her for the girl she was and seemed not in the least to care where she had come from. Gerald was to be her future and she would never be lonely again. The thought had brought tears to her eyes, and every night in the weeks after he'd left, she had daydreamed for hours in the tiny room she rented, imagining the home they would make together. Now all she felt was emptiness.

She pulled herself up sharply. She must shake off this crushing sense of disappointment. There would be an explanation for Gerald's conduct, she did not doubt, and in good time he would tell her. Meanwhile she must not fall into an abyss of self-pity, for India meant a new opportunity, a new life. She squared her shoulders and walked after her husband.

CHAPTER TWO

In later years, Daisy preferred not to think of the journey to Jasirapur. She noticed that most other Europeans travelled with a personal servant who brought them tea or soda or hot water for washing. She had not washed or changed since early that morning and once settled in their compartment, there was no chance of doing so. The floors had been swabbed by a brutal disinfectant and her head soon ached from the smell, and from the noise of passengers filling the train: soldiers returning to their barracks and civilians travelling she knew not where.

'Who are all these people?' she asked when they had sat in silence for the first half hour of the journey.

'Officers in the ICS.' Then, when he saw her confused expression, 'The Indian Civil Service. They push pens around pieces of paper.'

He had the soldier's contempt for men who spent most of their lives within four walls. Grayson Harte was to be a District Officer in the ICS, she remembered, his first posting in India.

'What does a District Officer do?'

Gerald seemed surprised by her question. 'He's in charge of a district. Collects taxes, settles disputes, does the paperwork — that kind of thing.'

Grayson had enthused over the role he was to take on but she wondered if he would enjoy the reality. She sensed he was a man who had come to India for adventure, and keeping files or adjudicating village quarrels did not seem quite to fit his personality. But what did she know of this immense country or of those who ran it?

She gazed out of the window. It was early afternoon and a white incandescence hung over the endless plain. From time to time toy villages sprang into being, barely distinguishable from the earth itself except for the occasional temple or mosque. On either side of the train, great dun landscapes rolled themselves out like an endless carpet, sometimes flat and featureless, sometimes rocky with small, spiky bushes, but always stretching to an unreachable horizon. It made her feel as small as the smallest of insects. Here and there, a few dusty trees broke through the monochrome beige and, more infrequently, a flaming patch of scarlet would flash into sight.

'They are oleander trees, aren't they?' She pointed through the nearest window but Gerald was plainly uninterested in the landscape.

They had never before had a problem with talking or at least Gerald had not. He had talked and she had listened. He'd kept her enthralled with stories of his childhood, his days at boarding school and most of all his tales of life in India. This new taciturnity was uncomfortable; it belonged to a different Gerald, belonged to a man she hardly recognised.

But perhaps she was being too harsh. She should not be surprised they found themselves so awkward with each other. After all, theirs had been a whirlwind romance conducted in snatched moments against the backdrop of a great city. Now they were meeting for the first time in four months, and meeting in a very different world.

She waited a while and when he said nothing, tried another tack. 'Have you known Mr Rana long?'

'Lieutenant.'

'Lieutenant?'

'Lieutenant Rana. He's a fellow officer in the 7th.'

'I didn't know your regiment had Indian officers,' she said humbly.

'We're getting more each year. It's called Indianisation.'

'And did Lieutenant Rana attend Sandhurst with you?'

Gerald shifted in his seat and looked out of the far window. 'He went to Dehra Dun.' Daisy heard the boredom in his voice. 'The Military Academy. It's an Indian version of Sandhurst.'

'He seems very nice.' It was trite, she knew, but anything more original might again betray her ignorance.

The conversation fizzled to a close and they sat once more in silence. At length, Gerald stood up and repositioned himself, stretching lengthways along one of the bench seats. 'We have a few hours to go, Daisy. Better try to get some sleep. It looks like we have the carriage to ourselves.'

'How many hours?' Already the journey seemed interminable.

'Fifteen, sixteen, I reckon.'

Her ears did not quite believe what they were hearing. Sixteen more hours imprisoned in this broiling square of tin. When they'd joined the train, she'd seen First Class stamped boldly on the bodywork and felt guilty. She had wronged Gerald, unwittingly it was true, but she was undeserving of such palatial treatment.

She need not have worried, however, since it soon became clear that First Class was no indicator of comfort in this confusing country. The seats were hard, the carriage creaked and jolted over old Victorian tracks, and the heat was utterly overpowering. Only the smallest respite came from the faint whirr of an electric fan, that played on the tub of melting ice placed between the seats in a vain attempt to keep the compartment cool.

Door and window handles were soon too hot to touch and the studded leather benches grew slimy beneath her sweating limbs. A film of red dust percolated through the closed windows and settled on everything it touched: blinds, seats, passengers. She tried to doze but whenever she felt herself drifting, she was jolted awake by the train grinding to a halt.

Stops were frequent, station after station seeming to have dropped from the sky into the middle of nowhere. As they drew alongside each platform, she could see long lines of sleeping men, swaddled in protective layers of white cloth, while their wives squatted patiently beside them. Once the train had pulled to a stop, the clamour was unbelievable. Passengers ran in all directions, trying to scramble onto the train, clinging to carriages, even clinging to the roof. Friends pushed each other through windows, families set up makeshift bedding in corridors. Vendors handed in trays with teapots and plates of bread covered with rancid butter and little green bananas.

At one stop, Gerald alighted and returned with food from one of the itinerant sellers but she could not eat it. Her throat was parched, almost closed, and all she could do was sip the water he offered.

Her new husband slept heavily. He had the soldier's ability to rest wherever he found himself, and he slept with barely a sound. His face had lost its earlier sallowness and the strands of fair hair falling over his forehead made him look very young. Daisy's heart stirred. She forgave him his indifference, his impatience with her, even his drinking.

He had so far offered no explanation for his discourtesy, but her mind had been busy supplying one. It was wedding nerves, she'd decided, that was all. Marriage brought change, a disruption to the world he knew, and Gerald loved his life in India, that was plain from every conversation they'd ever had. He was immensely proud of being chosen for the Indian Army, so competitive was entry. And proud of being a cavalryman. Whenever he spoke of his regiment, he lit with an inner glow. He must be worried that her arrival posed a threat to the life he loved. Her job was to reassure him, make clear that she had not come to unsettle his world but to build a loving home for them both.

By sunset, they were travelling through a different kind of landscape. In village after village columns of fire smoke wound their way upwards and spread out across fields of blue linseed. Preparations for the evening meal were clearly under way. She felt her heart open to the tranquil beauty of the land, to the thousands, no, millions of lives, lived beneath its broad skies. A pale, golden dust hung from above, outlining a straggle of cows making the slow journey back to their night shelter. In an instant it seemed the glittering heat of the day had been transformed into one of milky warmth. Darkness fell just as suddenly and, at last, through sheer exhaustion, she slept.

* * *

'We're here. Jasirapur.'

Daisy felt herself shaken awake and, with clouded eyes, looked out on yet another platform. It was early morning but already she could feel the sun gathering pace, its stealthy fingers probing the compartment's defences. *Marwar Junction*, she read.

'We get out here,' Gerald repeated.

Hastily she scrabbled her possessions together and in a few minutes had joined him on the platform. The train was already preparing to leave for its onward journey to Delhi. She looked around for her suitcase but the luggage had disappeared from sight. An aroma of cinnamon trailed the air, wafting in clouds from the steaming cauldrons scattered at intervals along the platform.

Gerald stopped in his walk towards the exit. 'The bags are already in the trap but would you like tea before we set off? The *chai-makers* are pretty good here.'

His kindness revived her as much as the tea. She sipped at the cup slowly, readying herself for this last part of the journey. She had been travelling for twenty-four hours with little rest, but she couldn't complain. She had come despite Gerald's warning that she would not be at all comfortable and her journey was unnecessary. He'd promised to return to England at the first opportunity and when he did, they would marry immediately. She could see she'd upset him by taking matters into her own hands, but he loved her, and he would understand why she'd had to come. With his support, she would make a success of this new life. For a while the country would be strange, but she would adapt, she would learn as she went along.

Though the sun shone hotter by the minute, the pony and trap set a brisk pace. The track they were travelling was little more than a dirt road, rough and unfinished, and she was constantly jolted from one side of the carriage to the other. She saw Gerald looking anxiously at her but she said nothing. It was not the right time.

'Won't be long now,' he encouraged.

This morning he seemed completely himself, looking and sounding the debonair young officer she'd met that morning at the perfume counter of Bridges. Debonair was not an adjective she could claim for herself, for the dress she had so carefully chosen for her wedding looked little more than a rag, and smothered now in the red dust that flew everywhere.

The driver swung onto a narrower track, following it down and round, the pony skilfully negotiating a series of corners and curves until they were at a rough mud wall enclosing what she took to be a compound. It was hard to discern how large the compound was or what lay within it, since weeds and grasses had been allowed free rein and were now almost thigh high. Patches of red oleanders here and there broke through the wilderness. And right in front of where Daisy sat perched on the trap's small seat, an enormous tree, its thick, drooping branches growing roots of their own and casting a circle of dense black shadow against the sunlight. Behind the tree and through its huge branches, she could just catch a glimpse of a whitewashed building.

Out of nowhere, it seemed, a light-skinned servant appeared at the side of the trap. He was dressed from head to toe in starched white cotton and was bowing his head in welcome. Gerald jumped down and clapped the man on the shoulder.

'Rajiv, this is your new memsahib. Daisy, you must meet my trusted servant, Rajiv.'

The man bowed his head again, but she was aware of his eyes sliding sideways and up, observing her, watchful, even hostile. No, she must be wrong. He couldn't be hostile since he did not know her. But if he had been with Gerald for years, she reasoned, he might resent her presence, might resent a woman stepping into his domain. She would need to make an effort to get to know him.

'I am very new to India, Rajiv, but I hope you will help me settle in.'

'Of course, he will,' Gerald said a little too heartily, and led the way into the building she'd seen in the distance.

A thatched roof sat atop its blinding white walls and a wide verandah wrapped itself around all four sides, the paint peeling from its decaying wood. She noticed a bicycle propped against one of the supports. It seemed as battered as its surroundings. Panels of plaited reeds had been hung at every window and, once inside the bungalow, she could see that though they made its interior overly dark, they also helped to keep it cool. Rush matting covered the floor, and the furniture was sparse: a horsehair sofa, several chairs made from wicker, a table, a desk. They appeared to be standing in saucers full of water and she bent her head to look.

'That's to stop the ants from climbing up and eating the furniture.' Gerald had seen her from the corner of his eye. 'You'll soon get used to the wildlife.' And as though to test his theory, she heard sounds of scratching and scurrying above her head, making her look upwards to the ceiling of whitewashed hessian.

'That will be the rats. We get the occasional bat too, but nothing to worry about. They won't find a way in. They live between the thatch and the ceiling.'

'But can't you get rid of them?'

'Not possible. Like I said, you'll get used to it.'

When her face suggested this was unlikely, he shrugged his shoulders and dug his hands deep into his pockets. 'I'm sorry this isn't the palace you might have been imagining. But you insisted on coming. And you can't say I didn't give you fair warning.'

'No, Gerald.' She walked up to him and took his hands in hers. 'You're right. The bungalow is delightful.' After all, what had she to compare it with, a bleak room shared with five others in the orphanage, a servant's attic in Miss Maddox's house or the miserable bedsit she had only just afforded in Paddington?

Without warning, Rajiv appeared once more at their side. He seemed to have his own peculiar form of locomotion, gliding out of nowhere, silently, effortlessly.

'*Chota hazri*, sahib.'

'Yes, of course. Daisy, you must have some food and drink and then I think a long sleep.'

Tea and fruit had been laid out on the table, which stood at the far end of what she imagined was the main room of the bungalow. The fruit and the small, sweet cakes that accompanied the tea were delicious and she ate with appetite. Gerald only picked at the food and was soon on the veranda giving instructions to his servant.

She wandered into the larger of the two bedrooms. It was another spacious room with a high ceiling, but once again the furniture was sparse: a three-drawer chest, a small chair, a narrow cupboard, which had seen better days, and two single iron bedsteads draped with mosquito nets crammed together in the middle of the room. Was that to avoid what might be tempted to crawl down the walls, she wondered.

Her husband came in while she was opening her suitcase. 'Leave that to Rajiv. He'll do it later. The bathroom's next door if you want to wash.'

'And the kitchen?'

'In the compound, separate from the house — more hygienic that way and no cooking smells. But that's Rajiv's domain. You don't go there. He sleeps in the room behind the kitchen.'

'What if I want—'

'Whatever you want, he'll get it. Just ring the bell,' and he pointed to a small brass bell on the chest. 'There's one in each room.'

'Shall I wash first then?' She felt shy. They were a married couple now and she need feel no shame at their intimacy. Ever since that night in her room, she had been reproaching herself, for try as she might she could not forget her mother's fate. But she was not Lily Driscoll; she had a husband, and she was free to love as she wished.

'I'll wash in the other bathroom,' he said quickly. 'You can have this one to yourself. I need to get moving.'

She blushed at the thoughts that had been going through her mind. 'But where are you going?'

'To camp, my dear. Work to do. I've wasted three days going to Bombay and back. I'll be home for lunch and, in the meantime, I'd advise you to get some sleep.'

'Gerald . . .' But he had kissed her on the cheek and gone.

CHAPTER THREE

Daisy sunk onto the bed, unable to prevent the tears. It was because she was so tired, she told herself, but she knew it was not the whole story. Since the accident on board she had held on to the thought that Gerald loved her, that he wanted to share his world with her, come what may. But he'd shown little sign of wanting to share, little sign even of wanting her here. She was trying to stay positive, but a deep hollow had settled somewhere in the pit of her stomach. What would he say, what would he do, when she confessed the truth to him?

She wandered back into the main room. Everything was quiet. The servant had retreated to the kitchen, busy with preparations for lunch, she imagined. In England she'd heard tales of families in India employing an army of servants but hadn't really believed them. The way Gerald ran his household certainly disproved it, since Rajiv seemed responsible for everything. She might, perhaps, take on some of his duties, if she could do so without offending him. There seemed little else for her to do.

Whatever coolness there had been in the bungalow had disappeared and beads of sweat began their slow trickle down her back. She wandered out onto the veranda, hoping to find a breeze, however slight. There was none, but there was a garden full of birds.

Familiar only with grey streets and grey plane trees, she stood entranced. Pigeons she could recognise, even the bright green parakeets from pictures she'd seen, but what were those golden creatures flashing through the treetops, and the smaller birds which flew in and out of the long grass, striped in orange, black and white, the crests on their heads opening and shutting like small black fans? She stayed for as long as she could, but eventually overwhelmed by the heat, she drifted back into the main room of the bungalow.

Gerald would return soon, she hoped and, in the meantime, she must find some distraction. A few books sprawled untidily across the desk and she picked one up, flicking idly through the pages, but it contained nothing to keep her interest. There must be something in the house that she could settle to read: a magazine perhaps, or a local newspaper or guide. She must learn as much as possible — about her new home, about the regiment, about India. She was painfully aware of the social gap that existed between her and the man she had married and was determined not to let him down.

A small pile of papers had been disturbed by her riffling, but they appeared to be correspondence rather than any reading matter. As she turned away, the address of a letter she'd dislodged caught her eye. It was a road in the East End she knew well. Did Gerald have friends there? That would be surprising since it was a very poor district, but for a moment she was overcome by a wave of nostalgia. She scolded herself for her stupidity. Eden House had been a harsh, unhappy place, unworthy of even a jot of remembrance.

She caught a glimpse of the salutation. *My dear Jack*, it read. That was strange. Why would Gerald have a letter addressed to a Jack? It was none of her business. She should leave the letter where it was, but then she could not quite stop herself skimming to the bottom. The final words gave her a jolt, and for minutes she stood staring, making no sense of them. The letter was signed by a Joseph Minns, but it was the line above the signature that mesmerised her. *Your loving father*. Why would Gerald have such a personal letter in his possession?

She scanned the page again, casting adrift her scruples and reading it quickly. It was a plea for financial help. The elder Minns had sold his business some time ago. He had been a master tailor, it seemed, and the entire proceeds of the sale had gone to pay debts he had incurred. But it had not been enough, and he was still in debt, forced to return to Spitalfields and live with his wife in a single rented room. He had done it all for Jack, done it so that his dear and only son could train to be the cavalryman he wanted to be. He hated to ask but could Jack please telegraph a little money to help his mother and father, since they had fallen into desperate straits.

She returned the letter to its place. This had nothing to do with Gerald after all. The letter evidently belonged to a private soldier, one of the young men in Gerald's regiment. He'd told her how close relationships were between officers and their men, how they knew where each man came from, what his family were, had maybe even visited his village. In times of trouble the officers would be relied on. Gerald was looking after Jack Minns, helping the boy to sort things out.

Feeling relieved, Daisy sank into one of the two cane chairs. It was as uncomfortable as it looked but tiredness was catching up with her and she hardly noticed. She should go to bed, but she wanted to be sure she would see Gerald when he returned for lunch. They had barely spoken since their wedding vows and she was hoping for time together, an hour or two to talk, to explain, to recapture the emotion that had made them lovers.

The silence in the room was complete and, despite her determination, her eyelids drooped. As she began the slow drift into sleep, a thought burrowed its way into her mind, and jerked her awake. It was a thought she didn't want but it would not be dislodged. Hadn't Gerald said that all the men under his command were Indians? They would be unlikely to have the name of Minns or to hail from Spitalfields. So why *did* he have this missive?

She got to her feet and walked back to the desk, fingering the letter again, turning it this way and that, trying fruitlessly to solve the conundrum. A wave of irritation hit and she wiped her forehead dry for the twentieth time that morning. She was getting obsessed by trivialities because she was too hot and too tired to think rationally. But, as she turned to replace the letter, the thought that she had married a man of whom she knew almost nothing, returned with unwelcome force.

* * *

'Lunch is ready, memsahib.'

She jumped at the sound of the voice. The man was only a few feet from her, his eyes fixed on the letter she'd been holding. She had not heard him approach on bare feet and had no idea how long he'd been watching her.

'Thank you, Rajiv.' It was a struggle to keep her voice calm. 'The sahib isn't home yet and I'll eat when he arrives.'

The servant bowed his head slightly, his eyes cast downwards, refusing to meet her glance. Then as quickly as he'd appeared, he vanished through the side door, which led directly out to the kitchen.

When he'd gone, she slumped back into the wicker chair, her heart thumping a little too loudly. She hadn't realised the man was in the room. Had he been spying on her? He had seen her hand on the letter, but did he realise she knew its contents? She must talk to Gerald as soon as possible, admit that she'd been reading his correspondence. There was probably no mystery to it, there was probably a simple explanation. But . . . a siren voice whispered in her ear. Her husband just might have some small thing to hide and if he did, it would make her own confession that much easier.

Another half hour dragged by. The ugly Victorian clock half-hidden in the corner of the room chimed twice and she made a decision. Rajiv appeared almost immediately she rang the small brass bell, as though he had been waiting just the other side of the door, and her feeling of disquiet intensified.

'I'll eat now, thank you,' she said briefly, 'but we should keep some food aside for your master. He'll be here soon, I'm sure.'

'The sahib does not come.' The man turned to go and she caught at his gown. He looked coldly down at her hand and she retrieved it immediately. 'What do you mean the sahib isn't coming. How do you know?'

'He send message.'

'When?'

'This morning.'

'This morning? You knew that he wasn't coming and yet you didn't tell me?'

He said nothing and his face was mask-like in its lack of expression. He would always win a contest of wills, she realised, and it was pointless to remonstrate. Instead, she gave him her first order and surprised herself with her curtness. 'When you've cleared the dishes, I would like to take a bath. Please see to it.'

She was perturbed by Rajiv's animosity. He was a servant with whom she must share her home, whether she liked it or not, and she felt troubled for the future. She knew just how awkward a difficult servant could be for those who shared the same roof. In Bryanston Square one diminutive maidservant had set the whole household by the ears. Ethel had taken the greatest offence when Daisy had been promoted to be Miss Maddox's personal attendant. As the longest-serving parlour maid, she contended, she was next in line for advancement and the job should have gone to her.

She swore she would make Daisy's life miserable and was as good as her word. Silly, trivial things like hiding Miss Maddox's special soap, or rumpling her mistress's silk underwear after Daisy had spent hours ironing it, or spilling coal dust on the carpet after she'd cleaned and tidied her mistress's bedroom. Worst of all, Ethel had caused division among the servants themselves; if you were for Daisy, you were against her. Daisy had never sought approval from her fellows, but the result of Ethel's poisonous campaign was to turn much of the household against her and make her life even lonelier.

At least Rajiv wouldn't be doing that in this household of one. And he was efficient, she had to grant. Within minutes she heard bathroom taps being turned and a pile of sparkling white towels appeared on her bed. Minutes more and she'd slid gratefully into the oval zinc tub and breathed a deep sigh of pleasure. The luxury of hot water! Her knees were bunched, the water barely covering her lower limbs, but she gave herself up gladly to its delights. She would put his unfriendliness out of her mind and savour the fact that, in the middle of a working day, she had the leisure to enjoy this slow bathe.

When finally she regained the bedroom, she saw that her soiled dress from yesterday was no longer where she'd abandoned it and the contents of her suitcase had been hung in the cupboard on an ill-assorted clutter of hangers. Perhaps it was a peace offering. She hoped so, though it no longer seemed to matter. She was utterly fatigued.

Outside the heat was reaching its crescendo but she hardly felt it. She sank limply down onto the bed. In the distance she thought she heard the sound of water, water splashing faintly over the hanging mats of fragrant grass. The slightest breeze was playing across their surface, sending a sweet-smelling coolness into the room, and rocking her gently to sleep.

* * *

It must have been the sleep of the dead, for when she next woke it was the middle of the night. She stretched her arms wide but there was no answering body lying close. She lifted her head from the pillow. Gerald wasn't there and in the stabs of brilliant light that stippled the room, she could see that the bed beside her had not been slept in. She panicked. Had he suffered an accident and this was another message Rajiv had decided to keep from her? She peered down at the watch she still wore on her wrist. It showed four o'clock, which meant she had slept at least twelve hours. But where was Gerald? Surely if anything bad had happened to him, she would have learned by now.

In the distance she could hear the screech of night birds and the barking of dogs, echoing from village to village for miles around. Should she go looking for him? He couldn't be too far away. But then another sound intervened, much closer this time. A rasping cough. Gerald? No, it couldn't be Gerald. It was the cough of someone who smoked heavily and it seemed to be coming from the garden.

She slipped noiselessly out of the bed and over to the window, guided by the pinpricks of light which shone through cracks in the woven tatty. Very carefully she rolled up the edge of one of the plaited blinds and gazed out across the veranda to the jungle of garden beyond. The sky above was black but studded with diamonds, the starlight piercing in its clarity and illuminating the scene as though it were the stage of a theatre. You could read by those stars, she thought. The garden stretched before her, silver and magical, the tall grasses erect and hardly moving. She must have imagined the noise after all and turned to go back to bed.

But there it was again. A harsh clearing of the throat and then the unmistakeable sound of someone spitting. She crouched down and pressed her face to the glass. There was a figure, she was sure, but she was granted a glimpse only, and then there was nothing but the grass and the deep velvet sky and the brilliant moon and stars. Could it have been Rajiv walking in the garden at this very early hour? She could not be sure as she'd seen virtually nothing. A faint outline only. But if it wasn't Rajiv, then it must be an intruder.

There were no other houses nearby and she felt suddenly vulnerable. Gerald needed to be here, holding her hand, reassuring her, and she couldn't understand why he was not. Had he heard the intruder, perhaps, and gone in pursuit? If so, he must be sleeping elsewhere in the house. More evidence of his indifference, if she needed it. Saddened, she padded back to the empty bed.

But might it be worse than indifference? Her stomach tightened at the thought. If Rajiv had alerted his master to the fact she'd read his private correspondence, Gerald might be extremely angry. She closed her eyes, determined not to indulge her misgivings. She badly wanted to believe that all would be well between them and in the moments before she fell back into sleep, she tried to find comfort. It was possible that when her husband had returned from work and found her sleeping so heavily, he hadn't wished to disturb her. It was possible he'd been thinking kind thoughts.

CHAPTER FOUR

When she woke again, the sun was already climbing the sky. She had forgotten in the night to roll down the woven mat and the room was awash with its glare, a searchlight striking her through the eyes and travelling like the sharpest of arrows to pierce the very back of her head. Swiftly, she moved to lower the panel. There was no sound in the house and she knew herself alone again. Another solitary day beckoned, another day of enforced idleness. Since the age of fourteen she had worked for a living; even as a small child at Eden House she had been given her daily chores, and woe betide if they were not performed to the superintendent's satisfaction. It felt utterly wrong to be this lazy. At least she could still dress herself.

She tugged open the door of the wardrobe and saw with surprise that her silk dress had reappeared, washed and beautifully pressed. How had that happened? She'd heard nothing and yet someone — Rajiv, it must have been — had glided in and out of her room, in and out of her wardrobe, and left not a hint of his presence. The sense of unseen hands ordering her life was disquieting. But for the moment there were more pressing worries. What to wear to stay cool, or what passed for cool. She shimmied herself into one of the only two light cotton frocks she possessed. The choice was sparse for she had been able to afford few clothes for her trousseau, and she could see now that those she had chosen were mostly wrong.

She wandered into the sitting room, as quiet and grave-like as the rest of the house. Gerald had come and gone without a word. A morning kiss, a fond goodbye, wasn't that part of being married? Not for Gerald, it seemed. She had realised yesterday, as they'd travelled in isolated silence, that it would take time for him to adjust to a new way of life and she must help him all she could. She *would* help him. But there was a growing emptiness that she couldn't repress, for the path ahead seemed so very steep — even before she'd told him the news he wouldn't wish to hear.

There was no sign of Rajiv and she wondered whether he, too, had deserted. It seemed an age since he'd surprised her at the desk, riffling through papers she had no right to read. The letter she'd found, though, had stayed with her, its memory lodged deep and only temporarily blotted from view by the overwhelming disappointment she'd been feeling. But it was back now, sitting squarely before her, and a thought caught at the edges of her mind. It trembled there for several seconds, then burst into full flowering. She had begun to think the unthinkable, Daisy realised, and found herself shaking her head as if to signal a warning not to entertain such ideas. Her suspicions had to be mere fancy.

But what if Gerald *were* the real recipient? If the letter had been meant for Gerald, what Pandora's box would that open? She knew all about Pandora, and where her curiosity had led her, from the reading she'd done with Miss Maddox. If Gerald had been the intended recipient, he must be the Jack Minns addressed. And that meant he must be two people. Which was absurd. Why would he be two people? She told herself not to go on with this train of thought, but somehow found herself continuing. If he were Jack Minns, which was quite mad, it would mean that Gerald had a mother and father alive. He had told her that sadly his parents had died together in a car crash five years ago. It would mean he had lied to her. And if he'd lied about something as important as his family, he might have lied about other things, too.

She would not think it, yet the notion continued to niggle. If he *were* Jack Minns, then some of his childhood at least had been spent in Spitalfields, a stone's throw from Eden House. He had not played in the spacious rooms of a manor house, as he'd told her, or run carefree through its Somerset estate. The repercussions of such a lie were too enormous to take in. So she wouldn't. She definitely wouldn't. She would dismiss them as ravings brought on by the sun. But she had enough of Pandora about her still, to want to discover why that letter was on Gerald's desk.

Except that it wasn't. Not this morning. The papers that were left were conspicuously tidy, a small, neat pile placed carefully in the middle of the desktop. And she could see at a glance that the letter from Spitalfields was not among them. She had been right about Rajiv. He had told his master what he'd seen, and Gerald had acted. He had squirrelled the document away to ensure there would be no discussion. And if she dared to ask questions, she felt sure he would deny the letter's very existence.

Rajiv came in bearing tea and fruit for her breakfast and she wondered if she dared mention her night-time experience. A mysterious letter and an unknown intruder were not the most cheering of introductions to her new life. Since she'd arrived, the sense of being watched had grown on her and, though she recognised that solitude and an unnerving servant could be making her foolish, a strange man in the garden did nothing to soothe. If, in fact, there had been a man. She was beginning to wonder if he was part of a dream, a figment of sleep, and decided to put it to the test.

'Were you walking in the garden last night, Rajiv?' She looked directly at him.

His eyes did not meet hers and his face was without expression. 'Last night,' she repeated, 'were you in the garden? I'm not cross. Perhaps you couldn't sleep. But I need to know.'

'No, memsahib.'

'You're sure you didn't walk there in your sleep?' This was getting laughable.

'No, memsahib.' Rajiv was looking decidedly anxious and no wonder. He must think he had gained a madwoman for a mistress.

'Thank you,' she said feebly. 'That's all I wanted to know.' He slipped silently away, leaving her no wiser but feeling a great deal sillier.

She had barely finished the tea and fruit when she heard footsteps on the veranda and a knock at the door. Anish Rana was standing on the threshold and greeted her with a smile.

'I hope you slept well, Mrs Mortimer.'

She was surprised at how glad she was to see him. 'Thank you, I've slept for hours Mr — Lieutenant Rana,' she corrected herself. 'I'm afraid I didn't give you your proper title yesterday.'

'That is no problem for me. I am an Indian officer, you see, and we do not stand on ceremony. My name is Anish.'

'And mine is Daisy,' she said shyly, aware of the slightest edge to his voice. But his smile appeared sincere and she thought him a most engaging character. 'Gerald is not home,' she continued. 'I'm afraid you must have missed him.'

'It's not Gerald I came to see, but you. I wanted to make sure you had survived the journey and your first day in India.'

'I did, as you see.' She pinned a smile to her face, unwilling to show how downcast she was feeling, and quickly changed the subject. 'Did you travel back with us on the same train?'

'No. There were people I had to see in Bombay. I decided to take the later train and return overnight.'

'You must be very tired then. Perhaps I can offer you some breakfast?'

'A cup of tea only. That would be wonderful.' He settled himself in a seat opposite her. 'So now that you are recovered from the journey, how do you intend to pass the day?'

She looked blankly at him. 'I've no idea except . . . if I could get to a shop, I might buy some material.' She saw him looking puzzled. 'To make a dress, you know. I've not brought enough lightweight clothes. It was stupid of me.'

'No one has sufficient clothes for this climate, so you are not alone,' he said easily. 'You must visit the bazaar, that's the answer. It is a paradise of materials. Why don't I take you? I've commandeered the regimental transport this morning, complete with chauffeur. If you crane your neck, you can see him through the window.'

'That enormous tree is in the way but I can just see him, I think.' Through the branches she glimpsed a flash of brass buttons and the very top of a turban sporting a highly starched and pleated plume.

'That enormous tree is a banyan. You will see them everywhere and know them by their forest of roots. But surely you cannot intend to sew your own dresses?' He sounded almost shocked.

'I'm not so bad with a needle,' she defended herself.

'An English lady sewing her own clothes! It is unheard of. You must employ a *durzi*. A tailor.'

'But won't that be costly?' Instantly she regretted the words uttered unthinkingly. She had no wish to advertise her poverty and Gerald would hate her background to become common knowledge.

'It will be very cheap, I promise. And very good. You will not be wanting to work in these temperatures,' he said in the manner of a reproving schoolmaster. He was probably right, though it would have given her occupation.

'Thank you, Anish, you are very kind.'

'Not at all, and it is a good plan.' He was warming to his idea. 'Simla is much cooler, of course, but you will still need plenty of summer dresses there. The social life is very jolly, I believe.'

She frowned at his words. She seemed to have missed a vital link in the conversation. 'Simla? I am going to Simla?'

'Everyone goes to Simla. All the ladies at least. It is in the foot of the Himalayas as you call them, a mountain paradise with magnificent views. And the warmth is of the gentlest.

There are gardens everywhere, filled with English flowers. You will love it. You will be able to ride out every morning and enjoy good company every evening.'

Daisy wasn't too sure about the riding but otherwise it sounded a paradise indeed and she was already looking forward to it. 'When does the regiment leave?' she asked innocently.

He laughed. 'The regiment does not leave, Mrs Mortimer.'

'Please, call me Daisy.'

'Thank you — Daisy. We men have work to do, we must toil on the plains. It is for the ladies to go. Some are already there but the rest of the womenfolk will leave shortly and you will be able to travel with them.'

'I'm not sure I understand. Are you saying I must leave Gerald behind?'

'He will come to see you, I'm sure, when he can take a few days' leave.'

'But . . . we are only just married.'

'Yes,' he said thoughtfully. 'It might perhaps have been wise to postpone your wedding until the cool season.' He looked searchingly at her and she felt her cheeks flush. 'But no matter, it is done. And you will love Simla and gain much benefit from being there.'

'Will you visit as well?'

'I have no reason to. No wife, no family. And though the mountain towns are beautiful, they are not for Indians. They have been built entirely by the British for the British. This is my place, Daisy, here on the plains. My family are Rajputs and Rajputana is our homeland.'

His voice rang with such pride that she could only murmur, 'Your family must have a splendid history.'

'We do, or rather we did. Now we serve the British. As a martial race, we are useful to them.'

'Do you serve them or serve with them?' something in his voice made her ask.

'It is a nice distinction. I have been educated by the British and trained by them, so clearly I serve with them — but only in India. My commission does not allow me to command outside my own country. But the situation in Europe is changing fast and new threats are emerging all the time. It is beginning to look as though our martial skills will be needed far beyond India. As they were in the Great War.'

She felt a small shiver of apprehension. 'I hope you're wrong.'

'I hope so, too, but the news is not good.'

'If Rajputana is your home, you must have family nearby.' It was an attempt to lighten the conversation but she knew immediately that she had said the wrong thing. When he spoke it was in a voice that lacked all emotion.

'Both my parents are dead and, as for my extended family, I have little contact with them. Our lives have taken very different paths.' But then he was smiling once more. 'You know, I am breaking rules by keeping a military vehicle idling outside, so if you are ready to leave, we should make tracks for the bazaar.'

She felt herself relaxing again. On closer acquaintance, she was finding Anish a strange mix of warmth and prickliness. For a while, she'd been tempted to talk to him about the letter and try to find out what he knew about the unknown Jack Minns, but she was glad now that she'd kept silent. She liked him, liked his frank face and his smiling eyes, but there were moments when she'd felt an invisible barrier slide into place between them.

'I'll get my bag this minute,' and she jumped up from the table and started towards her bedroom. At the door she was struck by an unwelcome thought. 'How will I find my way back from the bazaar? I imagine you must soon return to camp.'

'You're right. I must drop you and then leave, but I will let Gerald know where you are. He will make sure the *syce*, the chauffeur, collects you before lunch. If you're lucky, he may even come himself.'

CHAPTER FIVE

The jeep was retracing the road that yesterday she had driven along in the pony and trap. Daisy was struck anew at the isolation of the bungalow, for there seemed not a single habitation within miles. Just acres of dry, glistening grass and rock and red dust, and in the distance a range of hills, their rims fudged and melting in the haze. In twenty minutes they had reached the small town. Winding their way through narrow streets and past huddled dwellings and hidden courtyards, they reached a maze of small alleys milling with people and crowded with rickety stalls. Anish offered her his arm and steered her carefully through the mêlée.

Sanitation was rudimentary and there was a strong smell of open drains. But there were other odours too: aromas of spice and pepper and incense from the shops they passed. Crowds of hot, sweating people jostled their way in and out of the narrow alleys, gathering around stalls which appeared to sell everything that any one person could want: rice and chillies, spices and saris, leather work sandals and fragile glass bangles in rainbow colours. There were stalls piled high with fruit and vegetables and stalls with mountains of sticky sweets wrapped in silver paper. In the thin strips of space between, several old men sat cross-legged, stitching clothes or boiling things in huge cooking pots.

'They are called *dekshis*,' Anish told her. 'And the food is very good.' Everywhere, heat, movement, people, colour.

He came to a halt at a shop slightly larger than the rest, and with a banner overhead that read *Johari Bazar*. 'You will enjoy yourself here. The owner's name is Sanjay and he will look after you well. He will find you a trunk of materials for a few rupees, see if he doesn't.'

She felt a stir of panic and blurted out, 'I've been very stupid, Anish, and brought only a little money with me.' She did not want him knowing that all she had was a few grubby notes from her time on board ship, since Gerald had not thought to leave her anything.

'You won't need money. Gerald is sure to have an account and you must order what you want and the sum will be added to whatever is owed. This afternoon Sanjay will deliver your materials to the bungalow. It is all very civilised.'

'Yes, I'm sure it is.'

She thought she discerned that edge again but then wondered if she was imagining it. She wanted to reassure him that it was not the Indian way of doing things that made her hesitate but the fact that she had never in her life ordered anything on account. From where she came, you paid cash for whatever you wanted, and if you didn't have the cash, your wants went unsatisfied.

At Anish's call, the stallholder came forward, waving her proudly into the shop and ready to display every bale of material he possessed. She turned to thank her escort for his kindness but he was already halfway back to the jeep and waving her a cheerful farewell.

Before she'd taken two steps into the shop, a woman emerged from its depths holding a number of bright silk scarves in her large, capable hands. 'Sanjay, old chap, can you take for these?' She offered the shopkeeper a handful of tattered notes, then smiled across at Daisy.

'You must be a newcomer. Allow me to introduce myself. I'm Audrey Macdonald.'

'Daisy, Daisy Mortimer. How did you know?'

'That you were a newcomer? Easy,' and she nodded in the direction that Anish had taken. 'The mems wouldn't like it but you don't yet know that.'

'I'm sorry, I don't understand.'

'Indians, my dear. You can't fraternise. The mems will disapprove.'

'Who . . . who are the mems?' Daisy felt utterly confused. She hoped she was not always going to feel this much at sea.

'Memsahibs. The older ones, that is. They run the place — socially, at least. What they say, goes, and friendship with Indians is a definite no.'

She felt ruffled. She liked Anish and didn't want to be told she couldn't spend time with him. It gave her the courage to ask directly, 'Are you one of them, one of the mems?'

'Bless you, no. I'm not even married. I'm a nurse at the Infirmary. Sister Macdonald. But I've had enough dealings with them to know that newcomers soon learn to toe the line.'

'I'm not sure I like the sound of that.'

'You probably don't but if you want to live peacefully, you'll take heed.' She must have noticed Daisy's worried face because she went on with brisk reassurance, 'The women aren't all bad. And when they are insufferable, it's not entirely their fault. They're forced into pretty limited lives. There's no job for them here, you see, not even running the house. The servants do that. Days spent doing nothing with no end in sight saps the spirit. It's bound to leave you wearing blinkers.'

'Then perhaps they should try removing them occasionally.' The idea that her life was to be monitored and decided by others was frustrating.

'Perhaps they should, but this is an alien culture, and it can lead people to foster — well, let's say, an extra Englishness. And that's not all bad.'

Daisy took up the cudgels, though she had only the haziest notion what prompted her. 'On the contrary, it sounds a very bad idea to me.'

'That's because you don't know India. European women have to have guts to live here. They need that extra to stick it out and the mems are first class on fortitude. They have to be. To keep their children safe, they're forced to send them home to England at an early age. There are thousands of child graves scattered across this country, you'll find. But when parents and children meet years on, they hardly know each other. It's a rotten choice, don't you think? Return home with your offspring or slug it out by your husband's side.'

Daisy acknowledged the truth of this but she was still smarting. 'And what happens if you disagree and don't follow their rules?'

'You must, my dear, you must fit in. When you married, this is the life you chose. Attitudes may be changing. A few mems have taken up nursing or teaching, usually as voluntary work, but most are still stuck in the old ways. So be charming but vapid, that's the ticket. Remember, women who are difficult or cause a scandal, damage their husbands' prospects, and you wouldn't want to do that, I'm sure.'

She wouldn't, Daisy thought, but her new future was looking less than promising in all kinds of ways and by the time Sister Macdonald had pumped her hand in a hearty goodbye, she'd lost much of her enthusiasm for buying materials. But Sanjay was not about to allow a likely customer to escape so easily and she found herself spending the next thirty minutes in a daze, wandering back and forth with him among the rows of crowded trestles.

The building was long and narrow, stretching far back, and with every counter they came upon, her memory of the nurse's conversation faded a little, while her delight in the shop grew. So did painful indecision: cottons, fine lawns, embroidered materials and the most exquisite of silks all called to her. But the frugality she'd been forced to practise all her life prevented her losing her wits altogether, and she bought only cottons she thought would make into several frocks for the day and a length of silk for any formal occasion to which she was bidden. In the end, she found she could not resist the splendid array of trimmings that Sanjay showed her, and squirrelled away several ribbons and a card of silver braid.

Flushed with success, she asked the shopkeeper for his pattern book. She would make a start this very day, once the sun's warmth had begun to wane. Sanjay shook his head and instead showed her a picture from a magazine. She was repeating her request, thinking he'd not understood her, when a voice from the front of the shop called her name.

'Miss Driscoll?'

She was taken aback to see Grayson Harte standing a few feet away. When they'd spoken on the ship, he'd told her little of his plans and she hadn't realised that he, too, was headed for Jasirapur. If she'd thought about his destination at all, it would have been to imagine him many miles away by now. His tall, slim figure looked absurdly cool in linen slacks and a short-sleeved shirt, as though the punishing heat of the bazaar had decided not to take up his time but instead slide gently from his shoulders.

'Mr Harte, how nice to see you. But I'm no longer Miss Driscoll. I've become Mrs Mortimer since we last met.' If only in name, she thought, and blushed slightly.

'Of course, forgive me. You were to be married immediately we docked, now I remember.'

'Mr Harte . . .'

'Grayson,' he corrected.

'I wonder if you could help me, Grayson? I can't make this gentleman understand that I need paper patterns for the materials I've bought.'

He stepped forward and spoke in what Daisy imagined was fluent Hindi. 'You don't need a pattern apparently,' he translated. 'You choose a picture that you like, a dress you see illustrated in a magazine, for instance — like the one Sanjay was showing you — and the *durzi* will make it for you.'

Her mouth fell open at this news. 'It is pretty amazing, isn't it,' he went on. 'I knew you could get a suit made in that fashion, but I wondered whether ladies' clothes might be a bit more tricky. Not so, though.'

She turned to the stallholder to say goodbye and Grayson translated for her. 'He thanks you for your custom and he'll deliver your purchases later today. What's your address by the way? He probably has it, but better to check.'

She gave it and he looked surprised. 'You're not in the cantonment then? I would have thought you'd be living alongside the other military families. But perhaps your bungalow has its own attractions?'

She wouldn't have described the cheerless house as having any attractions, but felt compelled to defend Gerald's choice, though why if there was accommodation within the cantonment he'd not taken it, she was at a loss to think.

'I believe Gerald — my husband — chose it for its tranquillity,' she managed to say.

'It will certainly have that,' Grayson agreed. 'It must be the last building on that side of Jasirapur.' But he had a frown on his face as he spoke.

'How is your job going?' she asked abruptly, hoping she might deflect him from finding fault in Gerald.

'I have the feeling that it will suit me very well, but thank you for asking — Daisy? I hope I may call you that.'

They were standing outside the bazaar and Sanjay had retreated into his small, airless office.

'Yes, of course. I'm glad it's working out for you. I expect you much prefer it to sugar cane.' She remembered his telling her that one small personal detail, that he'd spent three years in a neighbouring region, working in the sugar business and hating every minute.

'I was never cut out to be a businessman but the experience hasn't been a complete waste of time. The languages I learnt eased me into the Foreign Office and then helped me land this job.'

'I suppose you'll use them when you start travelling. I don't expect you'll be staying in Jasirapur for long.'

He seemed uncertain of how to answer. 'At the moment, I'm not sure of my movements. But even in town, it can be useful to speak the local language. As we've just discovered.' He grinned and waved his hand towards the shop behind them.

She was following his direction when a severe crash from a stall several yards to their left startled her. The crash was followed by a body hurling its way towards them. A bare-headed man in a dirty white kurta came rushing down the alley, knocking everything and everybody aside, a uniformed policeman in hot pursuit. Grayson grabbed her arm and pulled her out of harm's way.

'You seem fated to attract wrongdoers. But this time fortunately you've stayed on your feet.' He was holding her in a loose clasp.

Daisy felt herself trembling and when she attempted to reassure him with a smile, it didn't quite make it to her face. Her memories were too painful to do better.

He let go of her arm but his expression was anxious. 'You don't look at all well. You should make for home.'

'I'm fine, really I am. Gerald is meeting me and he'll be here very soon.' She made herself say it with a conviction she didn't feel.

Grayson looked relieved. 'In that case, I hope you won't mind if I leave you. Please forgive the sudden departure but I should go. Have fun with your dresses.'

And in an instant he'd disappeared in the wake of the fleeing man and his uniformed pursuer. It happened so quickly that Daisy could only blink. One minute Grayson was standing beside her, shielding her with his arm, and the next he had melted into the crowd that had gathered to debate with great volubility the incident they had just witnessed.

Grayson Harte was in the Civil Service, a pen pusher, Gerald had said, but his conduct hardly seemed to match the job and raised all kinds of questions. What was he doing still in Jasirapur when rightly he should be miles away, dispensing justice to a clutch of outlying villages? And why had he taken off after the two running men? It seemed very odd and she could only conclude that somehow she'd got things wrong. Perhaps District Officers had to train in town before being let loose on the population, and today he'd simply remembered that he needed to be back at his desk for an important meeting.

From the corner of her eye, she caught sight of Gerald waving at her from a nearby alleyway. She felt real gratitude that he'd managed to come, and walked towards him as swiftly as the heat allowed. The burning air was dancing ever more energetically through the bazaar and she felt drained by its onslaught. Drained, too, by the recent unwelcome reminder of what had happened on board ship. The memory was never far away and for the moment she was thoroughly shaken.

Beneath the shade of his *topi*, Gerald's expression was unreadable, but his words made his feelings clear. 'Buck up, Daisy. I've been waving at you for an age. I borrowed a regimental motor to come, and it has to be returned straight after lunch.'

He marched forward, leaving her to follow meekly behind. In single file they retraced their steps to the road and the waiting car. She didn't see Grayson Harte, once more mingling with the crowd and all but invisible. Didn't see that from beneath the awning of a nearby stall, he was watching them and watching them intently.

CHAPTER SIX

Their journey back to the bungalow was conducted in silence, both of them exhausted by the oppressive atmosphere of early afternoon. The once bright blue sky had turned leaden but a pewter sun was no less powerful, bouncing its rays off the *topi* she'd remembered to wear. She tried to blot the discomfort from her mind and concentrate instead on gathering her thoughts into some kind of order.

She was looking forward to eating dinner with her husband that night. 'Looking forward' was perhaps optimistic; the prospect was making her apprehensive, even a little scared, but she knew she must make the attempt to clear the air between them, and very soon.

Daisy had been in India three entire days and the conversation she'd been waiting to have remained unbroached. She would have liked the meal to be special but this morning she hadn't felt brave enough to give Rajiv a menu. Ten to one he would pretend he didn't understand, or the food she chose would not be available. And then Anish had arrived and taken her to the bazaar and she'd pushed the thought of the meal to the back of her mind. So whatever Rajiv chose to cook tonight would have to suffice. And the food itself was unimportant, it was what she must say to Gerald that was vital.

What *would* she say? How would she say it? She could begin perhaps by recounting the details of her day. He wouldn't be interested in cottons and trimmings, she knew, but it might give her the confidence she needed, the courage to speak the difficult words.

The driver swerved to a halt in front of the bungalow and Gerald said something to him in Hindi.

'He'll be returning at five,' he explained. And before she could question him further, he strode up the front path and across the veranda, calling loudly for his servant.

'We won't require dinner tonight, Rajiv.'

Her heart gave a small lurch. There was to be no meal after all and the words she had been rehearsing dissolved into the sticky air.

'Where are we eating, Gerald?'

'At the Club. Sorry — I should have mentioned it but things have been a bit hectic at camp.'

She was tempted to ask what things. They might explain why Gerald had decided not to share her room last night, but he'd turned away from her and strolled across to the table to fill two glasses with the lemonade that Rajiv had mixed for them.

She felt an immense frustration. She needed to put things right as soon as possible and tonight had been her chance. But perhaps she could still persuade him to stay. There had been a time when he hadn't wanted to leave her side. Very deliberately, she walked towards him and laced her arms about his neck.

'Couldn't we spend this evening here?' she asked quietly, giving a little tug to pull him close. 'We could go to the Club another night.'

'Not possible, I'm afraid.' He was fidgeting beneath her touch. 'It's all arranged — I can't mess things up now.'

She tried to hug him tight, then stood on tiptoe and grazed his cheek with her lips, catching the corner of his mouth as she did so. 'Surely it won't matter if we miss one dinner,' she persisted. 'I'd like to stay home, Gerald. We've hardly spent any time together.'

'We will,' he said briskly, looking over her head at the wall beyond and unwrapping her arms from around his neck. 'But tonight it's important we go to the Club. You'll enjoy it. It's in the cantonment and the centre of social life on the station. There's lots happening. Dancing, cards, billiards. And a great bar. It's the Club dinner tonight — there's one every week — and everyone comes. I'll be able to introduce you around. It's a chance for you to meet the other wives. You'll want to do that.'

She didn't share his certainty, but as it appeared she was destined to spend a good deal of time in their company, it might be better to get the ordeal over as soon as possible. And the Club dinner couldn't go on for ever, she reasoned. When they returned, Rajiv would be gone and they would be alone. She would have the opportunity to open her heart. Gerald would be shocked at her news, but sympathetic, she was sure. He would soothe her with words and kisses. They would curl up in bed together and sleep in each other's arms. She sank down on the sofa, smiling softly at the picture she'd conjured.

The cold trickle of lemonade was reviving her a little. 'What should I wear?' she asked.

It was an important question. She wanted to make him proud of her and if she were about to meet the women she would live among for the next few months, it was essential she look her best.

'The dress you had in Bombay. The one with splashes of colour.'

So he *had* noticed. She felt her bruised soul sing just a little. Even in his disoriented state, he had noticed what she'd been wearing for their wedding. And that dress was now freshly clean and pressed and hanging in her wardrobe. Thanks to Rajiv, she thought. She must try to feel more charitably towards him.

'You need some company,' Gerald was saying bracingly. 'It's not good to be on your own too much. The mind can start playing tricks. Rajiv tells me you've been seeing ghosts in the garden.'

Daisy's impulse to charity withered. It seemed that Rajiv carried every tale he could to his master, but she was not going to be coerced. 'I did see someone,' she said firmly. The more she'd thought about it, the more sure she'd become. 'And it was no ghost. Unless ghosts are heavy smokers.'

'Unlikely. Almost as unlikely as seeing a real-life trespasser at that hour. You were overtired, Daisy, and when you saw what you thought was a figure, you could only have been half-awake.'

'I was awake enough to be scared that I was alone,' she retorted. 'You were nowhere in sight.'

'I slept in the other room — I didn't want to disturb you — and *I* heard nothing.'

It was just as she'd thought, and there was really no need for him to sound defensive. The mystery remained unexplained, but perhaps Gerald was right when he said she'd been in a dream.

He wandered to the table with the empty glasses and seemed keen to change the subject. 'It will be good for you to get to know a few of the wives before you travel up to Simla.'

There it was again, that place. First Anish and now Gerald. 'Anish mentioned Simla to me this morning.'

'I hope he painted its delights for you.'

'He praised the town highly.' She debated whether to say more. 'He also said I'd be going without you.'

Gerald looked taken aback. 'Whatever made you think I'd be coming? My work is here, you must see that.'

'And is that so for the other women? They don't mind leaving their husbands behind?'

'They're only too delighted to get out of this heat. You should be too. While you're there, you can think of me slaving away on the burning plains! In any case, I'll visit when I can, but it's a two-day journey and I'll need a block of leave to get there and back.'

She sat staring ahead, lost in a solitary future. He was watching her closely and an irritated frown furrowed the smoothness of his face. 'What's wrong? Why on earth would you not want to go?'

'I've only just arrived, Gerald, and we are only just married.' It shouldn't be necessary to remind him, she thought.

'I realise that. It's why I haven't packed you off immediately. By the time the last group of women leave next week, you'll have had ample space to recover from the journey.'

Was he deliberately misreading her concern? Making out that it was the travelling rather than their marriage that was worrying her. She couldn't be certain, but she *was* certain she had no wish to be 'packed off', no matter how enticing the place. The set look on his face, though, signalled it would be difficult to refuse.

'You'll try to visit while I'm there?'

'Whenever I can.' His response mixed relief with cheerfulness. 'But really you won't need me. The women get all sorts of things going. Parties, picnics, concerts, amateur dramatics. Even fashion shows. And every Sunday you can wear your best clothes for morning service — the cathedral is always packed — and be certain they'll stay crisp. The climate is wonderful.'

'So Anish told me.'

'He was right. The scenery is wonderful too. You can see the Himalayas through the clouds and they go on for mile after mile. Great masses of ice and snow almost hanging in the sky. It's majestic. The gods are supposed to live in the mountains, did you know that? And when you see them for the first time, you'll believe it.'

She smiled faintly. He was so enthusiastic and he was concerned for her. He wanted her to be happy and comfortable in her new life and that was reassuring; that was more like the old Gerald. She would do as he wished, she decided, and if she were ever tempted to waver, the thought of escaping an overpowering heat would be sure to persuade her back into line.

* * *

The driver was at the door at five o'clock sharp. She saw the pleat of his turban bend and flutter as he talked with her husband on the veranda. Gerald had warned her not to dress until the last minute and she was glad of the advice. Even though the early evening air was balmy, the warmth still bounced off the ground, hitting legs and body with unbelievable energy. Her entire skin was aflame and once the dress was on, the lightest of silks felt like a hot glove.

The Jasirapur station had so far been only a word to her but as they drove through what Gerald told her were the civil lines, she had a sense of the power and reach of the administration of which she was now a very small part. Row after row of bungalows spread before them, the homes of Civil Service personnel, of police and forestry officers and their families. On the other side of the road, further lines of bungalows stretched into the distance, each whitewashed and red-ochred and separated one from the other by splashes of tired grass. This was the cantonment, her husband told her, the home of the military. Beyond the bungalows, a hotchpotch of interlinked buildings signalled the barracks for the Indian soldiers.

Daisy glanced across at her husband. He looked splendid in blue and gold, his slim, upright figure admirable in the close-fitting dress uniform. For an instant she was filled with a surge of pure pleasure. It was wonderful to be dressed so prettily, to be sitting beside the man she loved, and to be going into company for the very first time as a couple. Her heart felt lighter than it had since those heady moments in London. These last few days, she'd become wary of betraying her ignorance and swallowed most of her questions, but a new sense of well-being encouraged her to ask, 'Have you always rented the bungalow, or did you once live on the station?'

'I lived in the Mess. It's over there.' And he pointed vaguely in the direction of the barracks. 'It's home to the unmarried officers. Some of the married officers too — if they want to get away from their wives. The centre of regimental life really. Everyone sleeps, eats, spends their spare time there.'

'Then Anish must live in the Mess. Will he be coming tonight?'

It seemed important that he was. His was a kind face, she thought, kind and familiar and friendly.

'He won't be at the dinner. Indians aren't allowed in the Club.'

She stared at him in astonishment. 'It's beginning to change but it's still difficult,' he said tersely. 'Last year the Colonel put up an officer for membership, a cadet from the Indian Military Academy — the same as Anish. He was turned down, so the old boy won't allow other Indian officers to apply.'

'But surely . . .'

'It's the way it is, Daisy.' His voice rose in annoyance. 'And you'd better get used to it. There are all kinds of distinctions to life here and it's important you learn them. The military and the ICS — the Civil Service — are on a par, top of the social tree, but planters and businessmen are not quite the thing. If you hear anyone called a box-wallah, that's who they're talking about. Tea and indigo planters have more status than the sugar and jute wallahs. They're trade and aren't allowed to join the Club either. They have their own place.'

Daisy knew all about distinctions. She had been on the wrong end of them all her short life and had had little option but to accept that was the way things were. But it didn't mean she was ever going to think them right. And certainly not a distinction that barred a man like Anish from mixing socially with those he worked beside day after day. But she knew, too, that she was helpless in the face of conventions she imagined had held rigid for centuries, so she said no more.

CHAPTER SEVEN

The Club was housed in a spacious, white building with a long, deep veranda running its full length. A sloping red roof provided shade and as much coolness as was possible. Cane tables and chairs were scattered along the veranda's expanse and several groups of people were chatting there, heads bathed in the light that spilled from open windows and doors. Drink was flowing freely and repeated calls of '*Koi-Hai*!' interrupted the buzz of chatter, as one or other of the Club servants was called to attend. The scratchy sound of an old record filtered through the air and Daisy felt her husband's arm guiding her towards the sound.

As they mounted the wooden steps, she felt the drinkers' eyes swivel in their direction, their stares variously curious and indifferent. A tall woman rose from a nearby table and came towards them. She appeared to be wearing a floral dressing gown, its skirts flowing around her ankles. At second glance, Daisy could see it was an opulent evening gown, and immediately felt underdressed.

'Gerald, my dear, how good to see you here. And with your new bride. Such a pretty girl you've found!'

'I'm glad to see you, Mrs Forester.' He certainly looked glad, Daisy thought. Glad and relieved. 'Daisy, this is Mrs Forester. Colonel Forester is my commanding officer.'

'Call me Edith, my dear. It's a great pleasure to meet you. You must let me take you in hand and introduce you to as many wives as we can manage. Gerald, get your wife a *chota peg*.' She saw Daisy's anxious expression. 'On second thoughts, a gimlet might be better — gin and lime my dear, most refreshing.'

Daisy felt a confusing mix of emotions as they passed into the Club meeting room. It seemed she was approved by this august matron and that had to be good, but she was not at all sure she wished to be taken in hand by her. It was Gerald who should be by her side. But where was he? Making straight for the bar, she saw, along with every other man in the room. And it was an enormous edifice, its huge, polished surface filling at least a quarter of the available space.

In general, the clubhouse was not inviting. Its walls were wood panelled and decorated with the heads of various dead animals, interspersed here and there with sepia-tinged photographs of past company. In the middle of the central wall was a full-length portrait of the new King and Queen, looking almost as nervous as Daisy felt.

At one end of the room a huddle of women bunched tightly together, and it was towards this ocean of floral silks and flashing jewellery that she allowed herself to be gently pushed. Edith was propelling her with one hand while with the other she waved to friends on either side, as the women divided obediently at her approach. Like Moses and the Red Sea, Daisy thought.

For the first few minutes, the excited babble of female voices would have blocked out Edith's introductions, even if Daisy's nerves had not. 'This is Rosemary Laughton, Daisy,' were the first words she heard. 'Her husband is the Adjutant.'

'Rose, this is Lieutenant Mortimer's new bride.'

She had a rank now, Daisy thought, she was the wife of a lieutenant. Sister Macdonald's stringent words came back to her: *the women have no role of their own, they are simply accessories to their husbands' lives*. She noticed that Rosemary had almost bowed to Edith Forester as the Colonel's wife and she supposed that, in turn, she should be bowing to Mrs Laughton, for it appeared that Gerald was a very junior officer.

Rosemary drew slowly on her cigarette and looked at her through the rising smoke. 'Well, you're a surprise, my dear.' She seemed to absorb Daisy in a single glance. 'We had no idea that Gerald had you tucked away somewhere — quite the contrary, in fact. It *must* have been love.'

Before she had time to puzzle the meaning of this, Rosemary was asking, 'And how are you settling in?' Her voice expressed a distinct lack of interest but Daisy tried diplomacy. 'It's very strange, of course, but I'm sure I shall enjoy living here.'

'You'll enjoy the regiment, my dear.' Her smile was superior. 'The cavalry is the cream of the Indian Army and *they* are the best of all soldiers. It's India that's the pits.'

The woman's rudeness startled Daisy and pushed her to a small challenge. 'Is that true of Simla. too?'

Rosemary looked taken aback. 'Not Simla, no. Certainly not Simla. Life is wonderful there and you'll enjoy yourself enormously. We leave next week, and I imagine Gerald will have made arrangements for you to travel with us. You'll need to nag your servants into action, though, or you'll find yourself packing for them.'

Confronting this frightening memsahib had made Daisy's heart beat too fast but now she saw the woman was simply ridiculous. How difficult was it to pack a suitcase? Of course, Rosemary Laughton couldn't know that the girl facing her had in all probability packed more suitcases than any Indian retainer. And she must never know.

'I don't think that will be a problem,' she said aloud. 'We've only the one servant and I imagine Gerald will wish to keep him here.' Leaving Rajiv behind was one delight of Simla she hadn't considered before.

'Only one servant! What is Gerald thinking of! What about the *mali*, and the *jemader* and a cook?'

'It's a very small bungalow.' She was once more driven into defending Gerald's housekeeping. It was becoming a habit. And what on earth was a *mali* and a *jemader*? 'Rajiv does all the cleaning and the cooking.'

Rosemary snorted. 'I shall speak to Gerald. It's quite ludicrous.'

The conversation had reached a dead end and Daisy was unsure how to restart it. Did these women talk about nothing other than their servants? Rescue appeared in the shape of Edith who returned to her side at that moment and whisked her away from the terrifying Rosemary.

'It will be good for you to meet some young women of your own age,' Edith enthused, her long skirts swishing in tune with a powerful stride. 'Amelia Simmonds married only last year and you're sure to have a lot to talk about.'

They arrived in front of a thin, young woman who had been lingering uncertainly on the edge of the group. Even in the dim light of the clubhouse, the vivid fuchsia of her tea gown was startlingly at odds with the pale, pinched face above.

'Daisy is Lieutenant Mortimer's wife, Amelia,' was all Edith offered, before marching away to join an exclamatory group of women gathered beneath the head of a particularly morose gazelle. Daisy was left to smile hopefully at the new introduction.

'My husband has just been made Captain,' Amelia said proudly.

There wasn't much you could say to that, Daisy thought, and retreated to the old, trite question, 'And how are you enjoying India?'

'I love it.' Amelia gushed enthusiasm. 'So will you, particularly when we get up to the hills. Such fun! So you're Gerald's wife . . . I'm so pleased to meet you . . . I'd thought that Gerald . . .' Her voice tailed off and then she repeated a little desperately, 'I'm so pleased to meet you. It can get a bit dull here to be honest, a bit claustrophobic. Same old clubhouse, same old activities. Of course, it's far too hot to do anything much at this time of the year.'

'I can imagine. I've found even reading to be a chore. But that's probably because I've had nothing very interesting to read. Is there a library in the cantonment?'

Amelia looked blank. 'Books,' Daisy prompted.

'Oh yes, there are books. There's an annexe somewhere around the back of the clubhouse, I believe. I've never been there myself. There are plenty of magazines hanging around the Club itself, oh and catalogues from the Army and Navy.' She paused looking doubtfully at her new acquaintance. 'You're not a blue stocking, are you?'

'I enjoy reading,' Daisy said simply.

She had never thought herself in any way clever. Gerald was clever, he had been to public school so he must be. Grayson Harte was clever. He'd talked to her of Indian history, Indian culture, and he knew all kinds of languages. That was clever in a way she was not. But neither was she as shockingly ignorant as these women appeared to be. Eden House had given her a decent grounding and Helena Maddox had continued her education, even though she'd been a servant in the house. And it had gone well beyond books. Miss Maddox had taught her to walk and talk in a genteel fashion; to appear as much of a lady, she thought proudly, as any of the women in this room.

'So what do the wives do all day?'

'Do?' Amelia shook her head slightly as though this was an extraordinary question. 'Oversee the house, I suppose, organise the servants. Give Cook the menu for the day, that sort of thing. Sometimes we have coffee together.'

'That's not likely to take up much time.' Daisy was regretful. She had genuinely wished for a clue as to how to fill her days, but Amelia was now staring at her as though she were a species she had never before encountered.

'I'm not used to being idle,' Daisy tried to explain.

Amelia considered the matter. 'I believe some women have become nurses or teachers, but only for a short while — to fill a gap maybe.' She moved closer and put her lips to Daisy's ear. 'If you want to be accepted, you had better stick to the house, that's my advice. The senior wives would hate the idea of you working.'

'The senior wives?'

Amelia looked around to make sure they were not being overheard. 'The Colonel's wife, in particular,' she whispered, 'but also the wives of all the senior officers. They run the show, you'll soon find out. And as wives of junior officers, you learn to let them. They wouldn't approve of you working.'

Daisy bristled inwardly but kept her voice even. 'What else might they not approve?'

'I'm making them sound horrid when they're not. They're very nice — really, they are. They're just keen on all the women fitting in and, as long as you do, there's no problem. You'll find the regiment is very close-knit, like a family. Everyone has an opinion so you have to be careful not to upset people. With the way you dress, for instance, or the friends you make.'

'And who shouldn't I have as a friend?' Daisy asked. But even as she posed the question, she knew the answer.

'Indians for one thing. And Anglo-Indians, too. Some of them are nearly white so you have to be careful.' The whisper deepened. 'They're not people we mix with, not now at least. It used to be different once, I think. But now too many lower-class British have married women from the bazaar, that kind of thing, and we don't recognise them.'

So that was Anglo-Indians as well as Indians and who else did Gerald say — sugar and jute planters? There was no end to the categories that were unwelcome. And she would be just as unwelcome if they knew the details of her history: a girl without parents, a girl sent into service when she was little more than a child, a girl who had burst with pride when she became a shop assistant selling perfume in a department store.

A loud gong cut their conversation dead, the sound outpacing the now raucous voices. Daisy drifted with the crowd towards an adjoining room where two long refectory tables stood parallel to one another, each bearing twenty place name cards and twenty sets of strictly ordered cutlery.

She found herself seated in yet another cane chair beside a man with a very large moustache. The cutlery bothered her but, by dint of watching her fellow diners, she managed to acquit herself without incident. The first course was soup but a soup she had never before tasted. She glanced sideways to gauge her neighbour's reaction. The soup seemed to catch in his side whiskers and Daisy had to stop herself from watching in fascination as bubbles of the dark liquid slid slowly down his moustache.

'As always, good mulligatawny,' he said at last, when he'd emptied most of his bowl, 'but God-awful bread, don't you think, m'dear?'

The bread was the least of Daisy's worries. The hot, spicy liquid was burning her throat and she had to force herself to finish what was in front of her.

'Made with yeast from Bombay, you know. Comes in the post every month — no wonder it tastes like dung.'

She laboured painfully through the soup and then it was on to tough, curried chicken and another helping of hot spice. She filled and refilled her glass with water but nothing seemed to souse the flames.

'Have you stayed on, then?' was her companion's next gambit.

'Stayed on?' That was a puzzle. 'No, I've just arrived.'

'Can't have done, m'dear. Wrong time of the year.'

She was minded to contradict him but then recalled the various pieces of advice that had come her way. The man might be an eccentric but she must try to suit his humour.

'Why is that?' she asked, as though she genuinely wished to know.

'It's April. You couldn't have arrived with the fishing fleet.'

'I didn't. I arrived with the *Viceroy of India*.' And what on earth was the fishing fleet?

'Bless your heart, the fishing fleet isn't the name of a ship! It's the girls. Girls just like you, husband hunting. They come out from home in the autumn and the young men go wild for them. Lots of 'em stay. Plenty of husbands to spare, you know. But come spring, those that haven't made it, go back. Returned empties, we call them.'

'I've not come to fish and I'm not a returned empty,' Daisy said with dignity. 'I came to India to marry. My husband is Gerald Mortimer.'

The man banged his spoon loudly on the table and laughed. 'Sorry about the mix up. Young Mortimer's gal then? Good! Difficult business but glad to see him hitched.'

She was unsure what he meant by a difficult business but he seemed well meaning. And now that the dessert had arrived, it was taking all her attention. She eyed it hungrily. Two delicious woven toffee baskets, each filled with fresh mangoes and cream. It was the only part of the meal she'd managed without her eyes watering, and she had to stop her glance wandering enviously towards her neighbour's plate. From several places along the table, she saw Gerald smiling. He was looking at her as though she had passed a test, though what that might have been, she had no idea.

Two decanters were placed in the middle of the two long tables, and she could just make out the writing on the silver labels which hung around each bottle neck: Marsala and Port. A duo of waiters made their solemn round of the guests, the women being offered the marsala and the men the port. When every schooner was filled, her neighbour stood with glass raised and all the men followed suit.

'The King Emperor!'

There was a muffled rumble as everyone mouthed the words and held their glasses aloft. Daisy took a cautious sip. The wine was thick and sweet and clung to her tongue. The other women seemed to have no problem with it, but she was delighted when she saw Mrs Forester rise from her seat at the head of the second table and could stop pretending to drink.

'Shall we, ladies?'

CHAPTER EIGHT

All the women stood up and Daisy followed uncertainly. Leading the way through yet another polished oak door to a much smaller room, Edith stood waiting on the threshold.

'This is the snug, Daisy. We have our coffee here, and the men will join us after the port has finished doing the rounds. How are you enjoying this evening?'

She managed to murmur something that sounded like enjoyment, and then she was being taken by the hand and walked up to yet another young woman. 'I would like you to meet my daughter,' Edith was saying.

A smiling fair-haired girl was at her mother's side. 'This is Jocelyn. Jocelyn, this is Gerald's new bride, Daisy.'

The girl's red lips opened to an even broader smile, showing two rows of perfect, white teeth. Her deep blue eyes sparkled with pleasure as she dispensed with the hand Daisy had offered and, instead, clasped her warmly around the shoulders. Immediately, Daisy smelled it. The perfume. She knew that perfume — *Shalimar*. The very perfume Gerald had bought from her counter at Bridges. Could you get *Shalimar* in Jasirapur? Somehow she doubted it. So where had it come from? Gerald had said the perfume was for his aunt and she'd thought then that it was a strange choice for an older lady. Now it seemed she might have an explanation: it had not been for his aunt, if indeed he had one, but for this girl. And there could be one reason alone for such an intimate gift, she decided, and that was courtship.

Jocelyn continued to talk cheerfully, but Daisy hardly heard her. Her mind was too busy roving over remarks that earlier had made no sense. Was that what Rosemary Laughton had meant when she'd said Gerald's marriage had come as a surprise, that the regiment had expected something else? Had they expected Jocelyn to be his bride? Surely not, for she was the Colonel's daughter and from Daisy's small experience of Jasirapur, the social hierarchy was even more rigid than in England. Jocelyn would be destined for a man of much higher rank than Gerald. She was allowing her imagination to run amok, she chided herself. Yet there was also Amelia Simmonds. She had been surprised by the marriage, so surprised that she'd been flustered into incoherence.

'And what have you been doing since you arrived?' Jocelyn was saying.

Daisy brought her mind back with a jerk and tried very hard not to show how bad she was feeling. 'Not a great deal. I'm still getting used to the weather. But I did go to the bazaar today and bought material for new dresses. I find I don't have sufficient lightweight clothing.'

'No one ever has sufficient,' the girl said, echoing Anish's words. 'Have you spoken to the *durzi*?'

'I thought I might sew the dresses myself,' she ventured, 'but I didn't think to bring patterns with me. Perhaps I can send for them.'

'You don't need patterns. All you need is a *durzi*, and I know the very man. I'll bring him to you — tomorrow if you like.'

Her first reaction was to refuse, to make an excuse, say anything not to spend time with the woman she was beginning to think of as Gerald's lover. But the girl was so pleasant and unaffected that rejecting her overture of friendship was difficult. She wondered if Jocelyn still cared for Gerald, and hoped it wasn't the case. *She* might feel badly wounded, but she had no wish for the girl to be hurt, too.

A second cup of bitter coffee was making the rounds before the men trooped through the door, some of them decidedly unsteady. Gerald was looking slightly flushed but came straight to her side.

'You did well.' She couldn't imagine why, but if her husband was pleased, she was happy. 'You were seated by the Colonel, you know,' he whispered. 'They must have thrown precedence out of the window tonight. Edith's doing, I imagine. A great honour, though. I guess it was because you're fresh from England. It won't happen again but the old boy seemed really interested in you.'

She was trying to think of a suitable reply when the room fell quiet. For some while it had been filled with loud chattering and the noise of chairs and stools being rearranged, until everyone was seated just where they wished.

Then, breaking through the sudden hush that followed this burst of activity, a voice drawled, 'She's quite dark, don't you think? Touch of the tar brush, I reckon.'

And what seemed like a hundred eyes swivelled in Daisy's direction. She felt herself turn hot and red, and wanted more than anything to disappear through the battered floorboards. What had the woman meant? For naturally it had been a woman's voice. The room buzzed furiously until Edith took charge of the situation, clapping her hands and silencing the wagging tongues.

'Don't forget, ladies, we'll be taking the six o'clock train on Thursday. Come prepared with food and drink. And not too much luggage, please. The last thing we want are corridors overflowing with trunks.'

Voices subsided and passed on to quieter topics. But Daisy could not pass on. She felt Gerald sitting rigid beside her and couldn't bring herself to look at him. The woman had meant her and everyone had known it. *Was* she too dark, too different? Her hair and eyes were a deep brown and her skin perhaps a shade darker than many of those she'd lived and worked beside, but she had never given much thought to her colouring. And neither had anyone else until this moment. What was the woman suggesting? That she was not English?

She was as English as any one of them in this room, she thought indignantly. She had only one keepsake from her mother, a faded photograph but, beneath the starch of a nurse's uniform, the woman portrayed was clearly English. But her father? Had he been English, too? She had no idea. And she never would, for there had been only one name on the tattered birth certificate the orphanage had reluctantly handed her when she left. She was an outsider and used to being so. As a poor girl without known family, it was inevitable. Miss Maddox's friends had counselled her against favouring Daisy, and her fellow shop assistants had looked down their noses at a girl they knew instinctively was not one of them. But now apparently there was another reason for her exclusion. She was the wrong shade.

Mortified, she found she could no longer make conversation, no longer mouth the trivialities that seemed necessary to the evening. But rescue was close. Colonel Forester announced that he and Edith were about to leave and, as their departure was a signal for the rest of the company to make their way home, it was only minutes before Daisy was able to hide her burning face in the darkness of the night.

* * *

Rajiv had primed a solitary kerosene lamp to light the bungalow and she undressed by its shadows. Her heart was so full she could hardly get the breath to her lungs and tears were constantly pricking at her eyes. It had all gone so horribly wrong. She'd been highly nervous, terrified of making a mistake, but she had been managing the evening well. She'd smiled, she'd listened, spoken a little and swallowed food that made her feel ill. She had made a good impression or so she'd thought, and Gerald had been pleased with her.

This moment would have been the time to tell him what she needed him to know. But then that one devastating remark and everything had been thrown into the air.

She unclasped the necklace she had been wearing and packed it carefully away among her clean underwear. Her only necklace, the string of pearls Miss Maddox had given her when she'd won the job at Bridges. How far away that seemed now. Then she hung the silk dress back into the wardrobe, feeling she never wanted to see it again. Despite all the hopes she'd invested in the garment, it had not brought her luck. Lifting her hairbrush, she began half-heartedly to pull it through waves that, as always, had grown limp from the sultry air. In the mirror she glimpsed Gerald framed in the doorway. He was fresh from the bathroom but his pyjamas were already damp with sweat.

'Just come to say goodnight,' he said awkwardly. 'It's hotter than ever, don't you think? Best I give you a bit of space, my dear.' And he turned to head towards the spare room.

'Gerald!'

He looked back at her, a frown carved into his forehead. It was clear he didn't want to stay and she felt too broken to try and detain him. But there was one thing she had to say before they parted.

'I'm not going to Simla, Gerald.'

The frown deepened. 'What do you mean, you're not going?'

'Just that. I can't bear to be with those women.'

'This is nonsense. What's got into you?' He leaned heavily on the doorframe and she remembered he had drunk lavishly.

'I don't want to spend the next few months hundreds of miles away from you and with no other company than people who hate me.'

'No one hates you. If this is about that stupid remark, you should forget it. Margot Dukes is a bitch and well known for her unpleasantness. Nobody will take the least notice of her.'

'It's not just her. It's all of them.'

And it was, she realised. Only a few of the women tonight had been unfriendly, several in fact had been amiable, but to be constrained to spend her days in such shallow, wearisome company was wretched. It would be weeks of trivia, of gossip, then if her knowledge of women living on top of each other was anything to go by, the inevitable fault finding, the backbiting. She would be the target, she was sure. And she was not strong enough to take it; she would buckle for certain. She'd tried telling herself that she was as good as anyone she'd met in Jasirapur; tried convincing herself that she should be proud of what she'd achieved against all the odds. But deep inside she knew she didn't really believe it.

Gerald started to walk towards her. She caught a glimpse of his figure reflected in the mirror and it was taut with tension. His voice, too, was tight and hard.

'That's ridiculous. I saw you talking quite happily with any number of the wives. You'll go, and you'll enjoy yourself.'

She shook her head and was near to tears again, but she was determined not to capitulate. As he drew closer, she rose to meet him. 'If I go, Gerald, it won't be willingly. You'll have to bind and gag me to get me on that train.'

'There's no need for these dramatics.' He shrugged his shoulders in a dismissive gesture. 'I know this country far better than you, which is something you seem to forget. And if I tell you it's for your own good that you go, you have to believe me.'

When she said nothing, his exasperation seemed to build in the silence and then spill over. 'I'm your husband, Daisy, which means you'll do as I wish.'

'Why is it so important to you that I go?'

The question had come to her out of the blue but it left him looking discomfited. She could see he was struggling with the situation and wondered why. He moved even closer and took the hairbrush from her grasp, then captured both her hands in his. His voice had a note of tenderness she hadn't heard before.

'If you won't do this for me, then do it for the baby. Simla is perfect. You must have heard that from everybody.

And there couldn't be a better place while you're in this condition. You'll love the gardens. You'll love the walking. There are dozens of gentle strolls to take. And when you get too tired, you can call a rickshaw. At night — think of it — you'll sleep soundly in cool air. How can you not want to go? How can you deny our child the very best start in life?'

His tone had grown more coaxing with every word and she felt herself warm against his body. She wanted his arms around her, wanted to hold him so tightly he would never escape. Instead, she eased her hands from out of his clasp. This was not the way she'd wanted to tell him, but she had no choice now.

'There is no child, Gerald. There is no baby.'

CHAPTER NINE

'What!'

'There was an accident . . .' Daisy faltered.

His face had turned ugly, contorted. 'So suddenly there's no baby. There was a baby when you needed to get married, though, wasn't there?' His normally slim figure seemed to grow bulkier, to fill the room with threat. He raised his hands as if to shake her, then let them fall slackly by his side. 'There never was a baby, was there?' he said bitterly. 'It was a tale you spun. A downright lie.'

No understanding then, no sympathy, no kind words. She tried to protest but her voice was weak, drained of conviction in the face of such hurtful injustice.

'How can you think that?'

He turned abruptly and strode to the door, then turned again and marched back to her.

'You've played me for a fool, that's how. You thought you'd catch yourself a husband and what better way to do it than pretend a pregnancy? And I thought you naive! You're a professional, Daisy, I underestimated you.'

'Don't, Gerald, please don't. You are wrong, very wrong. I was having a baby, I swear it, but there was an incident on the ship. There were prisoners, they were agitators — and they escaped from the ship's gaol and ran amok. They cannoned into me and I fell down a flight of stairs. The next thing I knew . . .'

Her voice broke. The whole dreadful scene was there before her. Flailing limbs, the sickening thump as she crunched onto the hard deck, pounding feet, loud voices and then a softer one in her ear — Grayson — and then the wetness between her legs and the dreadful realisation. Her eyes brimmed with tears at the memory.

Gerald was still smouldering, but her obvious distress silenced him for a moment. But only for a moment. 'If you really did have this accident,' he said roughly, 'then why not tell me about it in Bombay. Why not tell me before we married?'

'I planned to. I wanted to, but there was no chance.'

'What complete rubbish!' His scorn bit into her. 'You could have stopped the marriage at any time.'

'I was going to tell you what had happened when you met me at the port, but you weren't there. You didn't come as you promised. You sent Anish instead. And then when I arrived at the church, you were in no condition to talk.'

His face clenched. He did not deny the charge, but he seemed so overwhelmed with anger at the turn his life had taken, it was making him deaf to the truth.

'You could have found a way, if you'd wanted to. And if you hadn't sent that telegram—'

For a moment this new line of attack fazed her. 'But that was weeks ago.'

'It doesn't matter how long ago it was,' he said harshly, 'that did it for me. I was pushed into marrying, and you must have known I would be.' And when she stood looking blankly at him, he burst out, 'Don't pretend you don't know what you did. Sending a telegram to the regiment so every senior officer would read it and pass it to my Colonel. What chance did I have after that? I was summoned to account for myself — can you imagine what that felt like? Told the honour of the regiment depended on my doing the decent thing!'

'I had no idea that would happen.'

'Of course you hadn't. It's not an idea that would suit you. And it wouldn't suit you, would it, to know that junior officers need the Colonel's permission to marry? Though not this time, oh no. The baby saw to that. No questions asked, a wedding essential. Forester wasn't at all happy. The army pays no marriage allowance until I'm twenty-six and that's not until next year, but in the circumstances he had to agree.'

So that was what her companion at dinner had meant by a difficult business. She bowed her head, a small part of her appalled at the mayhem she'd set in motion. But the rest of her fought back. There had been a baby and it had been Gerald's, she insisted to herself, and as much his responsibility as hers.

'I wrote to you. The letters were addressed to you personally. I'm sorry if they never reached you.'

'They reached me,' he said grimly.

'Then why didn't you answer? It was only out of desperation that I sent the telegram.'

'I was thinking what best to do.' He looked down at the floor, refusing to look at her. 'You gave me no time to consider — and then you did this stupid thing.'

She walked up to him, forcing him to look at her. 'That's not true, Gerald. I wrote every week for a month. You know I did.'

But he was intent on his own injury and it was as though she had not spoken. 'Everyone on the station thinks I'm too young to be married. Did you know that? But I was forced into it. You forced me into it — and what was it all for? Nothing, absolutely nothing. No, I'm wrong. It has been for something.' His face glowered over her. 'It's been to make me look a complete fool. Word will get around, you can be sure, and when no child appears, I'll be the regimental patsy. How glorious that will be!'

In his agitation, he began again to pace up and down the room, his hands harrowing so fiercely through his hair she wondered that whole handfuls didn't come loose. She sank down onto the bed and her heart did a curious little plummet. Curious because she felt nothing. She should be distraught, weeping, wailing. His brutal words should have shredded her.

Instead, she was completely numb. The man she had thought her rock in life was nothing more than shifting sand; the man who had sworn to love her for ever was swearing now that he had been misled, manipulated by her, driven to actions he found repugnant. *Had* she pushed for marriage when it was something he hadn't wanted? No, he'd made the promise freely when there was no other reason to do so but love for her. She hadn't pushed him, he'd been the one doing the pushing. He'd been urgent in his wooing, drowning her in sweet words and sweet deeds.

She wanted nothing more than to hide away, pull the bedsheet over her face and forget the world existed. It was a struggle to speak, but she had to know for sure.

'Does that mean that you never loved me? That without your Colonel's order, you would never have married?'

Her voice was barely above a whisper and for the first time Gerald's face showed a fleeting guilt. 'It wasn't like that.' His voice dropped to a mumble. 'It's too soon. This was the last thing I needed.'

'But our time in London?'

'That was fun, Daisy, fun. That's all.'

He had come to a halt just feet away and she looked at him, a long and careful look. His face was mottled scarlet and the palest of whites.

'Was it fun to persuade me into giving myself to you, fun to promise marriage and not mean it?'

He had no answer and said sulkily, 'I had other plans.'

'What other plans?'

'It doesn't matter. They're dead in the water, destroyed, and all for nothing.' His anger was spent and he slumped wearily down on the fraying wicker chair. 'Do you know I came top of my class at Hanbury, top of my class at Sandhurst,' he said in a tight, high voice. 'That's how I got here against all the competition. I was going places and now I'm not.' Then, as an afterthought, he muttered, 'Every sacrifice made worthless.'

What was he talking about? Who had made sacrifices? Not his family surely, if he'd told her their true story. But if he hadn't . . . the letter from Spitalfields swam clearly into sight. To find the money for a boy to attend a top public school would be hard for an East End tailor, she thought, and then to equip that boy to become a cavalry officer in the Indian Army, even more so. Is that what had happened? Was that the sacrifice? Had Spitalfields not Somerset been Gerald's childhood playground and the Indian Army as far away from it as he could get? It seemed more than ever likely that he had lied to her about his past, just as he'd fed her fantasies during their weeks together in London.

If her suspicions were right, he had deceived her absolutely, yet a minute ago he'd dared to accuse *her* of deception. Her fault had been unintended, but his was squalid. He'd lied and then seduced her for 'fun'. She had been raised under a strict moral code and with her mother's dishonour ringing in her ears. So many times she had burned with shame when Lily Driscoll had been held up as a dreadful warning. The orphanage had made her pay for her mother's mistake. And she'd vowed that she would never repeat it.

But when she'd drunk alcohol for the first time that night, it had had all the effect Gerald could have wished. She'd known what was happening to her in that small room in Paddington but she'd pushed away the knowledge, wanting so much to please him, wanting to show him the depth of her love. Like a simpleton, she'd accepted what he told her — that they were simply anticipating the event, that they would marry very soon — and that was because they were words she'd wanted to hear.

They were both guilty of bad faith, she thought, but they were also man and wife and, whatever evils had passed between them, they must try to make some kind of life together. It was their only hope.

'Gerald,' she said gently, 'we've both been guilty of deception.' She felt his sharp glance, but said nothing of what she suspected. There was little point in unearthing what should stay buried. 'Perhaps we've been foolish in rushing into marriage but—'

'There's no perhaps about it.' His anger was back.

She tried again, keeping her voice as level as she could. 'Nevertheless, we are married and must make the best of it. So can we not try to put this behind us?'

It was no use. Her appeal vanished into the thick air that crowded in on them. His armour remained undented. When he rose from the chair, it was to stand looking down at her, his face a study of cynicism.

'You *are* naıve aren't you? My judgement was right the first time. As you helpfully point out, we're shackled together, and there's precious little we can do about it. But to ask me to put it behind me — how can you even think it? Don't you understand, you've ruined my life. Now tell me, how am I to forget that?'

He turned on his heels and marched towards the spare bedroom. His bedroom now, she realised with a shock. The door slammed behind him while she sat motionless, anchored to the one spot. In a few minutes, though, he re-emerged, this time fully dressed.

Seeing her startled face, he said brusquely, 'I can't stay here. I'm going out.'

'But it's eleven o'clock at night.'

He gave an irritated flick of his head and turned for the front door without another word. She heard his footsteps on the veranda, then the sound of the shabby bicycle being jumped down the steps. The image of Jocelyn Forester came to mind. It was difficult to imagine Gerald storming his Colonel's house at this late hour but perhaps the lovers had their own arrangement. And they were lovers, she was sure of that now. She had not been wrong about the perfume. Gerald had spoken of ruined plans and Jocelyn was part of them, while she was not.

She remained where she was for a very long while, trying to think her way through the morass. Whatever hopes he'd nursed, Gerald had married her and not Jocelyn. Married her, but not wanted her. Was she to be a wife in name only then, to smile and simper to the world, pretending that all was well? She could not bear to think it. A wave of weariness hit and she pulled back the sheet and climbed into bed. Her head found the pillow and she closed her eyes, listening hard for the song of the cicadas and hoping they might soothe her to sleep. But tonight there was no chance of that. Their scratchy chorus was soon overpowered, lost to the sound of the jackals that called in the dark.

CHAPTER TEN

When Daisy woke, heavy-eyed, it was to bright sunlight. It had been hours before she'd managed finally to sleep. After years of fiercely guarding her heart, she had opened it to Gerald. But even as she'd bathed in that happiness, she'd feared it was too good to be true. And she'd been right. From the moment they'd met again in Bombay, she'd felt him another man to the one she'd known, but she'd refused to think that he did not love her. Now it was out in the open. He had married her not from love but because the honour of the regiment demanded it. Last night she had barely been able to understand, but today the truth was scarred onto her mind.

It seemed she knew nothing of the man she had married, had not understood at all the passions that drove him. Passions that were strong enough to make him adopt another man's name. She guessed it was from shame, shame for his origins. It was an impulse she recognised: to adopt a new identity, to shrug off an earlier hated life. Hadn't she felt a similar desire every time the girls at Bridges had derided her for having been a servant, every time the servants at Miss Maddox's had taunted her for having come from Eden House?

But that was where the similarities ended. His mortification had led him to cut every tie, and that was something she couldn't understand. To belong to a family, to know the man and woman who had given you life, had been her dearest wish for as long as she could remember.

She was consumed with anger, not for Gerald but for herself. Anger at her own stupidity. He had called her naıve but she was beyond naıve. In the weeks before she'd left England, she had written constantly and when she'd received no answer, had thought her letters could not have reached him. She wondered now if they were hidden in the depths of his desk or had been straight away torn into fragments. In desperation, she'd sent the telegram with no idea that it would be read by anyone other than Gerald, no idea that it would lead to a passage on the *Viceroy of India* and a wedding at St John's. It was all so unbearably stupid.

How could she ever have imagined that a charming, successful, well-connected Gerald truly loved her? And how much less possible, then, was it to imagine the same of Jack Minns? If this were indeed her husband, then he was as burdened as she by the past. Jack Minns should have married for advantage; he should have made his family's sacrifice count.

Sounds of shuffling reached her from outside. Daisy staggered to her feet and slipped a wrapper over the flimsy nightdress. Peering through the plaited blind, she saw an elderly Indian sitting cross-legged on a small rug, which he'd spread across the width of the veranda. Half a dozen needles were stuck in his turban, each a different size and sporting a different colour thread. Head bent, he was busy looping a spool of cotton through an ancient sewing machine. Jocelyn had been as good as her word and this was the *durzi* she'd spoken of.

Daisy did not want to think of her, the English rose, the Colonel's daughter, an ample reward for any sacrifice. Jocelyn Forester had been Gerald's intended bride, it was clear, and everyone on the station knew it. No wonder the women at the Club had expressed surprise at the marriage he'd made so unexpectedly.

Still in her dressing gown, she drifted into the sitting room and sat herself down at the breakfast table. Pouring herself a cup of tea from the pot Rajiv had left, she managed only a few sips before there was a loud crash from beneath the sitting room window. A bicycle had been sent sprawling across the wooden planks of the veranda.

'Hallo there!'

It was the girl herself, bright and shining, her head craned around the door and a wide smile on her face. Surely no one could be that deceptive, but Gerald's bed had not been slept in and if he hadn't spent the night with her, where had he spent it? There was no time to think poisonous thoughts, though, for Jocelyn was already bouncing into the room.

'I'm sorry, Daisy. Did I get you out of bed?'

She murmured something about having had a bad night, and the girl nodded sympathetically. 'I can come back another time if you prefer. The *durzi*, too. I'll leave these catalogues with you.'

'No, please stay.' The words came out before Daisy could stop them. Strangely, she found she wanted the girl's company this morning but had no idea why. Perhaps it was a perverse wish to pick at a sore place or perhaps it was just that she was lonely and Jocelyn's was a friendly face. 'Rajiv has laid out some breakfast.'

'Wonderful! I can always eat a second *chota hazri*. And while we're eating, we can look through these.' She spilled the contents of a large canvas bag onto the table. 'I've brought the *Army and Navy* catalogue and the *Whiteaway and Laidlaw*. There's even a couple of *Vogues* — they belonged to my cousin who stayed with us over the winter. Julia is a walking fashion plate!'

In between mouthfuls of mango, they flicked through the pages of glossy images, immersing themselves in the serious business of choosing two or three styles suitable to give to the *durzi*. They shared a few grimaces for the more outdated fashions, and a few chuckles at the most ludicrous of the outfits and, despite Daisy's best efforts to remain distant, she found herself warming to her visitor. Eventually, several dresses were agreed upon and given mutual approval.

'This one is interesting.' Jocelyn pursed her lips. 'It may look like a shift but it should make up well in very light cotton and it will be ideal. Until you go to Simla, that is.'

Daisy felt herself being scrutinised and knew that her intention to stay in Jasirapur had already been relayed. Gerald was the only one who could have passed on that small nugget and she felt her mouth tighten at the thought. For a while, she'd forgotten what must lie between this girl and her husband.

'I'm not going to Simla — but no doubt you already know that.' Her voice was devoid of any warmth and Jocelyn flushed at her tone.

'I had heard,' she admitted, 'but I was hoping you would reconsider.'

'No, I don't think so,' and she got up abruptly to thrust the magazines into a rough pile.

'I'm sorry if I've upset you,' Jocelyn said awkwardly. Then, quite unexpectedly, she reached for Daisy's hand. 'I don't want to intrude, Daisy — it's your decision, obviously — but staying here is not the best idea. Really, it isn't. *I* lived through the summer in Jasirapur one year. Ma wasn't well enough to travel and by the time she felt better, it wasn't worth making the journey. But it was hell, I can tell you. You may be coping with the heat at the moment, but after weeks and weeks of feeling as though you're being fried alive, you can start to feel ill. At the very least, you'll feel utterly miserable.'

'I know it won't be comfortable, but Gerald and I are only just married and my place is beside my husband.' For the first time in her life, she felt a hypocrite. Watching Jocelyn very carefully for her response, she also felt devious. Was she hoping to beard the girl with the reality of Gerald's marriage or simply confirm her suspicion that they were something more than friends?

But Jocelyn's face showed only understanding. 'It must be awful to be separated so soon after your wedding, I can see that. I would hate it, too. But the menfolk usually manage to come up for a few days once or twice, so it might not be as bad as you fear. If you change your mind, let my mother know. We're not leaving for two days and she'll rustle up a ticket for you in no time.'

'Thank you, I'll remember.' The girl's seeming innocence confused Daisy and in the face of such evident goodwill, it was difficult to maintain her coldness. 'Tell me, does the *durzi* take my measurements, or does he just guess at them?'

Jocelyn giggled. 'He has a tape measure which he waves around, while rigidly averting his eyes. I'll go and get him. Have you given him the materials?'

'Not yet, I'm afraid. I overslept and I'm in a complete muddle.'

'Not to worry,' and Jocelyn was out of the front door and calling to the *durzi*.

Thirty minutes later the man had his measurements, together with instructions as to which picture went with which material.

'You'll look a star!' Jocelyn exclaimed, lovingly smoothing first one bolt of cloth and then another. 'You've chosen beautiful materials. Where did you get them?'

'Anish Rana took me to the bazaar and introduced me to one of the stallholders. His name was Sanjay, but I don't remember the name of the shop.'

Jocelyn was looking thoughtful. 'I hope you won't mind me saying this, but you shouldn't make too much of a friend of Anish.'

Daisy thought she knew what was coming, but she still asked, 'Why not?'

'He's an Indian.'

'But he's also an officer with the regiment.'

'I know but there are clear demarcations. It's fine to socialise with him on regimental occasions, but otherwise you should avoid being too much in his company.' A swift look at her hostess's face and she was constrained to add, 'It's wise to conform, my dear.'

Daisy knew it was pointless to protest. The arcane rules by which the army lived were as illogical as they were baffling.

'Is there anything else I should know — apart from not making friends with Indians?' She tried to keep her voice calm but she couldn't prevent a sharpness creeping in. Jocelyn looked at her a little warily.

'If you've never had servants before . . .' she began, and then tailed off, evidently uncomfortable. Daisy smiled encouragingly at her. 'If you're not used to servants, Daisy, you shouldn't be frightened of them. Make sure that Rajiv — it is Rajiv, isn't it — make sure that he boils all your water and washes the vegetables in *pinki pani*. And your *mali*, whoever he is, should be told to get on with the job. The garden is in a desperate state.'

'You're right. The garden is hideous, but we don't have a gardener.'

'No *mali*? How extraordinary!'

She allowed Jocelyn to exclaim for a while and then asked, 'Can you tell me what a *jemader* is?' She might as well learn as much as she could.

'He's the chap who washes the floors and cleans the bathrooms. I suppose you don't have one of those either.'

'No, I'm sorry to disappoint. Rajiv does it all.'

'Then you should talk to Gerald. One man can't do everything and it's essential you have help in this climate.'

She remembered that Rosemary Laughton also intended to talk to Gerald. It was hardly the best time and, in truth, she would rather things stayed the same. It would be unnerving to be surrounded by more servants, some of them no doubt as hostile as Rajiv.

But Jocelyn was now in full swing. 'And you've no electricity by the look of it. So that's a *punkah wallah* you'll be needing. too.'

'A what?'

'He's the man who sits on the veranda and pulls the rope to the *punkah*. That's a big frill of material that hangs across the room — just a very large fan. He sits on the veranda and pulls a string threaded through the window and that moves the *punkah*. Usually he lays on his back with the string attached to his big toe. Sometimes he pulls, but a lot of the time he sleeps.'

Daisy could not prevent a small laugh escaping. The image Jocelyn had conjured was comic.

'It works,' her visitor said seriously. 'Really it does.' Then she, too, began to laugh.

Halfway through packing the unwanted magazines back into her canvas bag, Jocelyn suddenly asked, 'How did you two meet?'

'It was in London when Gerald was on leave.' If Jocelyn were as close to her husband as she imagined, she should surely know.

'How romantic that must have been.' Jocelyn sighed. 'Usually it's girls coming out from England to bag a husband rather than a man carrying off his beloved back to India.'

She was beginning to feel less and less sure she'd been right about Jocelyn. The girl was so transparent, or at least she seemed so.

'The fishing fleet you mean.' Daisy was pleased that she'd remembered the Colonel's words.

'That's right. When we heard that Gerald was to marry, we knew it had to be true love. Daddy wouldn't tell us any details, though. He's as close as a clam when he needs to be.'

'There aren't many details to tell.'

'I'm sure there are. But I'm glad Gerald found you. He needs a wise woman.'

'He does?' This was a new idea. She was far from wise and she couldn't see how Gerald had any need of her. 'Why is that?'

'He doesn't always act sensibly.' Jocelyn's tone was tentative and her face flushed a bright pink. 'There are stories . . . but I shouldn't worry you. All young men can be a little wild, can't they?'

'I don't know many young men,' Daisy answered honestly.

'You soon will.'

'So how has Gerald been wild?' If she could persuade Jocelyn to talk, the girl might reveal more than she should of her feelings. Jocelyn was open and sunny, but Daisy couldn't forget she was also the woman that Gerald had wanted to marry.

'Wild is probably not the right word. Everyone drinks too much, of course, but sometimes Gerald overdoes it rather. I'm sure it will be different now that you're here. Everyone gambles, too, but . . .' She left the sentence unfinished and rose to go. 'I'll leave you in peace but I've enjoyed this morning tremendously. I'm sorry you aren't coming to Simla. I'm sure we'd have had fun.'

Daisy only smiled in response for she was already replaying their conversation in her mind. Gerald had been drunk at the altar, not with normal wedding nerves but because he dreaded going through with the ceremony. That was now horribly clear. But according to Jocelyn he regularly drank to excess. And gambled. That took money. Was that why there were no servants other than Rajiv, because he could not afford to pay their wages? And then there was the letter. His father, if Joseph Minns were indeed his father, wanted money, too. No wonder Gerald felt bitter towards her. She had been a huge disappointment; she had brought nothing to the marriage, not even a child.

She got up to see Jocelyn to the door and her knees buckled. The girl turned in concern and held on to her arm to steady her.

'I'm sorry.' Daisy said. 'I don't know where that came from.' Her head was spinning and she had to stand still for several minutes before she felt able to move again.

'It's the heat, my dear, unless . . .'

'No,' she said hurriedly. 'Nothing like that.'

'Remember what I said about the sun. You're very new to the climate. It can have some nasty effects. But I haven't given up entirely on your travelling to Simla. You've still got time, just about, and if you decide to come, send me a message and I'll come over and help you pack.'

Daisy murmured her thanks, though she had no intention of taking up the invitation.

'When I get back, we must persuade Gerald to move you onto the station, then we'll be near neighbours. There's a bungalow vacant, I know, and I can't understand why he didn't apply for it. This place is so remote and hardly "Ideal Home".' Then she looked crestfallen. 'I'm sorry, I shouldn't have said that.'

'Don't apologise. I agree with you. The house is certainly shabby and far too isolated. I find that quite worrying. There was a man in the garden in the middle of the night, you know.' She hadn't meant to say anything but somehow she'd blurted it out. 'At least, I think there was. I heard a noise, someone coughing and, when I looked out of the window, I saw a figure.'

Jocelyn's eyes widened. 'What kind of figure?'

'A man, I think. Dressed in white. A long top, maybe, over baggy trousers. Indian clothes.'

'Are you sure?'

'I should be. It was bright moonlight but, if I'm honest, I can't really be certain. It was only for a second that I saw him. It was like seeing a ghost.'

Jocelyn perked with excitement. 'You know, it might have been. Ages ago I was told this land was once a burial site.' Daisy's expression reflected her discomfort at this news.

'I'm sorry, that was thoughtless.' The girl patted her hand consolingly. 'But you don't really believe in ghosts, do you? It's much more likely to be a local and I'm sure he wouldn't have meant any harm. There's very little crime in Jasirapur — maybe he didn't realise the bungalow was inhabited. It was empty for a long time before Gerald moved in.'

Daisy grasped at the explanation. 'You must be right. That's just what it was. Perhaps someone looking for somewhere he could smoke in peace.'

'Whoever he was,' the girl said firmly, 'the sooner you move into the cantonment the better.' Daisy had to agree. Ghost or peace seeker, she would rather not have an unknown man wandering through her garden at the dead of night.

CHAPTER ELEVEN

She watched Jocelyn pedal out of sight and then turned her steps towards the bedroom. It was almost noon; the bungalow was oozing heat and she felt weak and faint from its effects. Lying fully clothed on top of the bed, she listened to the whirring of the sewing machine a few yards away. It was a drowsy, soothing sound. She heard Rajiv making his way around the house, throwing buckets of water at each of the woven blinds. Not at hers though. The *durzi* would not appreciate a drenching as he worked, and the thought produced a wry smile.

But why on earth was she smiling? What a mess she was in. A mess? The words were wrong. They were too mundane for the situation she faced. While Jocelyn had been with her, she had been able to forget her predicament. The girl was so natural, so friendly, that she'd largely disregarded the suspicions she harboured. But whether Jocelyn was involved with Gerald or not, last night's quarrel had happened and it had left her . . .

How had it left her? She was unsure. She should be broken-hearted but it didn't feel that way. She felt numb certainly, but not destroyed. Something had changed. Was it Gerald's behaviour since she'd arrived in India? Or had she just thought herself in love with him in London, carried away by the romance of being wined and dined by a handsome young man in a way she had never known before? She toyed with the idea that unaccustomed spoiling rather than true love had broken through the defences she'd built.

She supposed she would never know. The human heart was too complicated, and it was the here and now with which she had to contend. She wondered if there would ever come a time when they found a way of living together, of being truly husband and wife. A day when they'd become a family, a day when another baby would feel right for them both. Her body began to throb with a familiar pain. It felt like a physical wound, a bullet that had penetrated soft tissue and lodged there. That was the true meaning of heartbreak, she realised. It was the loss of the child that hurt her so much, not the loss of Gerald. He had rejected her and that was a humiliation, but she'd had plenty of those in her short life. She could overcome humiliation.

* * *

She must have fallen into an uneasy doze because when she heard the voice calling her, she started up in a daze. It was the *durzi* at the front door. She stumbled towards him, her head fuzzy with sleep.

'Dresses ready for you to try, memsahib.' The old man offered her a neatly folded pile of materials. 'You try,' he was insisting.

She took the clothes from his hands and held out each of the roughly sewn dresses, one at a time. She was amazed at how much he had done in the hours she'd lain sleeping. The clock showed her that it was well into the afternoon and Rajiv had not called her for lunch. Since his water-throwing activities, she had not heard from him at all. She walked past the *durzi* and out onto the veranda and looked around. There was no sign of cooking in the kitchen. No sign of Gerald either. Lunch must have been cancelled without her knowing.

'You want me to try them now?'

'I come back two days. You try before.'

'Thank you. I will. I'm sure you've done a very good job.'

He said nothing more but picked up the sewing machine at his feet and the large bag he carried containing all he needed for his trade.

'Two days then?' she checked. He nodded and walked down the path towards the road leading back to the town.

Out on the veranda, the air was blistering and the sun a pitiless glare. Quickly, she retreated into the darkness of the bungalow. The day's air was stale within and cloyingly thick, but she was beginning to feel a great deal better. After such a wretched night, she had needed to sleep. She would try on the clothes now, she decided, while she had the house to herself.

The first dress slipped over her shoulders. It was cut from a semi-sheer rayon, a pretty black and white print, and it felt cool and comfortable to the touch. A loose bow finished the V-shaped neckline, and the matching 'v' at the back of the dress was decorated with a beautiful black-crested button. Standing on tiptoe to see her reflection in the small mirror that hung high on the wall of her bedroom, she was disappointed she could barely make out the neck and shoulders. The bathroom was where she needed to be — its mirror was bigger and hung at a better angle.

The frock was a perfect fit for her slim form, its skirt cut on the bias, and flaring into a flattering arc as she twirled this way and that. Minutes passed as she continued to gaze at the figure reflected in the mirror. It was difficult to take her eyes from the girl who shone out of the glass, and an unfamiliar delight stealing through her. She had never before had such a pretty dress; she had never before looked like this. And there were two more such lying invitingly on her bed. She must try them while she could indulge herself in this wonderful new pleasure undistracted; with luck Rajiv would stay invisible for a while longer.

Eagerly she turned to go, but something bright and glittering caught her eye. It was on the floor beneath the washstand and she wondered if it was a broken ornament or glass that Rajiv had swept beneath the basin, meaning to clear it later. Her vision was slightly blurred by the heat and she bent down to examine the object more closely. Her hand reached towards it — then her heart almost stopped. It was a head that she saw, a head shining amber, amber and grey, now rearing upwards, its spreading hood a fearsome sight. It was a snake and it was ready to strike.

She tried to scream but no sound emerged. Her mind was telling her to back out through the open bathroom door, but her legs refused to work. The snake leaned in towards her, angry at being disturbed. Its neck was growing thicker and its tongue and head flicking in a dangerous rhythm.

'Rajiv!' Her voice croaked the name.

'Rajiv!' Stronger now, but still the servant did not come.

'Rajiv!' she screamed, and this time the sound pierced the air and caused the snake to rear its head even higher.

Then a sudden noise behind her, and she was pushed roughly aside. 'Go into your bedroom and shut the door. Stay there until I call you.'

Grayson Harte. Somehow Daisy found the strength to fight her paralysis and was out of the bathroom and into her bedroom in a matter of seconds, shutting herself securely away and sending up a prayer of thanks as she did so. But what was Grayson doing here? And where was Rajiv? Even if he'd gone to the market, he must have returned by now. But he had not answered her desperate calls.

She slumped down on the bed, her limbs shuddering uncontrollably. How long she stayed there she had no idea, only that her mind was filled with the most terrible thoughts. What was Grayson doing? Had he been attacked and was even now lying injured or worse on the bathroom floor? If only her legs would stop this agonising judder, she might gain sufficient courage to open the door and find out.

A soft tap made her sit up, her body stiff with alarm. The door opened a fraction. 'It's all right. It's safe to come out.'

With an enormous effort, she got to her feet and moved one small step at a time towards him.

'The snake is dead,' Grayson said bluntly.

'You killed it?'

'I had to. It wasn't leaving otherwise.'

She looked a little sick. 'I'm not a snake charmer, Daisy. I had to do it.'

'I know. I'm sorry. It's just horrible.'

'You were lucky that it didn't attack you when you first disturbed it. The bite can be fatal if you don't get help immediately. It paralyses the nervous system.'

'Then it's even luckier that you heard me calling. Were you walking by?'

'I doubt that you walk by this bungalow — it's way off the beaten track. I had the afternoon free and thought I'd look you up. See how India was agreeing with you. But are you on your own here?'

'I called Rajiv but he appears to have gone missing for the day.'

'So that's who you were calling. There was certainly no sign of him. In fact, when I pulled up, the place looked deserted and I was about to turn back. But something — I don't know what — made me walk into the house and I felt the danger even before I heard you.'

She managed a weak smile and, seeing her wavering expression, he took her by the arm and led her to the sitting room and into a chair. 'Snakes sometimes find their way into bathrooms,' he said thoughtfully. 'The smaller ones can crawl through the drainage hole, but a snake that big . . .'

'It must have crept in from the garden.'

Grayson was frowning. 'It would be unusual. Cobras are large creatures and need to go where there's plenty of food. Why come into the house when there's a huge unkempt space outside to feed on.'

'Perhaps it took a wrong turning.' It was an attempt at a joke, though she still felt extremely queasy.

'Perhaps it did.' He was willing, it seemed, to let the subject drop, gazing at her with concern. 'You're not looking well. Can I get you some water?'

'Thank you. I'm afraid I can't stop the shaking. It's making me feel very stupid. I'm obviously not brave enough to live in India.'

'Not so. You've had a tremendous shock.' He filled a glass from the carafe of water that sat on the sideboard. 'Most people finding a cobra in their bathroom would react the same. It doesn't help that you're on your own here. And the heat makes things worse.'

Daisy wondered if he was about to join the chorus, urging her to go to Simla. If the idea was in his mind, he didn't mention it and she was glad. Thankfully, she accepted the water and sat quietly until her heart had regained its steady beat.

'I don't want to stay here this afternoon,' she said at last. 'I'd really like to have a break from these four walls.'

He nodded his understanding. 'I think I can arrange that. In fact, I might know just the right place — *and* I've a horse and carriage to take us there.' He walked over to the table and picked up her discarded *topi*. 'So what do you say?'

CHAPTER TWELVE

Daisy's face was still frozen with shock when Grayson helped her climb into the carriage, and unable to stop herself grasping his hand as though he were saving her from drowning. But once the pony began its forward trot, she felt the tightness in her skin disappear and her colour return.

'Where are we going?' She wasn't really interested. Anywhere would do as long as it was far from a bungalow she'd been desperate to leave. But he'd done her an immense service and she must try to be good company.

'You'll have to wait. It's a surprise. But it's a peaceful place, I promise. Almost secret.'

They jolted their way along the narrow, curving lane leading from the house and were soon at the main road, only slightly wider and a little less rutted than the track they'd just traversed. At the junction, Grayson flicked his whip and the horse turned left, towards a rolling landscape of field after field of sugar cane, stretching flatly into the distance.

'It's pretty peaceful already, don't you think?'

She nodded agreement and settled back into the buggy's worn seat. They were travelling at a fair speed, whisking past clumps of tall sunflowers which clustered on either side of the road, yellow sentinels guarding the fields beyond. Brightness and warmth were everywhere, spilling over the world and into her heart. She could feel herself almost melting into the landscape and hugged the sensation close.

Grayson kept his eyes on the road, steering the pony clear of the steep ditch that ran alongside them and making a very good job of it. She smiled. 'You seem to know this route well.'

'I'm getting to know it. And most of the other tracks in the area that have the temerity to call themselves roads.'

'It's lucky for me you're still braving the byways, or you wouldn't have called today.' She glanced across at him, trying to decide whether to probe further. 'I was told that District Officers worked miles from town. But maybe I have it wrong.'

'No,' he answered easily, 'not wrong. I'm based in Jasirapur for the moment but I make regular forays up country.'

'And you're still enjoying the job, I hope?'

'I am. It's interesting. But then, India can't fail to be interesting, can it?'

They were passing through a village and, at its centre, a well was being worked by a patient bullock. Several women were collecting water and hid their faces behind saris. Despite their poverty, they walked with pride and with a lithe grace Daisy could only envy. On their heads, they carried brass pots, burnished by the sun. One shapely raised arm supported each pot as, bare footed, they glided through the dust. Several of the village children had spied the carriage and tumbled out of doorways to wave and begin an impromptu dance. Daisy clapped her hands to show her appreciation.

'Everything I see amazes me.' She looked back over her shoulder at the dancing children. 'Of course, you already know India, but it's all new to me.'

'I'm only familiar with one small part,' he warned. 'That's not at all the same as knowing India. Rajputana is very different.' They had left the village behind now and were once more on the open road.

'It was United Provinces you were in, wasn't it? Do you still have family there?'

'My uncle and great-uncle still run the business near Ayodhya. Herbert — that's my great-uncle — is really too old to do more than walk into the plant each morning, interfere for an hour or two, and then walk back.'

'But you could visit them?'

'It's difficult. UP may be a neighbouring state but it's a considerable distance, and at the moment work takes up all my time.'

'This afternoon though . . .'

'An exception. We're waiting on news from Europe but, in the interim, I've a few hours free.' He saw her look of surprise. 'We're not insulated from what's going on in the rest of the world, you know. If Britain is in difficulties, the entire Empire is affected, particularly India. It can be the perfect opportunity for anyone hoping to stir up trouble. And there are plenty of them. We've had one campaign of civil disobedience after another.'

Daisy was beginning to feel out of her depth. 'I'm not sure what difficulties you mean,' she ventured. 'We don't have a radio at the bungalow and I've heard no news since I left the ship.'

'It's probably just as well. The news from Europe isn't good. There are rumours of German troop movements on the Czech border, and confirmation that Germany has ordered an expansion of the Luftwaffe.'

'Does that mean there will definitely be a war?'

'Everyone hopes not but it seems to be coming closer. Memories of the last bloodbath might deter the hotheads, but Hitler is another matter altogether.'

'I hadn't realised the ICS had so much to do with politics.'

'Certain branches of it do,' he said vaguely.

'And it's where you've found your niche?'

'It seems that way.'

'Your family must be very pleased for you.'

'Let's say they're glad they don't have to scratch their heads over me anymore. I've been something of a problem for them in the past. Not that I'm ungrateful for the help they've given me — and my mother, too. They've been very good to both of us, particularly in the circumstances.'

She wished she knew him well enough to ask what those circumstances might be, and was glad when he seemed happy to talk on. 'I don't think they've ever forgiven my mother for marrying an impoverished artist. They're still prone to remind her of the "bad" match she made. But it didn't stop them buying her a charming flat in Pimlico and giving me a first-class education. It wasn't their fault I never quite came up to scratch. I simply didn't fit the moulds they saw me filling — as a military man or a business wallah.'

The road appeared to have tired of being straight, and for a while Grayson was taken up with manoeuvring the carriage safely around a series of severe bends. 'I guess I was a bit of a black sheep,' he said eventually, but his grin took the sting out of the words.

'I can't believe that. You look to me the perfect sahib!'

'You wouldn't be teasing me, would you?'

'Only a little.' And she had an answering smile on her face.

He was pulling off the road on to a thin, sandy path. It appeared to lead nowhere and after five minutes of bumping and jolting, he brought the carriage to a halt.

'I'm afraid we must walk the rest of the way. I hope you're up to it.'

He helped her down and for a moment his arm caught her round the waist. She remembered another time when his arm had held her. All those weeks ago, when he'd lifted her from the ship's deck and helped her back to her cabin. She'd stayed there for several days and when she saw him again, had invented a story about a stomach upset. He'd never appeared too curious, but she knew he'd probably wondered at the illness. She had looked little more than a ghost when she'd finally emerged.

They were following the path downwards, and more to deflect her thoughts from that dreadful moment than anything else, she said, 'Do your parents have connections with India?'

'Only through my mother's brother and uncle in Ayodhya. My father was a potter and India has sufficient potters of its own.'

'Your father is dead?'

'He died when I was a boy. He was on a train from Stoke, returning home. He'd been to a prestigious ceramic exhibition there and won third prize with a beautiful vase. It was red and white with a silver top and bottom. But there was a fault with the track and the train came off the rails. He didn't survive the crash but strangely the vase did.'

'I'm so sorry.'

'I don't remember much about him, to be honest. It's my mother I feel most sorry for. Whatever my uncles might claim, it was a love match. She was devoted to him and she's never remarried. I think she still has the vase, though she keeps it well out of sight. I imagine it brings back bad memories.'

The path had dwindled to nothing and they had to pick their way slowly between huge boulders which seemed to have been thrown at random, as though one morning a giant had woken in a tantrum and decided he didn't much like the house he lived in. The path became still more difficult when even larger stones rose up to bar their way. A veritable thicket of them, but this time carved into statues of Hindu deities. Together they inched their way past, Daisy giving the towering monuments a swift glance and, as swiftly, looking away. There were statues that were animated, dancing their way to heaven with bells on their toes, and statues that had lost their hands, their rough stumps reaching out in supplication. Others wore serene faces, filled with a knowledge of beauty beyond this world, and there were some that were quite terrifying, with bulbous eyes and a gash for a toothless mouth.

Once through the thicket, they were standing above the place Grayson had wanted her to see. Crumbling stone steps led down to a large paved rectangle, now dry and bleached, but once, she imagined, filled with water. At one end of the rectangle there was an uneven pile of rubble, all that was left of a once splendid building, but nearer to them the remains of a second temple were in better condition.

There were columns still intact and row after row of intricately carved figures looking out across a tranquil emptiness. The golden glow of stone, the shimmering blue of the sky and a hot yellow sun combined to make a gloriously vivid scene. Yet, despite its intensity, the site radiated the deepest sense of peace that Daisy had ever encountered. It was as though she had been born to know this place and this moment.

She stood wide-eyed, scarcely taking a breath. 'It's quite, quite beautiful.'

'I'm glad you think so. I've learned to love it since I've been here. There were two temples, I found out, one at each end of an expanse of water, and both built for a local deity, a goddess called Nandni Mata. The name means "daughter". I'm not sure what happened. The temples probably lost favour and over the centuries have been allowed to fall into ruins. Shall we walk down so you can have a closer look?'

He took her by the hand and led the way down the steps. It seemed a natural thing to do and she liked the feeling of her palm encased in strong fingers. They were soon at the bottom and walking towards the delicately carved columns of what was left of the temple. A flat terrace lay behind the columns, supported by one after another of fluted arches, echoing shapes receding into the distance with the bright blue of the sky encased within the final arch.

'The workmanship is superb.' He fingered the elaborate pattern of coiled rings and honeycomb spaces that covered the surface of each arch. 'And take a look at some of the gods that have been carved out of a different stone and somehow moulded into the arches. Their figures have been protected by the roof and survived pretty well.'

Daisy walked up to one of the arches. Something had attracted her to this particular one and, when she drew close, she saw the figure of a goddess emerging from the stone, triumphant and alive. A goddess with an ornately carved headdress and arms covered in bracelets. A girdle wound its way around her waist and her sinuous form moved as though it would dance out of the black, shiny stone. The eyes were closed in ecstatic appreciation.

The girl traced the line of the two necklaces that wound around the statue's neck, and stopped when she touched the centre of the lower chain and the pendant-shaped stone that hung from it. Her fingers passed over the emblem almost lovingly. She bent her head to it and her cheeks were flushed.

'What is it?'

'I remember this from somewhere. I don't know where.'

'A place you've visited?'

She wrinkled her nose. The flush had died, and she was intent on recovering a memory. 'No, not a place. A person. My mother . . .'

'She had a necklace similar to this?'

'That's it! Not a necklace though. A brooch. It's in the photograph. I've just one picture of her. She's in nurses' uniform but she's wearing a small brooch at the neck of the dress. I noticed it because I thought it strange to see jewellery. I've always imagined there were strict rules about what nurses could wear with their uniform. But there was a brooch, and I'm sure it looked just like this.'

'Do you have the photograph here with you in India?'

Of course she did. She had brought everything with her, every one of her earthly possessions.

'Yes. I can check when I get back to the house but, if I'm right, why would my mother have a brooch the same shape as the necklace of an Indian goddess? And a goddess from this particular district?'

'All kinds of motifs from temple carvings end up in all kinds of jewellery. Brooches, pendants, earrings. You can buy them in the bazaar any day, and not just the bazaar. I imagine Bridges — it was Bridges you worked for? — might even have some on their jewellery counter.'

'I suppose so.' Her voice was wistful. 'But it's a strange coincidence.'

'When you've been in India a while, you won't think so. Coincidence is only another word for fate.'

CHAPTER THIRTEEN

They turned to go, out from the shadowed arches and into the sun that blazed across the open space. As swiftly as they could, they retraced their path up the terrace of steps, and collapsed beneath the shade of one of the carved columns.

Grayson mopped his face with a large, white handkerchief. It was freshly laundered, she saw. He'd come well prepared, but then he would always be prepared for life's trials, Daisy was sure, whatever they were.

They'd rested a while before he said, 'Is that all you have of your mother — a single photograph?'

She nodded and looked across at the ruins of the temple, her mind for the moment elsewhere. The orphanage had been unwilling to give her even that, and one of the helpers who had a fondness for her had smuggled it to her the night before she left.

'And your father?'

She supposed it was only fair she answered him. She'd asked Grayson about his own father, though the case was not the same. At least, he'd known his parent. It was painful to confess how little information she had, yet she liked him well enough to confide what she knew.

'I don't know who my father was,' she murmured. Constraint gripped her for the moment and she found it difficult to continue. Her fingers began to pick at her dress, creasing its smooth folds into tiny lines, but then she volunteered, 'There's no name on my birth certificate, you see, and I never had a chance to ask my mother. She died before I was two.'

'And you have no other relatives who could tell you?'

'None, or at least none I know of. When my mother died, I was sent to an orphanage. Eden House, Cobb Street, Spitalfields.'

It was almost a mantra. She'd chanted it to herself so many times over the years and its sound was an echo of the loneliness that clung to her. She'd said too much though; what she had told him must remain between them.

'My husband knows nothing of this,' she warned.

'Has he never asked you about your family?'

'We haven't talked much of our families. I don't think Gerald was at home a great deal. He left as a young boy to go to boarding school.'

'I know. Hanbury.'

The single word startled her. Gerald had often spoken of Hanbury but her companion's calm announcement had shocked her. It was as though an explosion had been detonated between them. He saw her face and tried to explain. 'I was at school there, too. It's the kind of place you get sent if your family has military connections. Or wants them. Any connection in fact to the Empire, particularly to India.'

'So you knew Gerald?' She held her breath.

'I recognised him the other day in the bazaar,' he said carefully.

His tone told her everything. He knew of Gerald's double life. He had to. 'And what was Hanbury like?' She was playing for time, hoping she might lure him into admitting he'd known her husband as Jack Minns.

But if he had, he was keeping his counsel. 'It was like most such schools. There were good things about it and bad.

I remember a good deal of bullying, but then there always is at public school and some boys have a knack for it. It's not always the rough stuff either, the blows, the kicks, the hair yanking. But more insidious things like blackmail. Spying on you, for instance, watching your every move so that if you fall foul of a school rule — and there are plenty to fall foul of — you're threatened with disclosure. Unless, of course, you polish the boy's shoes or tidy his room or give him the rather nice cake your aunt has sent.'

It was clear Grayson was relating his own experience. But was it Gerald he was speaking of? His tale was too detailed, too specific, not to have one particular boy in mind. It might have been Gerald, she thought — she'd been on the receiving end of that same cold calculation — but Grayson was not about to enlighten her. She supposed it was not the kind of thing you said to a man's wife.

She shaded her eyes and looked up at the sky. 'The sun is much lower now.'

'It must be time to go then. Our journey back should be cooler.'

He offered her his arm and she felt the warm touch of skin. She looked up and caught his expression just for a moment, then quickly looked away. He was careful not to touch her again as they picked their way back through the scattered boulders to the pony who had been happily grazing by the side of the track.

By the time they approached the village once more, twilight was dropping fast, and wood smoke mixed with the beautiful smell drifting from the fields on either side. Neither of them spoke during the short journey and when they drove up to the bungalow, Grayson made no move to get down from the buggy. It was better this way, she thought; a meeting with Gerald would be too difficult.

She clambered down unaided and looked up at him, feeling a sudden shyness. 'Thank you, Grayson. Thank you for the temple. I shall remember it.'

She walked a little way towards the house while he remained where he was, watching her. But before she reached the veranda steps, a thought brought her back to the carriage. 'Thank you, too, for despatching the cobra.'

'I won't say it was my pleasure, but I'd urge you to tell your husband what happened. He should know there are cobras around. And he needs to make sure your servants come when you call them.'

'There's only Rajiv to come.'

'He's the only man you employ?'

'Yes. But I know all about *malis* and *jemaders* and *punkah wallahs*.'

'Do you indeed?' He sounded amused. 'Then you and British India are getting truly acquainted.'

* * *

Gerald arrived minutes after the pony and trap had disappeared in a cloud of red dust. He strode through the door, according Daisy a perfunctory nod, and then disappeared to change his clothes. They were creased and sweaty from several hours at the Club which she knew provided the afternoon's entertainment, though at this time of the year little more than billiards or cards. When he reappeared, Rajiv was already waiting to serve dinner. The man had arrived back at the compound as mysteriously as he'd vanished earlier in the day. She wondered whether or not she should tell Gerald of his absence. Grayson had advised her to but Grayson was not here, nor did he know the dire state of their marriage.

The meal was eaten quickly and in silence and, when the last plates had been cleared, Gerald stood up and stretched his long limbs. 'I'm off to the Mess. A couple of chaps and I have got a game going. Don't wait up for me. You look all in, you should have an early night. I expect you've had too much sun. I did warn you.'

So they were not to discuss their situation and she was to be left alone once more. Daisy's spirit hardened. 'Something happened today which frightened me a great deal.'

His eyebrows rose slightly but otherwise he looked less than interested.

'A snake, a cobra found its way into the bathroom. I nearly picked it up.'

'You would have had a problem. They weigh a ton.'

He went across to the desk and began gathering together several packs of cards and a small heap of notes and coins.

Daisy bounced up from her chair. 'I'm serious, Gerald. They're very dangerous, aren't they? It was only the fact that Grayson Harte decided to call that saved me.'

'Harte! What was he doing here?'

'You know him then?' He must do, she thought, but he wouldn't want to acknowledge it. That would bring him perilously close to declaring his true identity.

Her husband didn't answer and she went on, 'He came to say hello, nothing more, but it was fortunate that he did. He killed the snake.'

Gerald still said nothing but edged towards the door. She wanted to shake him. He seemed oblivious to the danger she'd been in. 'I called for Rajiv, two or three times, but he didn't come. He simply disappeared and for the whole day. At least I think he disappeared. I didn't go near his quarters so I can't be sure.'

'On no account should you. I don't expect he heard you calling.'

'I screamed. And if he was in the kitchen, he was only a stone's throw away. He must have heard me.'

'Then he wasn't there. He'd probably gone to the bazaar to buy food.'

'He didn't tell me he was going and he usually does. Grayson thought it odd that I was alone here.'

Gerald glared down at her. 'I find it odd that Grayson Harte has the time to pay social visits. I gather from Club gossip that he's a District Officer, or supposed to be. So why isn't he up country? What's he doing in Jasirapur?'

'I know nothing about his work, except that he appears to be very busy.'

'I bet he is, interfering in people's lives.'

'What do you mean?'

'Well, why was he here?' he repeated. 'Why appear out of the blue just when you needed help? Was it so he could rush in and play Sir Galahad?'

She looked perplexed, unsure of what he was getting at.

'You knew him on board ship, didn't you?' Her husband was getting into his stride. 'He was in the bazaar too, you told me. In fact, he's developing quite a habit of hanging around. Perhaps he's taken a fancy to you and it doesn't worry him that you're a married woman. It will worry everyone else though. If you hadn't noticed, this isn't London. You'll be a prize for the gossip mongers.'

'That's ridiculous, Gerald. He has no personal interest in me.' She wasn't entirely sure that was true, but she must banish the idea from both their minds.

He grunted. 'Maybe he's out to impress, then, and just likes playing at being a hero.'

'Are you saying that Grayson planned to rescue me from the snake, so he could show how brave he was?'

'Pretty much.'

'But then he would have to know I needed rescuing. He would have to know a cobra would find its way into the bathroom.'

Gerald shrugged his shoulders. 'Work it out for yourself.'

She gasped. 'You're suggesting that he deliberately left the snake there? That's even more ridiculous.'

'I'm not suggesting anything,' he backtracked. 'All I'm saying is that he's a pretty odd character, certainly nothing like any of the ICS chaps I know. He doesn't come to the Club and no one there knows him personally. They know his name but they don't know him. None of the Civil Service bods have a clue about his work. You should watch your step, Daisy, that's all I'm saying. It will do neither of us any good if you get talked about.'

'I don't think I'm in any danger from Mr Harte.' She wasn't entirely sure of that either, but she would do well to forget any attraction she felt. And well to say nothing of their visit together to the temple.

Without another word, Gerald strode past her. She was left feeling bewildered. The suggestion that Grayson would deliberately have put her in danger was too crazy to contemplate. And crazy, too, that somehow he liked her more than he should. He was an honourable man, a decent man.

Yet this afternoon at the temple . . . She'd been leaning against the boulder's warm surface, feeling herself merge with the stones and the statues and the setting sun. And then she'd become conscious of his eyes. They were of the deepest blue, eyes that saw clearly she was sure, but also eyes that were appreciative. She'd felt herself come alive beneath his gaze but had immediately suppressed the feeling. Whatever the truth of Gerald's absurd accusation, Grayson Harte was one complication she must do without.

She wandered disconsolately into her bedroom. She supposed she must have an early night. She was feeling weary from the heat and from the day's events and there was little else for her to do. Sleeping alone was becoming the pattern of her married life. The dresses she'd been trying on were still spreadeagled across the bed and she folded them into a neat pile for the tailor's next visit. She no longer felt happy and excited at the thought of them, for what use were pretty frocks if her husband would not even look at her? Somehow she must break the pattern, somehow recover the ardent lover she had known in London. Tomorrow.

Tomorrow a new Indian dawn, and despite her unhappiness she realised she was looking forward to it. She went across to the bedside table and took from its drawer a small wad of papers held together by an elastic band. From this, she extracted a worn photograph and nestled it on her lap. Her mother looked out at her but Lily Driscoll's expression gave little away. It was professional, businesslike, without a hint of the trouble to come. And there had been trouble, Daisy knew.

She'd told Grayson Harte that her father's name did not appear on her birth certificate. What she hadn't said was that in the space where it should have been, the word 'Illegitimate' had been scrawled in harsh black ink. Her mother had never married, despite the child she'd borne. Was that because her sweetheart had been sent to the Front and perished like so many others in the killing fields of France — the date was certainly right — or was it because she'd refused to marry, because her experience had been shorn of love and too much like Daisy's own, a night of false promises?

She looked again at the photograph, peering intently at the image. There was the stiff white cap sitting proudly atop her mother's soft waves, the sharp white cuffs, and the starched dress, caught at the neck with a pendant-shaped brooch. The very same emblem that she had seen this afternoon. She'd felt sure of it at the temple and she'd been right. So her mother had an association with this place, even though it was one bought in a shop on a distant shore. Nandni Mata meant 'daughter', and somehow that seemed significant.

It was part of that strange feeling of belonging that from time to time had washed over her since she'd arrived in India. It was a feeling she'd not known before. She had never belonged at Eden House and never belonged with Miss Maddox, though that lady had been so very kind to her. But for the first time in her life, here in Jasirapur, she was beginning to feel a sense of connection, a connection that went far deeper than disillusion over her marriage and terror at a rogue snake.

* * *

Daisy had fallen into a thick sleep and woke, bleary-eyed, several hours later. There'd been a noise, she was sure. Not from the cicadas and jackals and not from a man in the garden this time, but a noise loud enough to wake her from the deepest slumber. She tried to work out what she'd heard. It seemed to be coming from outside her bedroom door, a dragging sound across a wooden floor, something heavy, something too heavy to carry.

Her watch showed two o'clock, the middle of the night, and the room was inky-dark except for stabs of starlight that found their way through the woven blinds. She could just see the outline of the door and she padded across to it. The noise had appeared to come from directly outside. Grasping the handle, she pulled, but nothing happened. She repeated the action, pulling harder this time. But still the door did not budge. She peered through the keyhole but could see nothing. She should be able to see something, unless — unless there was a key on the other side. She'd not even known there was a key to the room but, surely if there were, it should be on this side of the door. Her dazed brain tried to make sense of what she was seeing. A key on the other side of the door, and a door that wouldn't open. She was locked in. Someone had locked her in!

CHAPTER FOURTEEN

After that there could be no sleep — she was a prisoner in her own home. Who had turned the key on her and why was a frightening mystery and, though her mind restlessly sought to uncover an explanation, she could find none. She dozed fitfully, always alert for any sound that might help make sense of her captivity. But nothing further occurred to disturb the peace of the night and, when she finally crawled from her bed early in the morning and stumbled to the door, it was to find it opened to her touch. There was no sign of a key on either side of the door.

She walked into the sitting room as Gerald was about to leave. He was silhouetted in the doorway, his khaki shirt and shorts smartly pressed, and a *topi* in his hand. From beyond the veranda, she heard the harsh churn of a car engine. He was in a hurry, ready to say a hasty goodbye, when Daisy moved with surprising speed towards him and clutched hold of a pristine shirtsleeve.

'I must talk to you.'

'Not now, I'm late.'

She gazed at the corner clock whose hands had barely passed seven. 'I won't keep you long.'

He shifted impatiently, but she was determined he would hear her out. 'I woke in the night. Something woke me, though I'm not sure what.'

'And you're keeping me from work to tell me that?'

'The noise isn't important. Well, maybe it is . . .' She encountered a scowl and stuttered to a close, but then gathered her forces again. 'It was when I went to find out where the noise had come from, that's what's really important. I couldn't get out of my room. The door was locked.'

'Locked, Gerald!' she repeated when he remained impassive. 'Somebody had used the key to my bedroom and locked the door from the other side.'

'That's impossible.' His laugh was not entirely easy. 'You must have been sleepwalking.'

'I wasn't. I was as wide awake as you are now.'

'Then if you weren't asleep, you were in some kind of daze. Your door couldn't have been locked. There are no keys to any of the doors. Even the front door has no lock.' He turned once more to go, but she moved in front of him.

'I was locked in.'

She felt vulnerable and slightly foolish standing there in her thin nightdress and bare feet, but Daisy knew she was right and she was not going to allow him to brush the matter aside. Hadn't she spent half the night in fear?

He took her by the shoulders, his voice a little softened. 'You *thought* you were locked in. Imagination, Daisy, very likely the effects of the sun. I warned you how bad it could get. You've been here a while and it's beginning to cloud your judgement.'

Her lips shut tight. It wasn't the heat playing with her mind, she was certain. But then, what else could it be? What other explanation? If Gerald were right and there were no keys at all in the bungalow, the door could not have been locked.

He seemed to sense his opportunity to leave. 'You probably tried the door and it stuck a little. Then you imagined you were locked in, tried to tug harder and made the door jam even more. That can happen. Maybe you started to panic and think you weren't going to get out.'

He was right. She had been in a panic. She'd crept back to bed, her pulse hammering and for a while hidden herself entirely beneath the bed's one cotton sheet.

'Now, can I go?' he asked, irritation in his voice.

She murmured a 'yes', unable to counter his argument. Perhaps he was right, too, about the heat. It was creeping up on her unnoticed, just like Jocelyn had warned, creeping up and slowly turning her crazy, fermenting her imagination to invent the silliest of dramas. She didn't know this country, didn't know its power. Thinking she belonged here was so much moonshine. She didn't belong, that was brutally clear.

* * *

Two days later, she rose even earlier than usual. The *durzi* was due today and she was dressed and waiting for him before the clock struck seven. But once she'd given him the dresses to finish, she was left with nothing more to do for the rest of the day except contemplate the bungalow's four walls. And contemplate them alone. The solitude was beginning to play more and more on her nerves and she wasn't sure why — the noises in the night perhaps, the locked door, a servant who was there and yet not there and, of course, the snake. She wanted to be as far away from the house as possible, but had no idea where to go. They lived a distance from anywhere she could name — from the civil station, from Jasirapur itself.

She wondered why Gerald had chosen such an isolated place when, according to Jocelyn Forester, he could have rented accommodation within the cantonment. She supposed it must have been for money reasons and felt a familiar heaviness descend. He'd accused her of forcing him into marriage at too early an age, when he was unable to afford a wife for several years. What he hadn't said was that he needed to marry money, or at least a woman with worthwhile connections. But Daisy knew it for the disagreeable truth.

She strolled onto the veranda. The morning was still early enough to be fresh and though she knew that would very soon change, the cool air on her cheeks reinforced her restlessness and made her itch to walk out. Except there was nowhere to walk and it would hardly be sensible to do so.

But a bicycle. Gerald had been collected by car this morning and the bicycle was still there, propped against the white plastered walls. He had no need of it so why could she not use it? She'd hardly ever ridden before, just a few wobbling yards along a London street beneath the wary eye of the senior footman, keen to protect his newly-acquired purchase. The tyres looked pumped, the chain greased, all things Robert had told her were important. She could see him now, urging her on, past the pillar -box, past the garden railings, his face puckered with concern. He'd been a friendly man, she thought, one of the few in Miss Maddox's household who had shown her kindness. Thanks to his instruction, she'd managed for a while to master the rudiments of riding, so how difficult could it be to try again?

Quite difficult, she found, but she persevered, teetering up and down the pathway until she felt competent enough to make a small journey. The *durzi* was still sewing furiously outside her bedroom window, but one dress lay ready and she slipped it over her shoulders, thinking herself sufficiently smart to visit the civil station. Ever since that dreadful dinner at the Club, she'd hoped to return but alone, when she could find the library and something new to read. And there was no danger now of meeting the women from that night since they would be on their way to Simla.

Calling Rajiv, she explained as simply as she could what she planned to do. As always, his face remained expressionless; he simply bowed and returned to his kitchen. At least they would know where to send a search party, she thought, and it had been sensible to tell him.

Dressed in the cream cotton sundress, *topi* wedged firmly on her head, she began nervously to cycle along the narrow lane towards the main road. She sensed Rajiv's eyes following her from his redoubt and was relieved to round the first bend. She had escaped.

It took her a while to navigate each of the curves in the lane but, once she reached the main road, she turned right onto the straight thoroughfare that led to the civil station. The road surface was slightly better here and her pedalling picked up speed. As she pushed forward, she could feel the breeze on her face and smell the aroma of hot, dried grass wafting upwards from the gully. From time to time, she passed tiny stones painted red and dotted along the roadside at intervals, shrines to one or other of the Hindu gods. Several rickshaws passed her travelling in the opposite direction, their bells ringing cheerily, and in the distance she heard the muezzin's call to prayer. Within minutes, the unaccustomed exercise had left her exhilarated but uncomfortably hot.

The civil station came into view and in her elation at reaching it, she lost concentration for a moment. It was enough for a peacock strutting across the road to almost unseat her. But she wrenched the bicycle upright and, by the time she turned into the main entrance of the station, she was again riding smoothly. The guard came out of his sentry box, a perplexed expression on his face. A lone white woman on a bicycle was not a familiar sight. But when she asked for directions to the library, it seemed to reassure him and he readily pointed out the route she should take.

* * *

Opening the door to the library, she was pink but pleased — there was no one in sight and she had the place entirely to herself. But a brief glance around the sparsely furnished room suggested she had expended a great deal of effort for very little reward. The far wall had been shelved from ceiling to floor, but elsewhere there were only crumbling cane chairs and an old oak table, whose surface told the story of a thousand scratched messages.

She began to take down some of the books, searching for something that might help her understand more of her adopted country, but she looked in vain. There were thrillers, romances, popular authors: Stella Gibbons, Djuna Barnes, Daphne du Maurier. Any of these would provide bedtime reading, she thought, but the book she really wanted was nowhere to be seen. All the way here, as her aching legs had turned the wheels, she'd been imagining a precious volume that would unlock for her the secrets of Indian mythology and, in particular, tell her the story of the goddess for whom she already felt an affinity, Nandni Mata.

She was about to select one or two of the lightest books to slip into the bag she had slung across her shoulders, when the door opened and Jocelyn Forester stood on the threshold. Daisy stared at her, uncomprehending. The girl should be travelling to Simla with her mother and the other memsahibs. How was she here? Why was she here? The old suspicions thrummed into life, so sharp and so strong that she was in danger of drowning from them. Then she noticed the crutches. Jocelyn smiled a wide, cheerful smile and waved a crutch at her.

'Can you believe what I've done, Daisy? I'm so annoyed with myself, I can't tell you.'

'What *have* you done? It looks painful.' She tried to infuse sympathy into her voice.

'I've sprained my ankle, that's what. And I did it the day before I was due to leave. We were packed and ready to go and then I had to fall through the front door!'

It seemed an unlikely accident. 'How did you manage to do that?' she asked cautiously.

'A letter came for me,' Jocelyn was blushing slightly at the memory, 'and I was so eager to get at it that I tripped over the doormat and this is the result.'

Daisy wondered what kind of letter could have been that exciting and, more interestingly, who its author might be. But she wouldn't allow herself such dangerous thoughts. Instead, she asked, 'Is your mother still at home with you?'

'No and it's so miserable, you've no idea. I can hardly move — certainly not out of the cantonment. Ma has gone ahead and I can't join her for at least another week. I tried to send you a message. I was hoping you could come over and keep me company, but the wretched servant delivered it to the wrong bungalow. I ask you. How could anyone get it wrong? But he did.'

'Well, you've found me now.'

Her mind was teeming. Jocelyn would have only her father for company and the Colonel was likely to be out most of the day and many of the evenings. It would leave his daughter free to pursue her own plans, even on crutches. Had she pretended an injury so she could stay behind and be with Gerald? Or had she deliberately tumbled? Daisy could not stop the thoughts after all. And if the injury were genuine, what was this letter? The girl had blushed when she'd mentioned it so it had to have been from a man, but was that man Gerald?

'I *have* found you,' Jocelyn was hobbling towards her, 'and I shall bag your company as much as you'll let me.'

Daisy smiled with what she hoped was sufficient enthusiasm. She couldn't help but like Jocelyn. The girl was a breath of fresh air blowing through the staid corridors of the civil station. But she couldn't trust her either, not entirely. The dreadful quarrel with Gerald had made clear that Daisy had spoiled his plans and those plans had surely included Jocelyn.

'How did you get here?' she was saying. 'Has Gerald been teaching you to ride? There are several horses in the regimental stables that aren't spoken for, I know.'

This time Daisy's smile was genuine. 'I did ride but on a bicycle.'

Jocelyn laughed out loud. 'Of course, it would be. I can just see you in that tremendous dress, head down and pedalling like fury along the road to the cantonment.' She leaned forward and smoothed the skirt of Daisy's dress. 'It looks wonderful on you. I couldn't begin to wear such a delicious cream, but you suit it so well.'

Because I'm several shades darker than you, Daisy thought, and then forced herself to stop. She would not allow that awful evening to shadow her life.

'I'm very pleased with it myself.' She tried to sound untroubled. 'And thank you so much for introducing me to your *durzi*. He's the miracle worker you said he was.'

Jocelyn smiled happily but couldn't prevent herself shifting from side to side on her crutches. It was clear her ankle was paining her. 'I'd be happy to ride over one morning to visit if that would cheer you up,' Daisy said quickly. She owed Jocelyn that at least.

'It would, my dear, immensely. But you shouldn't be out on a bicycle in this weather. I've got permission to use the Adjutant's pony and trap. Why don't I call for you at the bungalow and we could enjoy a whole morning together? Actually . . . I've just thought. Why don't we go to the parade? You'll love it — it's next Friday, a week today, if you're not doing anything.'

That was something she could be sure of, Daisy thought drily. 'I'd like that.'

'Wonderful! We'll have to leave pretty early. The parade starts just after dawn as it's too hot for the horses later in the day, but it's a splendid sight. You'll see. Every member of the regiment is mounted and rides through Jasirapur wearing his smartest uniform and finishing up on the maiden.'

Daisy's astonished look made her companion giggle. 'Not that kind! It's a large open area on the outskirts of town. The cavalry plays all their polo matches there but only in the cool season, of course. It's far too hot for polo now, but a parade works wonders. It keeps the regiment in shape and gives the locals a touch of colour. Helps to remind them who's in charge, too.'

The conversation with Grayson floated into Daisy's mind. He'd talked about nationalist protests and she wondered whether such a parade might be more provocative than helpful, but as usual she kept her thoughts to herself.

'I'd love to come. Next Friday you say?'

'Yes, but come over before if you can.'

Daisy nodded, but did not commit herself. She couldn't quite lose the feeling that Jocelyn was not as innocent as she seemed. 'I'll try, but there are several things at home that need my attention.' She hoped she wouldn't be forced to explain these non-existent tasks. 'In fact, I'd better be getting back there now.'

The girl looked disappointed but, after clasping Daisy's hand warmly, she hopped to one side to leave the doorway clear.

'See you next week,' she called after her.

CHAPTER FIFTEEN

'I saw Jocelyn Forester today,' Daisy said as casually as she could. They were seated at the dining table sharing the evening meal. It was fortunate that Gerald had decided not to eat in the Mess as he'd done the previous night; she wanted to see his reaction.

'Yes?' He sounded indifferent, deliberately so, she thought.

Daisy persevered. 'Did you know Jocelyn had an accident and wasn't able to leave with her mother? Apparently she tripped and sprained her ankle.'

'The Colonel mentioned something about it, but he thought she'd be well enough to travel very soon.'

Daisy laid down her knife and fork. Curried meat was losing what appeal it had ever possessed and this conversation was likely to prove more interesting than any chicken.

'She plans to travel the week after next, I believe. In the meantime, she's invited me to go with her to the regimental parade.'

'That's nice,' he said absently, and this time he appeared genuinely preoccupied. There were several minutes of silence before she became aware of his narrowed concentration. He'd pushed his plate aside and his gaze was intense. 'When she does leave, why don't you travel up to the hills with her? It's not too late for you to go.'

The suggestion caught Daisy unawares since she'd thought the notion of Simla truly buried. It left her flailing around trying to find a way to refuse, without provoking further ill feeling between them.

Gerald was swift to leap into the gap. 'You seem to have made a good friend of Jocelyn, so why not go with her? You can shelter under her wing if you feel the need. As well as being the Colonel's daughter, she's a popular girl. With her as a friend, the wives won't bother you.'

'I suppose so,' she said slowly, turning the idea over in her mind.

For some reason it no longer felt so objectionable. She wondered what had changed. Knowing Jocelyn, she supposed, was one thing but there was also the discomfort she felt at being here alone in the bungalow. An increasing discomfort. And then there was the stifling heat, which could only get worse as the plains turned into their summer inferno.

Gerald revved up his eagerness. 'Look, Daisy, we've got off to a bad start and I'm sorry for my part in it.' His tone was conciliatory and that was unexpected. 'I'm wondering, maybe, if we took a break from each other, it might help.'

He was hesitant and no wonder. How could a break help when so far they'd hardly seen each other?

'Just a short break,' he went on. 'If you're in Simla, I won't be worrying about you, and you'll feel a good deal better once you're in a more reasonable climate.'

'I feel fine,' she protested.

'You think you do, but consider what's been happening. You've seen a figure in the garden when there was no figure, you thought your door was locked when there's not even a key to your room, and you accused Rajiv of deliberately leaving you alone to face danger, when he assures me that he was delayed at the market that day. It all adds up to you not really being yourself, don't you think? But if you won't take my advice, ask any old hand. They'll say the same thing. People have to acclimatise gradually and coming out in April, it's not possible. You've been thrown in at the deep end.'

'You still want me to go away to Simla.'

She sounded more combative than she'd meant to, since the idea was beginning to grow on her. The women were still a problem, though. Apart from Jocelyn Forester, there was not one of them with whom she wished to spend more than five minutes.

'It's not that I *want* you to go. I think it's best — for both of us. I won't deny we've got problems, but they're not going to be solved while we're both sweltering. When you come back, it will be cooler, life will feel more rational. And there'll be months of entertainment to look forward to, and plenty of chances to enjoy ourselves.'

She had a lively idea of what winter in Jasirapur would be. Blissfully cool for one thing. She would learn to ride, perhaps sew curtains and cushions for the house to make it more homely, perhaps even tackle the garden if they couldn't afford their own *mali*. That was a life she could manage. But it wouldn't stop there. She would be expected to attend the Club regularly, go to the dances, the parties, the dreadful dinners, and be expected to mix with the same set of people day in and day out, people she already disliked.

This would be her life and, without Gerald's love, it was a depressing prospect. She needed him to feel close to her, needed him to care. Right now, he was being more amiable than at any time since they'd married, and part of her wanted to go along with this new mood of conciliation. But another voice was telling her not to agree to his demands just yet.

'I'll think about it,' she hedged.

'Don't think too long or a ticket could be difficult. And what's there to think of? If you go with Jocelyn, you'll have someone with you who's lived in India all her life and knows the ropes through and through. I'd feel comfortable knowing you're with her.'

She nodded, and he leant across the table and took her hand. It was a rare gesture of affection and she let her fingers lie in his. 'I'm sorry for what I said the other night. It was the shock, you see. Hearing that news — the baby — I just hadn't expected it.'

'I'm sorry, too.' She was eager to meet him halfway. 'I tried to find the right moment to tell you but it never came. Then when I did blurt it out, it was the worst possible time.'

Still holding her hand, he led her to the lumpy sofa and sat down beside her. Days of marriage and this was the closest they had been together. She allowed herself to lean very gently into him, and the action was sufficient to encourage him to talk.

'I know it's difficult for you to understand how I feel, and I know I've not been thinking straight. But I had such a devil of a job getting into the Indian Army, that getting on, being promoted, has become very, very important. Maybe too important.'

'Was it that difficult to get accepted?' She was genuinely interested. There was also a barely acknowledged hope that, if she could persuade him to talk, he might touch on that part of his life he'd kept so secret. It could be the beginnings of real honesty between them.

He lay back against the sofa and stretched his legs. 'It was immensely difficult. You have to graduate top of your class at Sandhurst to have any chance, and that means a lot of hard work. Getting into the Indian cavalry is even harder. The regiment recruits all the best people. Men from wealthy families, for instance, attracted by the hunting and the polo. And, of course, attracted by the uniforms — they're pretty colourful.'

'And romantic, too?'

'Yes, romantic.' He smiled at her, and it was as though they were back together in London, walking hand in hand by the Thames, talking, laughing. She held the feeling tight, longing for it to last.

'You see, I'm not naturally academic.' His expression had grown more serious. 'I found the studying very hard and when I succeeded against all the odds, and saw my name at the top of the list, that was only the start. There's a year with a British regiment in India before you're actually allowed to join the Indian Army. A year when you're watched very closely to see if you're suitable. That's not easy to take, being watched day and night, on and off duty. And you have to learn Hindi because you must speak the language of your men. Urdu as well — it may sound the same but it's different from Hindi when it's written — so that's two more exams to get through. And then when you've done all that and plumped for an Indian regiment, you get vetted there, too. You may think you've done the choosing, but in the end *they* choose *you*. The officers of the regiment give you a look over and decide whether they want you to stay or not.'

'It sounds horrid. But you must feel proud of yourself, Gerald. You've done so very well.'

He turned towards her, their hands still clasped. 'That's the damnedest thing. You can never feel proud, never relax. There's always one more fence to jump. When you wrote from England with your news, it sent me into a panic. It was one fence I couldn't jump.'

'I don't understand. What fence?'

'There's an unofficial rule of no marriage under thirty. The ICS have it, too. The army has a saying: *Subalterns cannot marry, captains may marry, majors should marry, colonels must marry*. If you want to marry before you're thirty, you have to have the CO's permission and it's usually refused. Or you have to send in your papers.'

Daisy looked baffled. 'Send in your papers?'

'Leave the regiment.'

'But that's so unfair.' She was indignant.

'It sounds it, I agree, but it's done for a good reason. If you marry early as a subaltern, you never have sufficient money. Regimental life is expensive. You're expected to stand your rounds in the Mess, expected to entertain regularly.

And, of course, while the older men have furnished their quarters, you have to start from scratch.'

She squeezed his hand. 'I appreciate we won't have an easy life, at least not for a few years, and I'm sorry for my part in creating the mess. Sending that telegram — I shouldn't have done it — I can see that now. But we still have each other and surely we can make a decent future together.'

He squeezed her hand back. 'We'll make a start on it, I promise. After you get back from Simla.'

* * *

Daisy felt happier than she had for days. At last they were talking properly. The evening's conversation had been open and sincere. It hadn't mended everything that was wrong, of course. She'd had a faint hope that he'd follow her into the bedroom, but when he'd said a friendly goodnight and disappeared along the corridor, she hadn't tried to stop him. The marriage was still fragile, she knew, and they must take things slowly. He'd been right when he said they'd had a wretched beginning and perhaps he was right, too, in thinking a break would help them start afresh when she returned from Simla.

This morning he'd left for the camp very early to supervise preparations for the parade, which was to be the grandest of affairs. She wondered how men and horses would stand up to the increasing temperature. Every day seemed hotter than the one before and the heat was gradually seeping into her very bones. For large portions of the day, she felt too dazed even to pick up a book.

She had risen early, too, when the sun was only just over the horizon and was now trying for the hundredth time to concentrate on one of the novels she'd borrowed from the station library. Sitting in the shade of the veranda, she gazed fixedly at the page but, despite the early morning cool, the words danced before her. Eventually she gave up the effort and sat quietly looking out onto the wilderness that was their garden.

She'd discovered a book on native birds in Gerald's small, rickety bookcase and now knew the names of several of the species that visited regularly. Cheerful little bulbuls with red and yellow rumps flew between the bushes and, in the furthest trees, she could see paradise fly catchers with tails like long, white streamers. She laid the book to rest on her lap and closed her eyes, then sensed rather than heard something watching her. A monkey — a black-faced langur monkey, she'd been taught — was peering at her between the posts of the veranda and behind him a whole troupe was gathered, watching her in silence.

Jocelyn had told her never to look a monkey in the face; if you didn't make eye contact with them, she'd said, they wouldn't bother you. She picked up her book, studiously ignoring them, but nevertheless feeling wary. Rajiv, of course, was nowhere to be seen. One of the monkeys started to chatter noisily, then others joined in, and soon the chatter had turned into loud shrieks. Several started to bound around the garden, flying at each other in mock charges.

She was about to slip indoors and out of harm's way when she heard footsteps on the path. Looking up, she saw two well-dressed Indians walking towards her. They waved their arms at the monkeys, who shrieked back at them before deciding it was safer to leave.

'Thank you for scaring them away.' She stood up to welcome her visitors. 'I wasn't sure what to do.'

'It is our pleasure, memsahib. But surely you have servants?' This was the older man, his grey hair and slim figure giving him an air of distinction. 'What are your servants doing? — they should be protecting you.'

She was tired of having to explain her household, so she simply smiled and asked them if they would care for a drink of water or for tea. She could feel the sun starting to throb and her head begin its familiar ache. They were clearly embarrassed by her invitation and Daisy knew she must have made a mistake, breached a rule of which she was not even aware. It was not customary, it seemed, for a lone woman to entertain Indian gentlemen.

'Thank you, memsahib.' The older man bowed. 'You are most kind. But we have come on business.'

Her face cleared. 'Then it's my husband you'll want to see.'

'Yes, indeed. Lieutenant Mortimer.'

'He's working. You'll find him at the camp.'

There was a moment's silence and the two men exchanged a look. Daisy began to feel uneasy.

'Alas, memsahib, but we cannot go there.'

'It is not possible for us to gain entry,' the smaller man said quietly.

This was yet another rule she hadn't known. 'Then perhaps I can help you.'

'Thank you, memsahib. My colleague and I would be most grateful.' And the grey-haired man handed her a sheaf of papers. 'Would you be so kind as to give these to your husband?'

'Of course, but what are they?'

The smaller man gave a faint cough. 'They are bills, memsahib.'

'Bills? You are owed money? Lieutenant Mortimer owes you money?'

Her plain speaking was evidently too much for them. They could not look at her, but bowed their heads in the same jerky movement.

'I'm sure he can't have known of these.' She was not at all sure but she must put on a brave face. 'I'm sure he'll pay you immediately, once he sees them.'

There was a slight pause and then another bow. 'Of course, memsahib. We must go now.'

Daisy watched them walk back along the path, the papers still in her hands, clinging stickily to her curled fingers. This could only lead to trouble, and just as she and Gerald had begun to grow closer. She looked up at the luminous sky and felt only sadness. He would blame her for the bills and for his difficult situation. If it hadn't been for her . . .

Walking back indoors, she placed the sheaf of papers in a prominent position on the desk. She would say nothing, she decided, but instead wait for Gerald to ask how they came to be there. But even that thought made her nervous. The men's visit had disturbed her badly and it was impossible now to go back to her book or even pretend to read. Her body craved movement. She began to walk rapidly up and down the room. But it was too enclosed, too limiting, and she knew she had to get out of the house.

The bicycle stood nearby, abandoned against the wooden posts of the veranda. She'd managed the trip to the civil station, so why not another expedition? But this one would be different. Today, she wouldn't be seeking distraction — it was peace of mind she needed. She would ride out in search of tranquillity. Without having to think, she knew where she would go. Since her visit with Grayson, the temple of Nandni Mata had never been far from Daisy's mind.

CHAPTER SIXTEEN

It took her nearly an hour to reach the ruined site, far longer than she'd anticipated. But the rising temperature had made cycling very difficult and she'd almost given up several times and turned for home. But something had kept her going and now she was pushing the bike down the sandy path and towards the temple.

At the top of the flight of steps, she stood looking out on the peaceful scene that stretched before her. It was much hotter than when she and Grayson had come and her skin was prickling badly. She chided herself for her stupidity — she should have realised that this was the wrong time of the day to visit, and that such a large, open space could only be an invitation to the sun's brilliance. She would go down to the temple for a short while only, just long enough to visit her goddess once more, then return to this vantage point and rest in the shade before she made the journey home.

Leaving the bike propped against one of the huge stones that littered the grassy ledge, she made her way slowly down the stairs, her limbs feeling uncomfortably weak — as though she were walking in slow motion, each leg hardly moving, yet somehow reaching down to the step below. Her *topi* protected her neck, but there was a burning sensation at her back and she quickened her pace to find shelter between the columns of the temple.

Walking up the steps to the temple's inner terrace, making for Nandni Mata, Daisy could still feel the same burning sensation. It seemed strange that the sun could penetrate this far into the building. It must do, for what else could be inflaming her body so oddly? She turned suddenly; she'd had the feeling she was being watched. Were they eyes that were burning into her back? Her gaze swept the empty space. Nothing but rubble, broken stone and shifting sand. It was the heat again. She was allowing the heat to get to her.

Nandni Mata was as beautiful as she had been days ago. Daisy stroked the shining black stone with gentle fingers, willing the goddess to come alive. It was foolish, but this statue was the only connection she had with her mother, this and a creased photograph. Lily must have bought the brooch in a shop or from a market stall, as Grayson had suggested, but what if the connection were closer than that? What if the brooch had come from here, from this very place? What if her mother had been here?

It was a fantasy, she knew, and she traced the necklace once more with her fingers, smoothing the stone pendant over and over, trying to feel her mother's presence. But she could not. All she could feel was the still, suffocating heat. She looked at the statue again and the goddess stared back. Her look was baleful. Daisy hadn't noticed that before and a strong impulse to leave flooded over her, for the temple hadn't brought the peace she sought and she didn't know why. It was as though the spirit of the place had withdrawn and left her exposed. Yes, she must definitely leave, and leave now.

She backed quickly away and walked through the regiment of columns to the top of the temple steps. A sudden noise above her head made her look skywards and there, held in suspension, was a stone, a very large stone, hurtling through the blue, hurtling towards her. She stepped back into the shelter of two columns a second before a deafening crack shattered the stillness of the arena and a rock lay in splinters on the steps below.

Oblivious of the sun and her pounding heart, Daisy raced down the steps and across the open space. The temple had seemed about to fall into ruins above her head and she must reach safety. Panting heavily, she ran up the far flight of steps to regain the grass ledge and, once there, bent double, her breath coming in short, sharp stabs. Her bicycle remained leaning where she'd propped it and she grabbed at its handlebars. There was no rest to be had here. She must leave now, no matter how hard the journey ahead. Frantically, she wheeled the bike along the sandy track, looking straight ahead. The most frightening of the statues loomed on either side and she dared not glance at them. As soon as she was able, she jumped on the bicycle and began to pedal.

The road was cruel, baked hard by the sun, and she would need every ounce of her strength to reach home. Yet even as she cycled herself into exhaustion, her mind would not be still. Could it really be that after so many thousands of years, the temple had been about to fall around her ears? Not today of all days, surely. Not the one day she had gone there alone. A piece of the roof must have sheared off, she consoled herself, and that could happen at any time. But it had happened just as she was about to leave. And the stone she'd seen falling had been irregular, uncarved, not seeming to be part of the edifice at all. A rough boulder plunging through the air. It could have hit her. If it had been a little more to the right, a little nearer to the terrace, it *would* have hit her. Even as her body vibrated with heat, she could not prevent a shiver of dread. It had been a lucky escape.

Escape! The rock had been meant for her. It was an absurd notion, but somehow Daisy was sure of it. She had sensed eyes on her, hadn't she, expectant, malevolent eyes? Even now she felt the spirits of the temple in pursuit. They had tried to kill her, her dazed mind was telling her, and she must get to safety, get to the bungalow. She had her head down, her legs racing and pedalling blindly, and saw nothing until suddenly a horse was rearing in front of her, and she fell from the bike.

'Daisy! My God, are you all right?'

* * *

Anish jumped from the saddle and rushed towards her, scooping her slight form into his arms and setting her gently on her feet by the side of the road. She hadn't seen him since he bid her goodbye in the bazaar but even in her badly shaken state, she felt a rush of pleasure at meeting him again. He continued to hold on to her, supporting her with his arm until she stopped trembling.

'I'm so sorry.' Her voice was little more than a whisper. 'I wasn't looking where I was going.'

He pointed to the abandoned bicycle, lying sprawled across the centre of the road, its wheels still ticking. 'You looked as though all the demons of hell were pursuing you. What happened to scare you so?'

Daisy flushed in embarrassment, unable to put into words the feelings that had sent her fleeing, oblivious of everything around her. She felt incredibly stupid, half-crazed. To imagine that the temple had changed its nature since her last visit, that it meant her ill and had sent avenging spirits to pursue her! How nonsensical. But the fear hadn't quite departed and, when she tried to reassure him that all was well, she made no sense.

Anish looked at her measuringly. 'We must find you somewhere to rest. There's a village a mile back and we can stay there a while. Just let me clear the bike to one side of the road. Gerald will have to collect it later but it will be safe enough in the ditch.'

When he returned to her side, he gave her a second long look. 'You're not in any shape to be walking, so it's another ride for you. Only this time, Gertie will do the honours.'

And before she could protest, he'd led the horse to her and tossed her up onto its back, adjusting the stirrups to suit her much shorter legs. Daisy had never in her life been on a horse, never in fact been on speaking terms with one, except for the coalman's faithful dray who had delivered rain or shine all the years she'd been with Miss Maddox.

Anish had taken the reins and was leading the mare forward. 'Just hang on tightly. To the saddle, to her mane, wherever you can — we'll soon be there.'

The village was small. No more than a dozen or so thatched huts, their walls plastered in clay and cow dung, and clustered around a saucer-shaped well. But a solitary shack of corrugated iron stood to one side, selling tea and soft drinks beneath its tattered, striped awning. Daisy almost fell off the horse into Anish's arms. As graceful as a sack of coal, she thought. He grinned and settled her into one of the stall's folding metal chairs. The owner brought *chai* for his two customers and water for the horse.

Anish leaned across the table towards her. 'Something happened to upset you badly. Tell me what it is.'

Daisy took a long gulp of the sweet tea, trying to find the courage to speak. She must tell someone; she couldn't keep this latest misfortune to herself and who else could she tell? It was unlikely Gerald would be interested, and Grayson Harte wasn't here. But Anish was and his kind, brown eyes were fixed on her.

Eventually she said, 'I went to the temple.'

'To the ruins? To Nandni Mata's shrine?'

'Yes.' She was grateful that he knew the place immediately. 'To Nandni Mata's temple.'

'I can't blame you for wanting to visit. It's very beautiful.'

'It is.' She nodded enthusiastically, for the moment forgetting her bad experience. 'I'd been there before, you see, and loved it.'

His eyebrows rose questioningly and she hurried on. 'Grayson Harte — he's a District Officer based in Jasirapur, I met him on the boat coming out — he took me. He knew the ruins well and thought I'd enjoy them.'

'I'm acquainted with Mr Harte,' he said thoughtfully. 'And how strange you should mention his name. I saw him only minutes ago. I was turning onto the main road. One of my *sowars*, privates that is, comes from a village just the other side and I was visiting.'

Daisy stared at him, her tale suspended. Anish had seen Grayson, so he must have been nearby, perhaps even in the vicinity of the temple. Had he decided to visit the ruins today? She recalled the uncanny feeling she'd had of eyes following her. Could it have been Grayson watching? But if he'd been there and seen what happened, why hadn't he rushed to help? Or . . . a cold hand laid itself across her chest. Was it what her husband had claimed — that the District Officer was following her around, stalking her for his own reasons? It had sounded absurd when Gerald suggested the man was trying to impress her, but it was beginning to sound a little less absurd.

He was hardly going to impress his victim, though, by sending her fleeing for her life. And how, in any case, could he have managed it? He must know the ruins well so perhaps there was a way to reach the top of what was left of the temple roof. But even if he'd climbed there, why on earth would he have sent that rock plummeting earthwards? It couldn't have been an accident, not a boulder that size. It had to be deliberate, but surely Grayson wouldn't want to harm her.

Yet she hadn't been harmed. The rock had fallen a yard away, perilously close it was true, but it could have come closer. It could have been aimed to kill. Had it then been targeted to scare but deliberately miss? Dislodged perhaps at an angle? If so, things had gone badly wrong. If Grayson had wanted to scare her and then rush to her rescue, she'd scuppered his plan by running away as fast as her legs could take her, running and cycling at full speed before he could find his way down from the roof and play the white knight.

Anish was looking at her, perturbed. 'Daisy?' She realised she'd been silent for minutes while her mind tossed crazy thoughts, crazy speculations, this way and that. 'What were you saying about the temple?'

'I'm sorry, I'm in a daze. I had a bit of a shock while I was there.' How understated, she thought, how English.

'Part of the roof fell down. I suppose it could only have been a small part but it was a pretty large chunk of rock and it crashed right in front of me. I thought the whole temple might be about to tumble.' She would be sure not to mention evil spirits and eyes that followed her. Anish would think she had completely lost her mind.

'It's an ancient building and it's slowly rotting. Pieces do break off from time to time, but I would have thought the temple roof secure enough.'

'Now we know, it isn't,' she said a little too brightly. 'But I don't think I was in any real danger. The rock fell a good yard in front of me. I'm afraid I got stupidly scared and jumped on my bike and rode without thinking. I'm sorry I frightened your horse.'

'Gertie is a good girl. Not much upsets her. But why were you there alone and at this time of the day? You should stay out of the midday sun, hasn't Gerald told you?'

'Yes,' she said miserably, remembering for the first time that morning what had driven her from home. 'But I had to get out of the house and the temple was so beautiful the last time I saw it and I thought it wouldn't take long to reach. But it did, and by the time I got there, the sun was too high in the sky.'

'I think you must be finding life in Jasirapur very tedious.' He weighed his words before he continued. 'There is little for ladies to do here in the hot season — that's why Simla is so popular. Perhaps you should have gone after all.'

She didn't answer, for her mind was elsewhere and in a burst of confidence, she said, 'Something unpleasant happened this morning. That's why I needed to get out of the bungalow.'

'More unpleasantness? You have been suffering.'

She wanted to confide in someone and Anish was a close friend of Gerald's. She thought he might already know something of his brother officer's difficulties and could give her sensible advice.

'Is army life very expensive?' she began.

The question appeared to disconcert him. It was evidently not what he'd been expecting. 'It depends on what you mean by army life.'

'For young officers, I was thinking.'

'There are certainly a good many expenses when you join the regiment. And the cavalry is one of the most expensive in which to serve. There's quite a lot that needs money. New uniforms, new equipment, gratuities to servants, that kind of thing.'

'I see.' There was a pause before she murmured, 'But don't most of those debts get paid from salary within a year or two?'

He frowned. 'What is this, Daisy?'

She looked down at her lap and fidgeted with her fingers. 'It's Gerald,' she confessed. 'He seems to be in debt.'

'Everyone is,' Anish responded cheerfully. 'An overdraft is normal. Unfortunately the Indian Army still has the attitude that young officers have private means, but nowadays that's true of only a few.'

'So Gerald isn't alone?'

'No.' His tone was cautious. 'Not alone. The temptation to spend is great, particularly if you're new to the regiment, or maybe if your background is slightly different. You have to fit in, you see.'

She felt his gaze keen, enquiring. Did he know the secret of Gerald's double identity and was he wondering if she knew, too? She hoped he wouldn't broach the subject, and was relieved when he went on, 'In the Mess you need to be seen to be generous. Anyone who is — shall we say careful with money — is treated with scorn. That doesn't mean you can get into serious debt, of course, but—'

'But?'

'Gerald has probably been a little more generous than most. And then he may have tried to salvage the situation, recoup some of the money he owes, and that's landed him in more trouble.'

'How could he recoup the money?'

'Oh, you know,' Anish said vaguely. 'This and that.'

Jocelyn's words sounded loudly in her ears. 'You mean gambling.'

Her companion looked uncomfortable. 'Yes, but everyone does it. The Mess is one enormous gambling den. It's a matter of degree.' There was a pause while Anish drank down his *chai*. 'This shouldn't be worrying you. All young officers have debts and, as long as they don't default, everything's fine.'

But everything wasn't fine, far from it. 'There were some men,' she faltered, 'they came to the house this morning looking for Gerald. They handed me bills they said he owed money on.'

Anish whistled. 'That's not good, I agree. Credit is easy to come by and the town's tradesmen are in competition with each other. But the moment one of the blighters starts pressing for his money, it's not long before the others join in.'

He saw her appalled expression and patted her hand. 'Don't fret. You won't suffer the entire bazaar descending on you, I promise. Gerald is sure to clear the debts very soon and as long as he does before it reaches the Colonel's ears, it won't be a problem.'

That was less than comforting, she thought. 'What would happen if the Colonel knew?'

'Gerald would get a severe dressing down and be ordered to pay immediately. Honouring your bills is all important. If you don't pay your debts, you let the regiment down, you see. Mess bills must be paid by the seventh of the month, no remission, though tradesmen can be made to wait.'

'These tradesmen aren't waiting.'

'You must trust Gerald to sort it out,' he said soothingly. 'And remember that a lot of the officers live as though they have the means when they don't. They live on credit.'

'And what about you, Anish? Do you live like that?'

'I can't afford to.' The smile did not quite reach his eyes.

Daisy looked puzzled. 'But surely — your pay — aren't you the same rank as Gerald?'

'I am an Indian Commissioned Officer and that makes a difference. We're supposed to be treated the same as British officers. That's the theory. But we're not paid the same so it really wouldn't be sensible to get into debt. British officers are serving away from home and receive an additional allowance, but we're reckoned not to need it because we serve in our home country.'

'That seems a little unfair. Doesn't it make Indian officers resentful?'

'Some. But it's largely unexpressed. Indian officers in British regiments are still on probation and it's not a good idea to voice criticisms too loudly.'

He'd said nothing that suggested his frustration, yet she knew he must feel it. 'Why are you on probation? Gerald told me there are more and more Indian officers in regiments like his.'

'I used the wrong word. And he's correct. There used only to be two Indian officers to each regiment but now you see nearly as many brown faces as white. It's still wise to walk cautiously, though.'

Once before, she'd had the impression that beneath Anish's calm facade lay a different man. But he was smiling again and this time she thought the smile was genuine. 'We should be glad of small mercies. Before the Indian Military Academy was set up at Dehra Dun, it was very different. But the IMA changed all that. We learned there how to be little Englishmen or rather public-school Englishmen. They taught us all that school stuff: our word must be our bond, we must own up to our faults, take punishment without a grudge and, of course, endure hardship without complaint — the stiff upper lip. What a wonderful phrase that is!'

'So you are all sahibs now.' She regretted the words as soon as she spoke them. They were trivial and thoughtless. Anish must feel the discriminations of army life deeply and here she was joking about them.

But he seemed not to mind. 'Not quite. We've come a long way and it can only get better. But what the IMA doesn't teach you is how to cope with the rules that aren't written down. Military life has some pretty strange quirks to it.'

'It's not just me, then, that thinks so?' She was relieved they'd found mutual ground again.

'Not at all. There are too many contradictions to count, shades of meaning that a newcomer will never fathom.'

'Tell me some.'

'Let's see.' He tipped his head to one side. 'On no account must a young officer be bumptious.' He sprang up from his chair and puffed his chest out to ludicrous proportions, his face one of perfect superiority. Daisy smiled broadly.

'But on the other hand, he mustn't be dull. That means he has to work hard at coming up with casual remarks that amuse. The kind of comment that's deliberately offhand but designed to catch attention — *my cook fell into the porridge this morning* — that sort of thing.'

She started to giggle.

'And, of course, he must never, ever wear brown shoes with a black suit!' His face pulled itself into an expression of horror.

She couldn't stop herself from laughing aloud but when he sat down, his voice was serious. 'It's silly, I know, but it has consequences that aren't so silly. If a man lives his life entirely within the regiment, he never has contact with an India that's real.'

Daisy thought she knew exactly what he meant and would have liked to tell him, but struggled to find the words.

'If you've finished your *chai*,' he was saying, 'I must be getting you back. Gerald will be home for lunch and you need some looking after.'

'Not really,' she protested, thinking it unlikely that Gerald would concern himself. She got up and followed him over the road to the shady tree where Gertie was lazily flicking her tail. 'I'm fine now. I was being stupid. It was the heat as much as anything. It always is.'

'So you make a habit of having large rocks nearly fall on your head?'

'No, but I don't make a habit of keeping a cobra in the bathroom either, and I seem to have survived that shock pretty well.'

She was watching his face for a reaction but he didn't seem surprised. 'They get everywhere,' he said placidly. 'But I can see it must have been frightening. I wonder you didn't turn tail and run for the hills.'

'I was tempted, but then Grayson took me to visit the temple and it was so beautiful and serene that I forgot how scared I'd been. I know Simla is part of India, too, and it's true I've never seen the town, but somehow it's this place that seems truer.'

'That's because it is. We are in a princely state, part of a proud and ancient land.' He was looking at her curiously. 'Have you travelled much, Daisy?'

'Not at all. Until I came here, I'd never been beyond London.'

'And you like being in India?'

'It's strange and wonderful but, yes, I like being here. It isn't my home but in an odd way, it feels as though it is. I'm happy — but I'd be even happier if the weather weren't so brutal.'

'I agree, it's a misery, even for Indians, but in a few weeks it will be gone. The monsoon will come and then you will see the land bloom again.'

Gertie turned her head and gave them an impatient look. 'She's ready to leave, I think,' Daisy said laughingly, putting her left foot into Anish's hand and allowing herself to be tossed into the saddle once more.

He gathered the reins into his hands. 'I'm glad you like Rajputana,' he said softly, 'but I wish you'd gone to Simla.'

CHAPTER SEVENTEEN

Gerald was standing on the veranda when they arrived looking irritated. 'There you are. I was starting to worry. Rajiv had no idea where you'd gone.'

Daisy felt a small pang of guilt, since this time she'd fled the house without leaving a clue to her whereabouts.

When Anish helped her down from the horse, she was thankful to plant her feet on solid ground once more. At that moment, she chanced to look up and saw the two men exchange a look. It was no more than a glance, but it signalled a private understanding to which she was not privy. She knew what they were thinking, though: they're worried I'm unstable, that I'm not coping well with the climate, that I've gone slightly mad.

'There's a bicycle to collect.' Anish grimaced at his friend. 'Daisy fell off.' She was glad he didn't mention the state he'd found her in. 'I think we should encourage her to ride, but a horse not a bike.'

'I'm not sure I could even stay in the saddle,' Daisy intervened. That was no exaggeration. Her fingers were numb from frantically clutching at Gertie's mane.

'Don't look so worried. A few practice rides and you'll be fine. I'll teach you.'

'Thank you, Anish, but—'

'We'll start small, walking the horses the first few times we go out.' He was not to be deterred. 'And we've plenty of land to walk in. Then once you're feeling more confident, we can venture further afield. Maybe head for the river. I'm sure you'd like it there and it makes for a good ride — as long as we leave first thing in the morning.'

'But the horse . . .' Daisy was looking for a way to escape.

'Leave that to me. There are several in the regimental stables that will be fine. Nice docile ladies, happy enough to plod quietly along while you learn. What do you think, Gerald?'

'It's an excellent idea. Daisy will need to ride sooner or later. But it will have to wait until she gets back. She's going up to Simla in a day or so.'

Anish looked across at his friend, clearly surprised. 'That's even better. Much easier to learn in the cool season. But don't forget, Daisy, we have a date when you get back from the hills.'

Her mind was spinning from Gerald's pronouncement, but Anish was about to remount and she must say goodbye. She held out her hand to him. 'Thank you for rescuing me.'

'You rescued yourself, but I was glad to be on the road.'

* * *

She walked back into the house, trying not to feel angry but hating Gerald's high-handedness. He'd had no right to tell Anish that she was leaving Jasirapur. She had been wavering on the brink of agreeing, but she'd made no decision. At the bathroom door, she scanned the floor before going in. She could never enter this room without her heart giving a small lurch. Splashing her face with water and patting it dry with the thin, cotton towel, she raised her head and saw her face in the mirror. Her eyes still had a hunted look. She was not easily going to forget today's fright. The more Daisy thought of it, the more she was sure that someone was trying to scare her. And succeeding, it seemed.

She walked back into the bedroom, thinking she might change into one of her new dresses. She wanted to look as attractive as she could since lunch was likely to be a difficult meal but, in the end, she simply smoothed out the creases of her old cotton frock and steadied herself for what was to come. A determination was forming in her mind; she might be scared, but she was not going to be scared away. Whoever was doing this, she intended to confront them.

And she had a pretty good idea who it might be. She couldn't work out what Grayson Harte had been doing near the temple nor whether he might have a connection to Rajiv. That seemed far-fetched. But she was almost certain that the servant had been behind the attack. He had been hostile since the moment she arrived. He was jealous of her, possessive of the house and of his master. He wanted her gone, and he was doing all he could to make her leave.

It seemed unlikely he could have got to the temple before her, but it was possible he had an accomplice — that man she'd seen in the garden — the man Rajiv had sworn didn't exist. Ever since she'd arrived, she'd felt herself being watched, but had shrugged it off as imagination. Now she was beginning to think that she hadn't been mistaken. If the man had been watching her and followed, he might know the temple site well enough to climb onto its roof without showing himself. It was improbable but not impossible. And there had to be some explanation for the unpleasant incidents that had begun to dog her, incidents that were gradually becoming more serious in the attempt to dislodge her. But she wasn't going to be dislodged. She was going to stay and find Rajiv out. She was going to show Gerald just what kind of servant he employed. He refused to believe any wrong of the man, but she was determined to prove that false.

* * *

'I've got your ticket.' Gerald waved a slip of paper at her as she came to the table. 'Only just, though. I was lucky.'

She sat down and ate a first mouthful. Then true to her resolve, took a deep breath and said in a quiet voice, 'I never promised I'd definitely be leaving, Gerald. I said I would think about it.'

'There's nothing to think about. And after this morning's mishap, you're surely glad to be going.'

It was this morning's mishap, as he termed it, that had finally decided Daisy against going, but that was something she couldn't say. She took another deep breath. 'I've decided to stay.'

'You can't.'

She looked astonished. 'I mean,' he amended, 'I've got the ticket now.'

'I'm sorry you've gone to that expense but I did say I would decide later,' she reminded him, 'and now I have. I'm staying.'

For a moment, he stared unbelievingly at her across the table. Then he thrust back his chair and stomped to his feet. His face was a mottled red, the same angry colour she had seen when she'd told him about the baby. 'You're impossible! This—' he waved his arm to indicate the house, their life together, she imagined — 'this is impossible! I'm going to work and then on to the Mess. Don't wait up for me.'

He pushed past the table, sending his cutlery clattering to the floor. Without bothering to retrieve it, he stormed out of the house and yelled at the driver who'd been waiting patiently for his passenger to finish lunch. A last rev of the car engine fading into the distance and silence fell across the bungalow.

Daisy remained at the table but managed little more of the meal. Her head was throbbing badly and pushing her plate aside, she went to her room and flung herself down on the bed. A half-sewn summer bag, which she'd begun to fashion from the remnants of material left behind by the *durzi*, was thrown to one side. A book followed. She was too hot to sew, too hot to read. Too hot, too hurt to do anything.

She had crossed Gerald again and his reaction had once more been violent. She was to do what he said or else. Last evening, they had begun to build a bridge of understanding and now she had broken it. Should she try to mend the pieces, agree after all to go to Simla? She couldn't, she was too far into this horrible chain of events to turn tail. If she was in any doubt, she had only to think of the mayhem that had overtaken her just a few hours ago. Something or somebody was sabotaging her life, was trying to make her believe there was something wrong with her.

There was nothing wrong with her, she thought fiercely. What was wrong was the life she was forced to lead, cooped up in this solitary house with a malicious servant living just feet away. Even if she went to Simla, he would still be here when she returned. If she were to prosper in this new life, she had to uncover what Rajiv was plotting.

* * *

That night, Daisy didn't wait up for her husband. There was little point since she had no idea what time the Mess bar closed, and that was where she guessed he'd be. And she was so weary from doing battle with the rising temperature that, despite the discomfort of a sticky room, she fell asleep almost immediately.

She must have slept for several hours when she heard stumbling footsteps in the sitting room. A chair scraped across the floor as though someone had bumped into it and there was the sound of something falling off one of the small tables. Gerald had returned and evidently not stopped at one *chota peg*. A loud curse and a clunk of leather against the hard floor. Boots, she supposed. She hoped he wouldn't be too long finding his bed; she felt desperately tired and wanted nothing but to sleep.

Her bedroom door banged open and, alarmed by the noise, she jerked her head up from the pillows. Between half-closed eyes, she saw the dim outline of a swaying figure. He staggered a few feet into the room and stood, legs splayed, unsure it seemed of where he was going or if he was going to get there. She wondered whether she should go to him and help him to bed. Rajiv would be the right person to do that, but Gerald had not called for his servant and might not wish to be seen so thoroughly intoxicated. She would have to do her best. But before she could slide out of bed, he had begun to unzip trousers and unbutton his jacket and shirt.

'Are you awake, Daisy?' he shouted. 'Better be awake, girl.'

'Yes, Gerald. I am awake. You woke me,' she said pointedly.

'Good, good. That's what a wife's for, eh. I've got myself a wife, might as well use her.'

She was no longer shocked by the sight of his drinking and her practical nature took over. 'Tell me how I can help you.'

'Help me! You think I don't know what to do. Should know better than that, Daise — you of all people. Knew what to do last time, eh?'

So this is what his intrusion meant. How stupid she was not to have realised from the outset. She thought of the times she'd longed to lie close to him, night after night of longing, but not like this. He was wretchedly drunk, even worse than when he'd stood by her side at the altar. It seemed to be the only way he could face any form of intimacy.

'You're beautiful,' he slurred. 'Just as well — least I get something out of it.' She quailed as his glazed eyes scanned her body.

He saw her shudder of revulsion. 'Wassa matter? Gone coy all of a sudden? No problem in London, was there?' The jeers shrank her soul and Daisy found herself hating him, hating where she was, hating what she'd done in marrying him.

Bunching the sheet, she tried to make a shell in which to hide. Gerald slumped back against the doorframe, watching her with the exaggerated intensity of the drunk.

'Don' worry,' he slurred again. 'Go back to sleep. You may not be a lady but I'm a gentleman. And don't you forget it!'

She heard him banging his way along the passage, then the crash of his body as it met the bed. The sound of loud snoring was almost immediate. She listened for several minutes as the snores continued to vibrate through the bedroom's thin walls, then swung her legs out of the hot, crumpled bed and tiptoed into the bathroom. Splashing her face with cold water, she stood for a long time looking at the drawn face in the mirror.

Once again, Gerald had been someone she hardly recognised. Daisy had used to think him tender and kind, but there had been little kindness on show tonight. Quite the opposite. It was part of a recurring pattern, she thought miserably. Since she'd arrived in India, he'd shunned all attempts to rekindle the feelings they'd once shared. Pushed her away in the most brutal fashion, left her solitary, hour after hour, a girl thousands of miles from home and cut off from familiar surroundings. And now he'd threatened her with assault when he was too drunk to know what he was doing. She felt hopeless and defeated. And the love she'd nurtured so diligently began its slow seep away.

CHAPTER EIGHTEEN

When Daisy woke next morning from a disturbed sleep, he'd already gone and she was left to spend the day wondering how they could bear to look each other in the face again. But she need not have worried. When Gerald returned home well into the afternoon, he appeared to have no recollection that anything untoward had happened.

She had been dozing over a book in the sitting room, but came fully awake when she saw her husband coming towards her chair, cup in hand. She wondered if she were dreaming.

'Rajiv has made *chai*. I thought you might like some. There are cakes, too.'

'No cakes, thank you, but this is very kind.' If he was making an effort, so must she. She sat up and took the cup from him. 'I thought you'd be at the camp for the rest of the afternoon. I didn't expect you back until dinner.'

He looked a trifle shamefaced. 'Thursdays are half days.' That was news to her. He had never seemed to have an afternoon free before. 'Normally we use it for sport, but there's not much you can do in these temperatures.'

He crouched down in front of her. 'I'm sorry about yesterday, Daisy. I shouldn't have ruined your lunch in that way, going off at the deep end. You'd had a tremendous shock. When I got back to camp, Anish told me about the scare. What on earth were you doing at that temple on your own?'

'I had a fancy to see it, that's all,' she said mildly.

'Next time you have a fancy, tell me. You shouldn't do that kind of thing, you know. It's not right for an Englishwoman to be roaming around the countryside unescorted. And you were lucky to get away without injury. The temple is nothing more than a ruin and I've heard that bits of it regularly crumble. It's definitely not safe to visit.'

If that were the case, she wondered why Grayson hadn't thought to mention it, but aloud she promised, 'I won't do it again.'

He got up and sat a little way off. There had been no mention of the drunken abuse. Was it possible he didn't remember, or was it that he didn't want to? If so, he might be right; it might be wiser to go along with the fiction that last night had been like any other.

'It's cooling off a little now. If I order up a tonga, would you like to take a drive?'

She wondered if she'd heard aright. Gerald was willing to spend time with her, and not just time, but was going out of his way to plan an excursion. 'Unless, of course, you'd rather stay here,' he finished lamely.

'No, not at all.' She was swift to set his mind at rest. 'I'd like that very much. Thank you for thinking of it.'

He seemed relieved. 'Rest a while more then, and we'll leave around five.'

When he'd gone to shower, Daisy lay back in the chair, feeling lightheaded and very slightly confused. She was finding it difficult to keep pace with her husband's rapid shifts of mood. Not that she wasn't grateful for his goodwill, but she couldn't help wondering if his change of heart was part of a plan to wear her down, an attempt to get her to change tack and agree to move to the hills. Threats hadn't worked and now he was trying to persuade her with gentle indulgence. Was that it? Even if that were true, she mustn't allow it to cloud her mind. She must think only good thoughts and, if he were trying to make amends, she must meet him halfway.

* * *

By five o'clock she was dressed in the prettiest of the frocks the *durzi* had made, a flimsy cotton in the palest pink, clinched at the waist with a belt made from the same material, and with a lace collar and cuffs to the puff sleeves. She looked in the mirror and was pleased. Her dark hair and eyes were a perfect foil for the dress; her eyes in particular had recovered their old sparkle. Gerald was waiting for her in the living room and when she saw his look of approval, her spirits rose even higher.

'Is that new?'

For a moment her mood faltered. She had spent only a small sum of money on the clothes but now that she knew their true situation, she reproached herself for it. Automatically her eyes swivelled towards the desk but even from where she was standing, she could see that the sheaf of bills was no longer there. They had vanished, in the same way she imagined as the letter from Joseph Minns had vanished. It seemed that anything disagreeable, anything that Gerald wanted to forget or keep from open discussion, was swallowed by his desk.

She wondered if he'd done anything about the bills or whether she was likely to receive another visit from the two Indian gentlemen. She wondered, in fact, if he'd done anything about the letter from the man she now thought of as his father or if Mr Minns was still struggling to survive in the poorest of circumstances. But Gerald wouldn't speak of either problems and she couldn't ask. At least not yet. If this afternoon were to mark the beginning of a happier relationship between them, she might one day be able to talk to him about the things that really mattered.

The tonga was at the door, the driver snoozing contentedly in his seat. Gerald gave an instruction in Hindi. 'I've told him to drive to the river. I saw how your eyes lit up when Anish mentioned a ride there.'

She could hear the old Gerald in his voice, the Gerald who had won her heart all those months ago, walking together through the streets and parks of London. 'I'd love to drive there,' she responded warmly. 'I caught a glimpse of the river when I was in Jasirapur, but only a glimpse.'

'The spot I've chosen is nothing like that. Where the river flows through the town, it's heavily polluted. Just about everything goes into it. But we'll be driving into open countryside and there are few animals and even fewer people to despoil it. We should find a small amount of shade there, too. Several trees, nothing much, but enough shelter from the worst of the glare.'

'It's already much cooler.'

'Maybe, but it stays hot for an hour or two, and you don't look well.'

She must have looked upset for he said quickly, 'You look very nice in that dress but your face is strained, that's what I mean. I'm not surprised. You're finding the climate difficult and you've had a few shocks. The snake, and now this incident at the temple.'

He didn't mention the locked door, she noticed, but then the snake and the rock were incontestable facts and the door had only been her illusion. As he'd said, it had probably never been locked.

'I'm not ill, just a little weary. It's difficult to sleep. You warned me how horrid it would be but—'

'—but you can't ever imagine the discomfort. Perhaps tonight you'll sleep better. I forgot to mention that Grayson Harte called at the house yesterday. Rajiv has just told me. He left some goji berries for you.'

'Goji berries?' She was surprised, and not just by the strange name. Disturbed, too. Grayson had been close to the temple when she'd made her ill-fated visit but had he first called at the bungalow with the excuse of a gift of fruit, then finding her gone, had guessed her destination and followed?

'You can squash them down into a juice and then make a drink from them. They're supposed to be good for your health and for sleeping. I've told Rajiv to prepare a glass for you at bedtime.'

'That's very kind.' She seemed to be saying that a great deal today.

He shifted uneasily in his seat. 'I haven't been very kind, and I'm sorry for that. Sorry for my outburst yesterday. I was convinced a break was the right thing for us and when you decided otherwise, I lost my temper. That was wrong. Whatever you decide about Simla will be fine. I know things are difficult for both of us, but we've just got to get on with our lives as best we can.'

It was hardly a ringing endorsement of marriage, but it was reality and one she'd begun to accept. Last night's hateful advances were only a mask for the real problem — the fact that he didn't love her. Even the days they'd spent together in London had a shadow over them now. He'd taken her dancing, taken her to the cinema, once even to a fancy restaurant. She still had the keepsakes he'd bought during their wanderings. They'd cost little but she had treasured them. He'd made her feel special and she'd fallen in love.

But his verdict on those times had left her flayed. She had been nothing but 'fun', a pick-up if you were to speak the vulgar truth. And she'd behaved like one, hadn't she? That last night in her room when he'd plied her with drink, she had become silly and flirtatious and willing. She'd listened to his promises and believed them. She'd surrendered her body and with it, her heart and soul too. It was still difficult to accept that it hadn't been that way for Gerald, that her feelings had been so very different from his.

'There's the river, straight ahead.'

She craned her head forward and saw a wide expanse of water curving a path through the flat landscape. The sun was low, and its rays were catching at the river's edge as it meandered right, then left, glittering and golden in the dying light. A boat drifted a little way offshore dragging a length of mesh behind it. A fisherman called out to his mate and she saw the glint of a body, scales gleaming in the sunset, then a loud thump as a large fish was ejected from the net and joined the wriggling heap on the boat's deck.

'Here, sahib?' the driver asked.

'Yes, here.' They drew up beneath the shelter of a small cluster of trees and she breathed in the sweet smell of the fuzz buzz flowers, warm from the day. 'We could watch the river from here, if you like — the shade is sufficient. Unless you'd prefer to walk a little.'

'Yes, let's walk. It's cool enough, I think.'

She was eager to go. The landscape was different here, its smells and colours newly thrilling. They sauntered along the riverbank, walking in harmony, bodies close but not touching, as the huge disc of sun slipped slowly downwards behind the horizon. When the last streaks of gold had disappeared from the sky, they turned back towards the tonga, for in no time twilight would be over and the inky blackness of an Indian night would be upon them.

'We should have done this before,' he said, as the tonga whisked them back to the bungalow.

'You've been busy.' She wanted to excuse him, to save this happy afternoon from recrimination.

'Not so busy that I couldn't take you out and about a little.'

She reached out for his hand and he let her take it. 'Don't let's think of the past,' she pleaded. 'This afternoon has been good, and we can do it again. Whenever you have another Thursday free.'

'That will be soon, I promise.' He allowed his hand to stay in hers, helping her down from the tonga and only releasing her when he turned to pay the driver. The smell of chicken curry greeted them as they walked into the house and for the first time in a long while, she felt hungry for it.

Dinner was a great deal more companionable than yesterday's lunch. And when Rajiv came in with the drink he'd made from Grayson's goji berries, she was relaxed enough to drink it down without a thought.

'You should get to bed,' her husband urged. 'Those berries should send you off to sleep in no time.'

It was only then that she felt worry strike. Should she have taken more care and not drunk them? What if these berries were like the snake and the rock, a possible means for Grayson to 'rescue' her? But she dismissed the thought almost as soon as it arose. Gerald had voiced no qualms and she was sure that Grayson Harte wished her nothing but well. It was simple coincidence that had found him close by when things had gone awry. It was what he'd said himself, 'fate'.

When she rose to go to the bedroom, Gerald made no attempt to go with her, but contented himself with a chaste kiss on her cheek. She wasn't surprised. In minutes she had undressed and hung her frock in the battered cupboard, safe from any marauding ants. She was glad that Gerald had liked the dress. One day things might change between them, but their estrangement no longer had the power to hurt and for that she was grateful. The sheets were cool to her touch, at least for the moment, and she stretched out between them, her head slightly fuzzy but her limbs completely relaxed. Grayson's drink seemed to be working. In a few minutes she was asleep.

CHAPTER NINETEEN

Over the next few days a wind began to blow, a searing blast which felt as though every oven in India had been opened simultaneously. Although Rajiv ensured that windows and doors were shut by seven in the morning, he spent much of the day wetting the plaited screens while the bungalow broiled. At night, it was once more difficult to sleep, despite Daisy dutifully swallowing a glass of goji juice before going to bed. Noise as well as heat was intensified: frogs croaked louder, cicadas sawed relentlessly and jackals shrieked rather than howled, setting in motion the frantic barking of stray dogs from villages for miles around.

For three days the wind raged and Daisy did not dare venture outside, but life within doors was almost as miserable. The air was a solid mass, and as its temperature rose, so did the number of insects. The floor came alive with black beetles and green flies heaped in every corner, while flying ants and bluebottles nightly incarcerated themselves on the kerosene lamps.

Gerald was largely absent. He was heavily involved in preparations for the parade and Friday's was the last of the season, and destined to be by far the most splendid. How the event was to take place in such weather, Daisy found difficult to imagine, but he insisted that it was certain to go ahead. His whole attention was focused on getting his troop in tip-top condition — men, horses, uniforms, weapons — for what was to be a huge occasion. The regiment had been told that a very important person, a 'bigwig' as Gerald put it, was travelling from Delhi to hold the inspection and they could not afford for anything to go wrong. He seemed to worry that it might.

'I don't like the stories we're hearing,' he fretted over dinner one night. 'There's always been the odd agitation demanding independence but since that chap, Gandhi, put in an appearance, it's got worse. And now the local trade unions have joined with the peasants, both bellowing at the top of their voices. That's serious — there's an awful lot of peasants.'

'They're demanding independence?' From what Daisy had seen of village life, it seemed unlikely.

'Not in so many words. They're asking for control over their rents and taxes, which is as good as. In my book at least. It all adds up to a bad situation and not what I thought I'd ever see.'

'But why do you think the parade will be affected?'

'I don't, not particularly. But the senior officers have received reports of unrest in and around Jasirapur, and there's some nervousness about how things will go. Nothing solid, just vague threats of disruption. It's unfortunate given that we've learned General Pearson is our guest of honour. If there are difficulties, it won't reflect well on the regiment.'

He relapsed into silence as Rajiv clattered their empty plates together and made for the kitchen. Then, still silent, he took his seat on the lumpy horsehair sofa and looked blankly into the distance.

'There may not be anything to worry about,' she said coaxingly. 'The police will be there, won't they, and they'll surely stop any trouble.'

He turned his head to look at her, a flicker of the old irritation in his face. 'They'll be there, of course, but they're not always able to hold the line. Then it's the poor bloody army that has to step in.' Gerald's language was a measure of his anxiety. 'We can't be sure what might happen and we need to be prepared.'

* * *

As soon as the wind died, Daisy began to look forward to the parade, taking little heed of Gerald's gloom. When she woke on Friday morning, it was to feel a small tingle of excitement. She dressed carefully in the cream cotton sundress, arranging her hair in a topknot rather than the loose waves she usually wore. The *topi* would make short work of the style, she knew, but she had the satisfaction of at least starting the day looking her best. She was ready for the occasion and Jocelyn would be here very soon.

The girl was as good as her word, arriving at the house with pony and trap just as Daisy finished a hurried breakfast. She got up quickly, wanting to save her visitor from a painful walk to the door, but Jocelyn beat her to it.

'See, I'm crutches free!' she exclaimed. 'Limping, but otherwise perfectly fit.'

'Is your ankle still painful?' Daisy hauled herself into the passenger seat.

'A little,' the girl admitted, 'but nothing to stop me from going to Simla. I'm off tomorrow. I must admit I'm not sorry to go. The heat has been horrendous, hasn't it, and I'm even beginning to miss Ma! I do so love going back. It's like being a child again. I remember how pale I'd grow after months on the plains but then we'd go up to the hills and in a short while, lo and behold — red, rosy cheeks.'

She cracked the whip and the horse turned obediently back along the overgrown path and out of the garden. 'So what have you been up to since I saw you at the library? That was days ago.'

Daisy wasn't sure how much to confide. Her solo visit to the temple had faded a little from her mind and she had no wish to bring the memory back, certainly no wish to confess the panic she'd been in that day. She decided on caution.

'I haven't been out for days — the weather has seen to that — but just before the wind arrived, I did get back on the bike. Or I did until I came a cropper,' she finished brightly.

'What happened?'

'I fell off. Something scared me as I was riding. A peacock, I think, flying up into the trees.' A white lie was permissible, she told herself. 'Anyway, the noise startled me and I skidded across the road and ended upside down.'

'How dreadful! Were you badly hurt?'

'Only my pride, but it did put paid to any more rides. On the bicycle at least. I've other plans now. I'm about to learn to ride a different beast.' She wasn't sure, in fact, if Anish's offer still held.

'You're going horse riding! That's wonderful. Learning to ride is essential, but who's going to teach you?'

'I'm not sure,' Daisy answered carefully. 'Probably Gerald — when he can.' It was better not to mention Lieutenant Rana, knowing how disapproving Jocelyn would be.

'Perfect, my dear.' Her evident relief that Gerald would be spending time with his wife made Daisy wonder how much the girl knew about their marriage. If Jocelyn suspected problems, she might be feeling guilty for her part in any estrangement.

'I have to admit I'm a trifle nervous,' she said, 'but I'm determined to give it a try. I'm not sure what I should be wearing, though.'

'Jodhpurs, of course.' Jocelyn smiled. 'But I don't suppose there's much call for jodhpurs in London. That's where you've come from, isn't it?'

'I haven't seen a pair walking down Oxford Street, that's for sure.'

The girl giggled. 'Would you like to borrow some, until you can get your own made? I've three or four pairs and I won't be needing them in Simla, it's much too steep for any decent riding. Rickshaws only. Unless you're the Viceroy, then you get a car.'

'Thank you, I'd be really grateful. We're much the same size.'

'Wishful thinking on my part, Daisy. You'll find them a bit big, but you can always put a belt around the waist so you don't lose them mid-ride.'

They both joined in the laughter, then settled to a discussion of Jocelyn's plans once she arrived in Simla, which lasted until they reached the outskirts of the town. The smell of mustard cooking oil was everywhere in the streets, mingling headily with the smoke of burnt cow dung. The smell of sunshine, Daisy thought, vigorous, intense, alive.

'We'll need to wind our way round to the maiden through some of the alleyways,' Jocelyn said, 'and I thought we'd park up beneath the trees when we get there. There are several on the south side where we can watch the parade from the buggy. The ground is sure to be very crowded and we'll get a much better view from the carriage.'

Daisy was disappointed. She'd been looking forward to mingling with the crowd, which was already beginning to spill out of the narrow streets, making its way towards the large open space on the southern edge of the town. But she bowed to Jocelyn's experience and, within a short while, they'd found a niche between several of the open air stalls, already doing a brisk business in fritters and fried chickpeas. An appetising aroma floated their way and, after a small breakfast, Daisy was tempted.

Her friend was quick to dissuade her. 'You should never eat from a roadside stall, even if the food is hot. You can't count on the hygiene, and you could end up very ill. Dysentery would be the least of your worries. Cholera is a real threat — you can get it from any water they may have used — and it's deadly. It can kill within a few hours.'

The British were evangelical about hygiene, Daisy already knew. Even though Gerald appeared to trust Rajiv implicitly, he still insisted on checking daily that the milk and water had been boiled, the fruit peeled, and the vegetables washed in permanganate of potash, the *pinki pani* of every European household.

She tried to forget her rumbling stomach and settled to watch the magnificent pageant unfolding before her. It was a moving caravan of dazzling white kurtas massed against a kaleidoscope of saris. Brilliant oranges and reds, shrill pink, and every shade of green and blue. Such beautiful people, she thought, all smooth brown skin and black hair ashine with coconut oil.

Very soon the small space in front and either side of the pony trap had been filled by an eager, excited audience. From the corner of her eye, Daisy caught sight of a face she thought she knew. She looked again, and was certain. He was one of the Indians who had come to her door days ago. The older man, the one with such a distinguished air. He must have felt her gaze for he looked across at her and bowed graciously in her direction. She'd had no further visits from Gerald's creditors and the man seemed genial enough. Did that mean her husband had paid his debts? If so, Daisy had no idea how he'd managed to do so.

Where could he have found the money? The first answer that came to mind, her first fear, was from gambling. According to both Jocelyn and Anish, gambling in the past had landed him in worse trouble. But, almost instantly, she dismissed the idea. Gerald had not visited the Club for days: he had been too taken up with preparations for the parade. So where *had* the money come from? It was yet another mystery.

The first strains of music sounded across the arena and the lead musicians of the regimental band wheeled into view, heading the parade and marching directly to the centre of the maiden. The music was followed minutes later by the sound of hundreds of horses' hooves beating a tattoo on the rough ground. The regiment had arrived, and in full regalia. Blue and gold uniforms with pennants flying from lances, and magnificent horses gleaming in the early morning sunlight, their harnesses jangling as they tossed their heads in a cloud of dust. On and on, the double line of mounted soldiers rode past, a conveyor belt of military splendour.

By now, the maiden was throbbing with hundreds, if not thousands, of people: eating, drinking, chattering, jostling for room. An ant heap come alive. From the road that circled the arena, a car swept into the one remaining open space and pulled to a halt just short of a white dais erected at a distance from the parading soldiers. A portly man clambered from the vehicle's back seat. He smoothed the creases from his uniform jacket, tucked his military baton beneath one arm and offered a smart salute to the Colonel.

'Doesn't Pa look magnificent?' Jocelyn whispered.

But Daisy's eyes were not on Colonel Forester but on Gerald riding at the head of his troop. He, too, looked magnificent, but distracted. His face was half-turned towards them, the slightest of movements, which did nothing to disturb the symmetry of his troop's line but, as his gaze focused, Daisy realised with a crushed feeling that his eyes were not seeking her, but Jocelyn. They rested on the girl for a second only, but the tell-tale flush on his cheeks told its own story. She tried not to notice and Jocelyn, sitting close beside her, seemed completely unaware. She was intent on watching her father accompany the General on his tour of inspection, a proud smile on her face.

General Pearson, acting as the King's representative, addressed the mounted lines of cavalry. He spoke at length, praising the men for their sterling work and looking forward to many more years of the regiment keeping the peace for India. The crowd listened politely, though Daisy suspected they understood little of his speech and were interested in even less. They had come for the spectacle, for the colourful uniforms and the magnificent horses.

One or two of the beasts began to fuss and shy as the General reached his peroration. The regimental sergeant major called for three cheers and then, the climax of the ceremony, the presentation of new regimental colours. The old flags were folded and laid to one side, the lances raised in salute, and the order given for the cavalry to march again, back once more through the town to the cantonment. There had been a hushed silence during the short ceremony, but now the crowd burst into a noisy hum of gossip and laughter.

'We'd better wait for the place to clear a bit,' Jocelyn advised, 'unless you're in a desperate rush to get back.'

'No, not at all.' Daisy's mind was still on the glance she'd intercepted. She hoped very much that Jocelyn wasn't involved. She'd made a rare friend and didn't want to lose her. 'But are you packed and ready to go?'

'More or less. I—'

She never finished her sentence for the happy buzz of the crowd had given way to a more sinister noise, the sound of loud shouting, and of people pushing their way forcibly through their fellows. The shouts were repeated. Slogans possibly, Daisy thought, but in a language she didn't understand. The sun was now almost vertically above them and the shade they'd enjoyed was rapidly disappearing. She held her hand up to ward off the glare. She could see figures moving through the crowd, mowing a path towards the soldiers who had turned in unison and were now riding forward and away from the maiden. The figures were waving flags and holding up banners. She heard what seemed to be a rallying call — in English this time — 'Mother India!'

Jocelyn was looking perturbed but kept the horse calm, soothing it in a quiet voice. A police superintendent appeared from their left and faced the crowd. He was dressed in full ceremonial uniform and wore a revolver on each side of his body.

'He'll be sufficient to settle any disturbance,' Jocelyn said comfortably. 'And look. He's brought several constables with him.' A couple of uniformed men had waded into the crowd and were busy confiscating the banners and flags.

But it wasn't enough. The protest continued and the shouts became louder and more forceful. The atmosphere had changed from carnival to ugly in a matter of minutes. Women wrapped their arms around their children or cradled babies tightly against their saris. A larger group of police arrived, ready to fortify their colleagues, and ordered people to disperse. A good number of the crowd slid quietly away, but there still remained a sizeable group. Without further delay, the police strode directly into them, *lathis* raised.

CHAPTER TWENTY

One of those who had been shouting loudest was caught, the policeman grabbing him around the waist and felling him with a loud crack of the long, wooden pole. From her vantage point, Daisy could see the scuffle unfolding. The body lying prone on the ground seemed little more than a boy's but, as he lay motionless, a much larger form intervened and pushed the policeman roughly out of the way. Screwing up her eyes, she tried to see his face. Something about him seemed familiar.

She dredged her memory and then it came to her. He was the man who'd run through the bazaar on her very first day in Jasirapur, the man who'd been chased by a police officer and was again their quarry. The policeman turned his attention from the boy on the ground and began to beat the would-be rescuer around the head with his fists, then took the wooden pole he carried and brought it down in a cruel arc across the man's back.

Those nearest in the crowd sent out an angry mutter and, when the other police joined in the mêlée and began to labour the crowd indiscriminately, the mutter turned to a howl. As one, the crowd turned on their tormentors and several of the policemen disappeared in a welter of blows, their *lathis* useless on the ground. At that, their fellow officers waited no more and made for cover, the crowd swallowing them as they ran.

'We must try to get out of here,' Jocelyn said, her voice a little shaky. 'I don't like the way things are going.'

But they were still hemmed in on all sides, and the horse, docile until this point, began to toss his head impatiently and paw at the ground, clearly unsettled. There was now a pitch battle going on just yards in front of them. Bodies threshed in anger and curses were hurled, along with bricks and soda water bottles, while sticks cracked down on unprotected skulls with a sickening crunch.

A figure caught Daisy's eye. It was Grayson Harte. He was not engaged in the fighting, but seemed to be trying to find a way through to the small circle of protesters who had begun the mayhem. A slightly built young Indian was by his side, and neither of them was making headway through the sprawling mass of fighting men.

Then soldiers appeared out of nowhere. Not mounted, for the cavalry had left the maiden before trouble had taken a real hold, but soldiers with rifles. The police had been unable to quell the disturbance and they had been summoned, no doubt unwillingly, to restore order. They made no attempt to infiltrate the crowd but instead herded them, pushing them back into a tight circle by dint of dropping their rifle butts on thinly shod feet. The once belligerent crowd were cowed, and began to file away as the soldiers directed.

But then one of the crowd disentangled himself from his fellows and, escaping the circle, began again to shout the inflammatory slogans that had started the riot. The soldier nearest him swung his rifle butt and the air echoed with the thud of wood on bone. The man slumped to the ground. For a minute, the crowd held its breath, then that howl of anger again, and people surged forward, fists and feet flying.

Jocelyn was shaking and Daisy held tightly to her friend's hand. The people on either side of them had faded away, trickling from the maiden in ones and twos, intent on escaping the violence that had shattered the day's pleasure.

'We should be able to get out now,' Daisy urged the girl.

The carriage might just squeeze through the space that had been left. It would mean executing a sharp right turn into the road, but Jocelyn was no doubt an accomplished whip. Daisy strained her eyes, trying to chart a passage for her friend, and there coming towards them was Grayson Harte, supporting the young Indian who had been by his side. The boy had blood trickling down his forehead and matting his hair, Grayson half-pulling, half-carrying him to safety. Jocelyn hadn't noticed. She seemed numbed with fear. This was something she had never before encountered, Daisy reasoned, and as the only two European spectators left on the maiden, they were clearly vulnerable.

In an almost hypnotic trance, the girl took hold of the reins just as Grayson arrived at the side of their vehicle, blue eyes blazing. He appeared uninjured, but his shirt was plastered to his body by sweat and his face looked grim.

'Daisy, Miss Forester,' he panted. 'My colleague — he's been hurt quite badly. Could I impose on you? I must stay, but would you take him to the Infirmary? He needs immediate treatment.'

Jocelyn looked blankly down at him. 'You know the way, Miss Forester?' he said urgently. 'If I try to keep the crowd back, you should be able to turn the carriage.'

The girl didn't answer, seeming to be in another world entirely, and Daisy felt forced to pinch her hard. Jocelyn sat up, suddenly alert.

'Mr Harte, what are you doing here?' It was a question that Daisy herself would have liked to ask.

'It's no matter. My colleague needs to go to the Infirmary,' he repeated. 'Can you help?'

'Yes, yes of course. Daisy, if you could clamber into the back . . .' Her wits, it seemed, were returning.

Daisy wedged herself into the rear of the trap and, with some difficulty, Grayson Harte heaved the young man into her arms. The crowd was very much thinner, but those who remained had nothing now to lose, their voices thrumming in anger, their faces set in retribution. Grayson managed to clear a space to one side of them and Jocelyn, her face tense, manoeuvred the pony and trap backwards and forwards until they were facing the narrow street they had travelled only a short while ago.

'Take this. It might help.' He passed Daisy a large, white handkerchief and then turned to go.

Her last sight of him was plunging back into the rioting crowd, this time accompanied by two burly soldiers, their rifles raised. She heard shots ring out, but there was no time to worry over what was happening. She had a more urgent concern. As Jocelyn concentrated on driving as fast as she could along the narrow street, Daisy used the square of linen to try and staunch the boy's blood. It was flowing far too freely and she resigned herself to the ruin of her dress. But it was the young man who took all her attention. His face was waxen and he appeared to have lost consciousness. She felt thoroughly scared, for she was not sure they would get to the Infirmary in time.

It was fortunate the building was situated on the very edge of the civil station and a notice announcing Indian Medical Service was reached within minutes. That was just as well, Daisy thought, cradling the boy's limp form in her arms. She had tried to keep the blood from trickling into his eyes and mouth, but she could see that beneath the dark plaster of his hair the wound he'd received was very deep.

'Hallo there,' Jocelyn was calling out. 'Dr Lane, we need help please. Help!'

Her voice crackled through the silence that lay over the civil station. Surely, someone must hear. She called again and again until finally a harassed-looking man, grey-haired and spectacled, emerged from the door and looked at them in surprise.

'There's been an accident,' Jocelyn began, and then without warning, tears flooded down her cheeks. The fright she'd suffered was taking its toll.

'I can see that.' The doctor's tone verged on irascible. At least, Daisy imagined, he must be the doctor. He called to some people behind him, and two large orderlies appeared and very gently extricated the young man from the back of the carriage.

Daisy climbed down from her seat but when her friend, still tearful, made to do the same, she stopped her with a grateful clasp of her hand. Jocelyn had been scared half to death but had driven them out of danger.

'You've done enough today. And you've a long journey tomorrow. You should drive home and get some rest.'

'But the man . . .'

'He's in good hands. The doctor will put him right in no time, I'm sure. And I'll stay for a while in case there's anything I can do.'

'I have to return the pony and trap to the Adjutant.'

'Of course you have. Go now before he gets worried. News of the riot will already be circulating.'

Jocelyn nodded, but still seemed reluctant to leave. 'How will you get home?'

'I'm sure I'll manage. I'm on the civil station, not in the wilds of the jungle.'

Her companion smiled weakly. 'If you're really sure.'

'I'm really sure.'

The girl picked up the reins and then smiled down at Daisy, almost her old self again. 'I do wish you were coming with me. To Simla, I mean. Promise that as soon as I get back, you'll come over and see me, or invite me to tea at the bungalow.'

'I promise. You'll have plenty to tell me.'

'I certainly will, though I won't be home for long to do the telling. Just a few weeks.' She said it with regret. 'But we'll make the most of them.'

'Why, where are you going?' Daisy was disconcerted.

'Back to England. Once we've returned from Simla, I'm to be packed off again. To Sussex this time. Ma has family there, and I'm to spend the winter enjoying myself. Or at least that's what she says. I'm sure there's quite a different scheme though. One that involves me finding a husband!'

'Wouldn't India be a better place to find one?' That seemed to make a lot more sense. 'There must be plenty of young officers desperate to marry.'

'That's the problem. I can't be seen to favour anyone in the regiment, not with Pa as the Colonel.' She screwed up her nose. 'And to be honest, none of them interest me sufficiently.'

'None of them?'

'There *was* a young man a few years ago.' Jocelyn's cheeks grew pink. 'He was on the Unattached List. He was with us while he decided which regiment he wanted to join. In the end, he got into Skinner's Horse. He *was* very good at his job. Either that or he had the right connections.'

'Did you lose touch then?'

'Yes, at least we did until a week ago. He wrote to me out of the blue.' The pink had changed to a fiery red. 'Actually, that was why I fell over the doormat. I saw the envelope lying there and recognised his writing — he'd written me a few notes while he was here. I couldn't quite believe he'd got back in touch.'

'And where is he now?'

'Well, that's the thing. He thought I was back home. I was supposed to be returning to England when I last saw him but, for one reason or another, I never got there. Anyway, he was waiting until he got home leave before he contacted me. He'll be in England next month.'

'So you'll meet up?'

'That's the plan. I don't know if anything will come of it. It's ages since we saw each other but I liked him enormously.'

'I wish you luck,' she said with sincerity, for every one of Jocelyn's words had made plain that the girl cherished no feelings for Gerald and never had.

'You can wish me double luck when I get back from the hills. And you must help me choose the clothes to take to England. It could be a very important journey.' The tears and fears of a few moments ago had been forgotten in the swirl of a likely romance.

'You should go now,' Daisy urged. 'You must still have plenty to do before you leave.'

Jocelyn bent down and planted a kiss on her cheek. 'Thank you, Daisy, and thank you for being with me. I couldn't have got through it without you.'

CHAPTER TWENTY-ONE

Daisy watched the horse out of sight as it trotted towards the straight lines of the officers' bungalows. Then she walked into the Infirmary. No one was around, and she took a seat in the small, stuffy waiting room, not quite knowing what she was doing there. But she'd promised Grayson, if only implicitly, that she would look after his colleague, and she must keep that promise. She sat staring at the faded cream walls for what seemed a very long time before, at last, the doctor appeared from his sanctum and told her that the patient would need an operation. A small operation, it was true, but a delicate one. Splinters of wood had become lodged in the deep wound in his skull and each fragment would have to be extracted before they could begin to stitch him together. If Daisy were willing, could she sit with the man while he and his nurse made their preparations? The boy had regained consciousness and was restless and in pain, and needed to be watched. There was no one in the hospital Dr Lane could trust to do it; since Sister Macdonald's departure, they'd been very short staffed.

The name rang a bell. The bazaar. She'd met the woman in the bazaar, a jolly down-to-earth character, who had spoken baldly of the difficulties Daisy might face with the mems, as she'd called them. Daisy had liked her, and hoped she might get to know her, but that had never happened. The bazaar was to be their one and only encounter.

The doctor was ushering her through the green-shuttered door into another small room, which was almost filled by the stretcher on which the young man lay. Someone had covered him with a blanket — to ward off shock, Daisy guessed — but his hands were all the time grasping at it, twisting it this way and that between his fingers. A ceiling fan turned slowly overhead, but every part of his body that was visible was covered in sweat.

She found a chair and pulled it up beside the stretcher, taking his shaking hands in hers, trying to calm him. The bleeding had stopped, thank heavens, and she felt brave enough to blot his forehead with a moist pad that had been left on the small table nearby. He couldn't speak but looked at her pleadingly. She tried to tell him that everything would be fine, that the doctor was coming soon and all would be well. She hoped fervently that she would not have to sit with him while they picked the pieces of wood from his wound but, if she had to, she would. When the doctor came, though, he was accompanied by the two orderlies who had come out to the carriage. Together, they wheeled the man into an adjoining room she hadn't noticed before and, through the open door, she caught sight of a nurse standing beside a fearsome tray of instruments.

Quietly, she walked back to the waiting room, and took her seat again. She felt exceedingly sorry for the young Indian, but it was a compassion mixed with relief — every time she thought of Jocelyn's words. In a stroke, it seemed, she'd lost at least one of her burdens. It was clear that though Gerald might still hanker after Jocelyn, that young lady had quite other ideas. Whatever fondness he'd imagined the girl felt for him, it had been just that — imagined. An illusion, a fantasy that he'd hoped would come true.

Daisy wondered at the nature of his fancy. Did he really love the girl, or was it ambition alone that had led him to think of her as a future bride? She was the daughter of the regiment's most senior officer and would be a prize for any young lieutenant. But it hardly mattered now. Jocelyn would very soon be on her way to England to find a husband for herself. She may already have found one. And Daisy's friendship with her could remain unclouded.

An hour passed, then two. She was beginning to think the doctor had forgotten that she was there. It had grown even hotter in the waiting room despite the unaccustomed luxury of an electric fan. But, with its endless churning of the same fusty air, it made little difference and she felt trapped in a bubble of stale heat. It was only a sense of duty that kept her in her seat.

Her eyes had closed against the suffocating atmosphere when a step sounded, not from the rooms beyond the green door, but from outside. Grayson Harte sat down, and she felt his warmth settle against her. He was creased and tired. When he leaned forward, she saw that he was covered in blood, and her hand went to her mouth.

'Don't worry, the blood isn't new,' he reassured her. 'It's Javinder's.'

A strong brown hand reached out to her. 'I want to say thank you, Daisy. Thank you for rescuing him and then staying.'

Her palm nestled in his for a few seconds, and she wished she didn't look quite as ragged. But he seemed hardly to notice the crumpled and blood-stained dress. 'Is there any news of him yet?'

'Your friend needs an operation. The doctor said it was only a small procedure, but they have to make sure the wound is clean before they can stitch it. They've been a very long time. I think Javinder was badly concussed, so perhaps they're doing tests for that, too.'

Grayson nodded. 'He's young and fit. He'll recover well, I'm sure.'

'Who is Javinder?'

'I'm sorry, I should have told you, but there was no time. He's been assisting me in some of my work and was unlucky enough to get caught in the violence today.'

'But you were lucky — to escape. I heard shots as we left.'

'The soldiers fired in the air, thank God, and that was enough to scare all but the diehards. They were rounded up shortly afterwards.'

'But what was it all about? One minute we were watching the parade, and the next we were in the middle of a riot.'

'It was the parade that triggered the trouble. It was too much of an opportunity for the protesters, particularly with General Pearson there.'

'The men with the banners — were they followers of Gandhi?'

'In all probability. But he's been around a long time and he preaches non-violence. Today's agitators were intent on trouble. Gandhi doesn't explain why the clamour for independence has become so much more strident of late.'

'It's what's happening in Europe, isn't it?' She was recalling Anish's certainty that war would bring change to India.

Grayson looked at her speculatively. 'Wherever you got that from, I think it's right. Europe is the key. The danger of war is growing all the time and these people know it. They hope that Britain will be too busy putting out fires in its own backyard to defend its possessions overseas, even the jewel in its crown.'

'It looked a very dangerous confrontation.'

'It's getting more dangerous certainly. Agitators are getting arms from somewhere. We were lucky today. Sticks and bottles were the weapons, but it won't always be like that.'

He seemed remarkably well-informed for a District Officer and she wondered if it was usual to have such a deep knowledge of a region's politics. But then Grayson Harte was no ordinary District Officer. People knew his name, but not the work he did. No one at the Club had any idea of his role, and she'd noticed that he was careful never to volunteer information. Just now, for instance, he'd given her no clue as to how Javinder was assisting him.

She was pondering whether or not to ask him outright what he was doing in Jasirapur, when he broke through her thoughts. 'I haven't seen you for days. How have you been since our visit to the temple?'

'Well, thank you. I've been sleeping soundly, except for when the wind has been particularly fierce. The fruit you sent has helped a lot.'

He looked gratified. 'Goji berries don't always work but I'm delighted they're doing you good. I'll be sure and send you some more. Just as soon as I clear this mess up.'

Daisy didn't ask what the mess was. Nor did she tell him of her misfortune at the temple. If Anish were to be believed, and why wouldn't he be, Grayson had been nearby on that day, but he'd made no mention just now of his visit and surely he should have done. If he'd been close by, as Anish contended, he must have seen her at the shrine, yet he'd said nothing. They were shadow boxing, she thought, and though she was not as good at it as he, she wouldn't give herself away. She might be drawn to this attractive man, but that didn't mean she entirely trusted him.

'Javinder will be fine.' The doctor appeared through the green-shuttered door. 'A trifle sore for a few days, and with a monumental headache, but otherwise he'll be fine. Do you want to see him? Just a few minutes, mind.'

She got up immediately. 'I should go now. He'll want to see you alone.'

Grayson put out a hand to detain her. 'You must let my driver take you home. And thank you again for staying.'

'Yes, thank you, Mrs Mortimer.' The doctor's gruff endorsement surprised her. 'You did us a good turn. It's been a madhouse here without sufficient staff. The orderlies are well enough for the heavy stuff, but they're not too adept at the hand-holding.'

'I take it that you've not yet had a replacement for Sister Macdonald?'

'No, Mr Harte, we haven't, despite my fulminations. But we certainly need one.'

'There you are, Daisy,' Grayson joked. 'Something to keep you busy.'

Dr Lane was quick to follow his lead. 'If you could spare the time, Mrs Mortimer, we'd be grateful of some help.'

'But I'm not a nurse,' she stammered.

'I'm not suggesting you fill in for Sister, but you could sit with the patients — as you've done today. That frees up the one nurse I do have, and it means a lot to people who are sick. And then there are their friends, their colleagues, who come to visit. They all need to be dealt with and it's the small tasks that take up my nurse's time.'

Daisy felt awkward. It seemed the Infirmary might offer her something useful to do at last. Yet Gerald would almost certainly veto the idea and it would become another source of tension between them.

Grayson was looking at her enquiringly. 'Didn't you tell me you were bored with having nothing to fill your days?'

'You could come in the early morning and be home by noon,' the doctor chimed in hopefully. 'We might even find the funds to pay for your tonga.'

'I'll think about it, Dr Lane,' was all she would promise.

But on the way home, she was already deciding. While the doctor was so short staffed, shouldn't she try to help? Gerald wouldn't like it and, if she told him, he'd probably forbid her from setting foot in the place. But her mother had been a nurse and the idea that she would be following in Lily's footsteps warmed her heart. She would definitely do it, Daisy decided, and somehow make sure that Gerald knew nothing until she was ready to tell him.

* * *

He was at home when she arrived and must have seen the ICS jeep bumping its way along the garden track, because he strode onto the veranda as the vehicle pulled to a halt. Even at a distance, she could see that he didn't look happy.

'Where have you been?' was his terse greeting. 'You should have been back hours ago.'

She thanked the driver and clambered down from the open car. 'I'm sorry if you've been worried. I've been at the

Infirmary and couldn't get word to you. Someone was hurt.' He stared at her impassively. 'There was a riot,' she added, hoping this might work some magic, 'at least I think you'd call it a riot. But it happened after the cavalry had left the maiden.'

'I know. Some kind of disturbance. The news is all around camp. But I can't see how that stopped you from getting back. You should have returned as soon as the parade was over. How was I to know what was happening?'

Daisy found herself apologising again. 'I would have come straight back, of course, but Mr Harte's assistant was badly injured in the fighting and Jocelyn drove us to the Infirmary and I stayed — with Javinder.'

'You should have come back here,' he said doggedly. 'You shouldn't be babysitting Harte's crony. And what is he doing even asking you? It's a damn cheek.'

'The boy was badly hurt, Gerald. He was only half-conscious and Dr Lane asked if I would sit with him until he was ready to operate.'

'Lane's an old woman,' he grumbled, unappeased. 'And as for Harte, didn't I tell you to be careful? I don't care how badly hurt the boy was, it had nothing to do with you. Getting you involved is another ploy by Harte to ingratiate himself. I told you to stay clear of him, didn't I?'

Daisy felt a slow sadness overtake her. It seemed impossible ever to draw close to Gerald before he pushed her away again. Hers had been a simple, benevolent impulse, yet he'd made it sound suspect. 'I think Mr Harte's only aim was to get his assistant help,' she said mildly. 'There was turmoil after you rode away and it was truly frightening.'

He sniffed disdainfully. 'A few lunatic Indians shouting the odds. Hardly stirring stuff.'

'It wasn't just shouting. There *were* slogans and a few men were waving banners, but it didn't stop at that. The mood was very ugly. When the police tried to arrest the protesters, the crowd turned on them. People were throwing bottles and sticks and there were dozens of injuries. Javinder's head was cut open.'

He sniffed again. 'It sounds like a storm in a teacup.'

She felt a stir of irritation. 'You said yourself that you were worried about trouble erupting,' she reminded him.

'Well, it didn't. Not while we were on parade, and that's all that matters. The regiment got a sterling report and my troop received a particular commendation. If you'd been here, I could have told you about it.'

She saw that he'd been itching to pass on the regiment's success, but rather than the audience he had expected, he'd returned to an empty house. She'd failed to be a good wife and she ought to feel guilty. Instead, she felt repelled by his disregard for the fighting and his complete lack of sympathy for Javinder.

'Rajiv has had lunch ready for the last hour,' he grumbled. 'You'd better come in and eat. I haven't much time.'

A delicious smell floated through the living room and she realised that she was extremely hungry. Rajiv might be her enemy, but he was also an excellent cook and conjured the tastiest of meals from a shelf of handleless saucepans and an oven that was little more than a hole in the ground. As they ate, Gerald recovered his spirits a little and started to talk. He seemed unusually voluble, evidently still boosted by the morning's triumph. Daisy nodded in what she hoped were the right places and let him talk on without interruption. Her own feelings were very different. She had seen the way the police wielded those terrifying long sticks of theirs, not caring who or where they hit. She could still hear the crack of skulls, see the bleeding faces, the maimed hands. It had been deeply upsetting.

Gerald had hardly paused for breath during the meal but still managed to finish way ahead of her. He put down his fork with a bang and took a last gulp of water. Then, abruptly, pushed back his chair.

'Now I know where you are, I must go,' he announced. 'I have to get back to camp. I've already been away too long.'

She was still eating as he strode to the door. There had been no farewell gesture, not even a kind hand on her shoulder.

Was this punishment for her decision to help Grayson Harte? Or was Gerald once more slipping back into unkindness?

Over the past week, she'd been made subtly aware that the delicate harmony they'd established on their river drive had begun to fracture. It was a slow, steady process but also inevitable. She was not to blame. It was nothing she had done, she reasoned, not until today at least. It was simply that Gerald was unhappy with the marriage he'd made, unhappy with her being here, and nothing was going to change that.

He turned at the door. 'I forgot to say that since you're staying on, Anish will be round in the morning. He's got a pony lined up for you. He'll be with us at six — you'll need to ride early.'

That came as a surprise and her reaction was to back-pedal. 'But won't teaching me take up too much time? He must be as busy as you.'

Gerald pursed his lips. 'He's plenty of free time. He doesn't have my responsibilities.'

She wondered whether those responsibilities really existed, or were simply an excuse for him to stay away.

'Then please thank him for me.'

Her voice tailed off. No definite promise had been given to Dr Lane but, as she'd journeyed home, she had started to make plans. Tomorrow morning early, once Gerald left for the camp, she'd thought to take the bike and find her way back to the Infirmary. If eyebrows were raised at her visit, she had the perfect reason to be there; she was enquiring about Javinder. Then. if the doctor thought she might be of any use that day and wanted her to stay, all well and good.

But now the plan must be put on hold. For a while she toyed with the idea of sending a message to delay the ride, but there was only Rajiv to take it and she couldn't trust him. In any case, she couldn't turn Anish down, not after he'd gone to the trouble of finding her a horse. When a few hours later, a pair of jodhpurs arrived with a friendly note from Jocelyn, she banished the idea of the hospital from her mind altogether and instead braced herself for the trial ahead.

CHAPTER TWENTY-TWO

As promised, Anish was outside the house at six the next morning. She went out to meet him, feeling almost a horsewoman in Jocelyn's jodhpurs. As her friend had prophesied, they were too large and she'd had to tie a scarf around her middle to secure them. Daisy hoped it gave her a rakish air. With her *topi* crammed firmly on her head, and Jocelyn's bamboo riding crop in her hand, she felt she might at least mimic a memsahib.

Anish came forward, a wide smile on his face. 'To the manner born, Daisy. You look as though you've been riding for years!'

He helped her up into the saddle and she sat stiff and ungainly, not daring to look down at the ground. It seemed a very long way beneath her, even on this small pony.

'You're being kind,' she said. 'I've never felt more awkward in my life.'

'You soon won't, believe me. Just try and relax into the saddle. It's fortunate that women can ride astride now — even here. You would have found side-saddle the very devil.'

No doubt, she thought, but it was unlikely she'd find riding astride much better. Anish mounted his horse effortlessly and sidled up to her. 'By the way, your pony's name is Rudolf and he's a docile beast. In fact, he's far more likely to stand still than he is to move. You'll need to be firm with him.'

Rudolf swung his head round and looked at her. She felt like reassuring him that if he wanted to stand still for the next hour, that was perfectly fine with her. But Anish was having none of it. He smacked the pony on the rump and Rudolf ambled into a sedate walk, Daisy rocking from side to side and hoping she didn't resemble too closely a sack of potatoes on its way to market.

They walked together, horse by horse, along the path and out of the garden, moving off into the dawn mist along the pale, dusky lane. When they reached the road, instead of turning right or left, Anish led them over it and onto a small path she hadn't noticed before.

Already small boys with little sticks were driving cattle from the thorn enclosures of night and into the fields that spread into the distance on either side of them. The boys shouted and whacked the still-sleepy cows as they stumbled along the lane from the nearest village. A smell of dung fires and coffee greeted them as they drew nearer. Dim figures emerged from thatched huts. Daisy saw the women standing at the village well, waiting to draw water. When their pots were full, they took them to the men sitting nearby, who gargled and spat and rinsed their faces, before tying their turbans in preparation for the day's toil in the fields.

Once out of the village, the horses continued to amble side by side along the lane they'd been following from the main thoroughfare. The colours of the earth, its texture, its smell, slowly infused Daisy's mind and body, inviting her into the landscape she was travelling. Very gradually, she began to relax. By the time they had passed through a second village, she felt sufficiently at ease to string a few words together. Yesterday's events were still vividly in her mind and she wondered if Anish would talk of them.

'Did you hear what happened after the parade?' she asked.

'You mean the protests? I heard you were caught up in them.'

'For a while.'

'Then you know more than I do. Tell me what you saw.'

'There was a lot of shouting, political slogans I think, although most of it was in Hindi and I didn't understand. Police officers ordered the crowds to disperse, but a large group of them refused and then the police charged with *lathis*. That sparked the riot. When the army came — soldiers on foot but with rifles — they fired. Into the air, I think.'

'And did it work?'

'I believe so. I wasn't there at the end. Fortunately, Jocelyn and I managed to escape. I didn't want to see what would happen if the crowd refused to disperse.'

'Artillery would have been brought in. Tanks, probably.'

'That would have been dreadful.'

'It would, but you shouldn't be surprised. The army is the last resort and can't be seen to back down. Otherwise, how would a hundred thousand Europeans control three hundred million Indians?'

She was spared a reply for they were passing through yet another village. Dogs rushed out and barked around their legs, but when Anish cracked his whip at them, they disappeared as quickly as they'd arrived. Peacocks strutted by the side of the dusty lane, and a woman came out to greet them and offered them a glass of milk. Anish declined with thanks and Daisy could only be grateful. She would not have dared to lean from the horse to take the glass and, worse, if she'd had to dismount, she would have found it almost impossible to get back into the saddle again. Already, the whole of her lower body had set up a dull ache.

She was finding the ride uncomfortable but Anish was a pleasant companion. They barely knew each other, but somehow it seemed not to matter. She felt more than ever that she could talk to him and be completely honest. And when they were once more in open countryside, she returned to yesterday's events. She wanted to hear what he'd made of them.

'Gerald didn't seem to think they were important, the protests I mean.'

'Gerald sees what he wants to see, and you'll discover the entire Indian Army is the same. Its soldiers are insulated against politics. Their interests lie in gaining promotion or being successful at polo or taking part in military displays. Everything else is ignored.'

'But judging by yesterday's events, the soldiers know there's trouble in the country and surely it must affect them.'

'Everyone feels a sense of strain on occasions,' he admitted. 'But it never lasts. It's simply an undercurrent running quietly beneath what really matters: polo tournaments and parades.'

'Even now, when the situation seems to be getting worse?'

'There's a conspiracy to keep a stiff upper lip and behave as though loyalty to anyone but the King Emperor could never arise. It won't last for much longer. Things will change, must change. There have been protests for two hundred years, but they're getting more frequent and more furious. Too many Indians have suffered loss and been humiliated and they want recompense. Of course, there are grander motives, too.'

'Grander? You mean independence?'

'I do. Self-determination is a powerful notion.'

He was smiling at her, no trace of bitterness on his face, and she was encouraged to say, 'Grayson thinks like you, that resistance can only grow, now that England is almost certain to be plunged into war.'

'Grayson? Ah, yes, the estimable Mr Harte.' She flushed slightly and hoped Anish had not noticed. 'He's right, of course. War will bring enormous upheaval, and not just in Europe. Indian resistance is already looking east for help with its struggle. The Japanese are in China, did you know? I understand they've captured a number of key cities.'

He was as well-informed as Grayson, Daisy thought. But unlike Grayson, independence was a deeply personal matter for him. He spoke of loss and humiliation and she knew that must come from his own experience. He worked alongside British officers and, if needed, he would fight alongside them, yet he was not considered their equal. He was not good enough to be paid the same or good enough to be welcomed at their Club.

The prejudice was stark and Gerald was part of it. She wondered at the way he'd encouraged her to ride out with Anish, since he was eager for advancement, and friendship with Indians was deeply frowned upon. But perhaps their alliance was strong enough to override such snobbishness or perhaps it was simply that Gerald wished to spend as little time as possible with her, and was more than happy to delegate his responsibilities to a man he could trust.

They had fallen silent, relapsing into their own thoughts, with Daisy concentrating hard on holding tight to the saddle. When she looked up at last, it was to see a broad, brown river appearing through a bank of trees.

'We're there,' she exclaimed. It was a different spot to the one she'd driven to with Gerald, but it was the same wide, muddy drift of water.

'We are. Here, let me help you down. You must be feeling stiff. We'll sit for a while until you get your breath back.'

Daisy giggled. 'It was hardly a breathtaking ride.' With some difficulty she slid from the saddle, and he caught her deftly and put her on her feet.

'Any time you feel the need to travel faster, just let me know. We might have a bit of a problem with Rudolf, though.'

'No,' she was quick to say, 'no thank you. I find walking perfect and I'm sure Rudolf does, too.'

'Actually, he prefers to lie.' Anish shook his head, making Daisy giggle again. 'But maybe next time we ride out, you'll feel like risking a gentle trot.'

'Will you mind bringing me out again? This can't be much fun for you.'

'On the contrary, I'm enjoying the morning immensely. You're good company, Daisy, and I like being with you. You're hardly a typical memsahib.'

'Is that a compliment?'

'I think it must be.'

They sat for long minutes beneath the shade of a line of peepul trees, Daisy watching as the sun glinted on and off rucks in the flowing water. Above them in the branches, green parrots chattered noisily to themselves.

'One day, I hope you'll visit some of our palaces,' Anish said out of the blue. 'I think you would love them. They are truly magnificent.'

'I've never been to a palace, though Miss Maddox — my mis — my friend,' she corrected herself quickly, 'was invited once to Buckingham Palace. She told me about it, and I wanted very much to see it for myself.'

'Our palaces are nothing like your King's residence.'

Daisy leaned towards him. 'Do tell me about them.'

'For a start, they're built around endless courtyards with arch after arch of carved stone. And every piece of stone is decorated and every small piece of decoration is inlaid with gems. In bright sunlight, the walls flash a rainbow of colour.'

'You're right. They sound magnificent.'

He nodded, his eyes half-closed. 'That's just the exterior. Inside there are huge audience halls, every wall mirrored and with silk carpets on the floor and tons of crystal hanging above. And the rooms lead out on to broad terraces where you can walk and view the sweep of the mountains or the curve of the Ganga itself. One day I'll take you to one, if you're still here.'

'Why wouldn't I be?'

'You may decide you don't like India after all,' he answered easily.

The sun's rays had begun to probe their shade and creep stealthily through the gaps in the dusty leaves. Daisy felt her neck grow uncomfortably hot and changed her position several times. Noticing her discomfort, Anish jumped to his feet. 'It is getting too warm for you. We should start back.'

It was none too soon. She found the return journey torture and, by the time they rode up to the bungalow, every part of her body hurt and she was white with fatigue.

'We've been out too long,' Anish confessed. 'Forgive me. I should have made sure we turned for home earlier, but we were talking and I forgot the time.'

'Don't say that. I loved the river and I loved talking with you. I shall be fine, once I've rested.'

'You don't look fine,' he scolded. 'The heat has done for you. Or Rudolf has. I should have known better.'

She almost fell from the horse and into his arms. Mounting the veranda steps, she tried very hard not to wince, or even worse, faint. He was looking at her with concern. 'You know you really shouldn't be here in these temperatures. And it's not too late to go. Miss Forester has only just left, and Gerald could organise transport for you.'

It was true she was growing more tired by the day, and the battle against the heat seemed interminable. For an instant, she was tempted, but only for an instant and when she spoke, her voice was sure.

'I can't go.' She would trust her companion with one small but important confidence. 'I've half-promised to help at the Infirmary and I don't want to let Dr Lane down.'

Anish's eyebrows rose. 'And what does Gerald say to that?'

'He doesn't know. At least, not yet. I thought I'd see how I got on, and if I'm no help to them or I don't like the work, there won't be a problem. Gerald need never know.'

'And what if you do like it and decide to be the new Miss Nightingale?'

'Then I'll tell him, but only when I think the time is right. You won't say anything?'

'We're friends, aren't we? You can rely on me.' And with a slight smile, he turned his horse and trotted back up the garden path, leading Rudolf by the bridle.

CHAPTER TWENTY-THREE

Daisy went to the Infirmary every other day for an entire week without Gerald knowing, following him out of the bungalow early in the morning but always making sure she was back in time to welcome him home for lunch.

She'd thought Rajiv might be a problem, but if he'd noticed her constant absences, he had evidently said nothing to his master. Her earlier conviction that he'd been trying to scare her into taking the first ship back to England had begun to fade — she'd watched him closely for days and seen nothing to disturb her. His time was spent cooking and cleaning and, if he left the house, it was to go to the market for an hour at most. For a while, Daisy had toyed with the idea that he might have an accomplice, but she soon realised she was chasing a phantom. There was no evidence to suggest that such a person existed and she'd had to accept her suspicions were wrong. She should have known better than to think she could play detective in a country she hardly knew.

She might not be about to unmask a criminal, but she was still glad not to have travelled to Simla. Her life had quite suddenly become full and a great deal more interesting. On the two mornings she didn't work, Anish called at the same early hour, leading the docile Rudolf. He considered a return to the river too ambitious, at least for the time being, but was happy to escort her on whatever gentle ride she chose. Instead, they travelled local paths, crisscrossing their way over fields of soya bean and oil seed, and passing through a sprinkling of small villages.

The women of the regiment would have disapproved highly. Spending time alone with a man not your husband was bad enough; spending it with an Indian officer was beyond the pale. But the women of the regiment were miles away and Daisy settled to enjoy herself.

Now that she no longer ached quite as badly, she began to take a real pleasure in the rides. For an hour or so she could forget the unhappiness that too often crept up on her while she was alone in the bungalow. And Anish was fast becoming as much a friend to her as to Gerald. If she asked for advice, he gave it. If she needed information, he talked to her of India. If she wanted to laugh, he related silly anecdotes from the Officer's Mess.

'Barton or Richards or Walker,' he'd begin. And then the story would follow. 'Walker is on secondment to our regiment and he's greedy. Always has to have the fullest plate, so we decided he needed punishment. At lunchtime, we have to carry our food from the cookhouse across an open space to the dining room. Which is fine, except for the kite hawks nesting nearby.'

Daisy had heard of kite hawks and smiled.

'You know what I'm going to say, don't you?'

'I've a good idea — but go on please. The detail is lacking.'

'Well, here's the detail. Lunch is a brilliant chance for the hawks to supplement their diet and, because of that, we have a klaxon to scare them off. Last week, one of the chaps managed to delay Walker for lunch and then hide the klaxon. When he finally came puffing across the yard, desperate to get stuck into the mound of food he'd shovelled onto his plate, a kite hawk struck. I think it got his potatoes. Walker went very red in the face — redder than usual — and scurried back to the cookhouse for a replacement. Out he came again, with another plate, but this time he made sure to scan the skies. Sure enough, a kite hawk sailed into view but, as it came from over his shoulder, Walker wasn't watching.'

Daisy began to laugh and had to cling on to Rudolf's saddle to stop herself slipping. 'What did it get that time?'

'The meat, of course. The bird had to have something to go with his potatoes. Anyway, Walker rushed back to the cookhouse again but, as he came through the door, the Adjutant stopped him and told him he was wanted immediately in the front office. He wasn't, but it was easy enough to pass on a false message. In the end, he missed lunch completely. We thought he was going to burst into tears.'

'You're very unkind.'

'You haven't met Walker.'

'But no food at all, Anish!'

'Poetic justice. Isn't that what you call it?'

And so they would meander along the lanes, joking, talking, discussing, with Daisy growing easier in the saddle and Anish quietly encouraging her. She was doing well, he said, it was all coming together, and she wanted to believe him.

Her work at the Infirmary was also progressing. Dr Lane had not exaggerated when he said he was badly understaffed. He was the sole medical practitioner and could call on just one permanent nurse to assist him in the minor operations he performed. Patients with more serious problems endured a long and painful journey to the British hospital in Delhi.

Daisy had imagined she would be making tea, tidying beds, greeting visitors, but almost immediately she found herself helping the medical staff in the several small wards the Infirmary boasted. She would stand a step away from Dr Lane and Nurse Adams as they worked their way through the day, constantly watching them, constantly learning.

Her chores were menial, but when a patient smiled as she changed his bandages, or another held her hand when she offered him a cooling wash, a small kernel of self-belief emerged and began slowly to grow. It was a novel experience.

She'd always known herself determined, dogged even, but now she began to feel differently about the person she was. For the first time in her life, she began to feel valued. She wondered what it would be like to be a real nurse, but it was unlikely she would ever find out. Her life was already mapped out — she was a wife, Gerald's wife — and she must remain content with being a volunteer who 'helped'. It was a helping that tired her considerably. When she returned home at lunchtime, she had to force herself to a liveliness she was far from feeling in order that Gerald's suspicions were not aroused.

Towards the beginning of her second week at the hospital, she wheeled her bike from its shelter and made ready to return home. She was always concerned that Gerald might arrive before her and question where she'd been, but today she was in good time. As ever, a blanket of silence lay over the cantonment. The Infirmary was on its outskirts and generally very peaceful but, at this time of the day, the quiet intensified even further and an almost eerie hush descended. For several hours, all activity was put on hold, and people variously dozed or read their way through the worst of the heat until it was again bearable to begin work. The ride home at this hour was always an effort and though the journey was only a couple of miles along a straight route, the sun's clamour was unrelenting.

She launched herself forward, eager to be on her way, but almost immediately the bicycle began to wobble in an unnerving fashion. Daisy ignored it. She must be more tired than she realised and was riding badly. It was only when she hit a particularly rough piece of ground a few hundred yards from the hospital, that she saw too late that something was very wrong. The bike stumbled into a hollow in the road and she crashed to the ground, winded but otherwise unhurt. She was scrambling to her feet when she heard footsteps pounding the road. They were running towards her.

'What happened?'

It was Grayson Harte, and he'd arrived out of nowhere.

'Whatever made you fall?' He repeated his question, at the same time pulling the bicycle upright and looking closely at it. 'You've got a puncture, that's what. Two, in fact, by the look of it.'

What was he doing here? She noticed his arms and legs were deeply tanned and that thick red dust clung to his boots. He wasn't spending a great deal of time indoors, she thought, despite the pen pushing that Gerald scorned.

'I can't have,' she stammered. 'The bike was fine on the way here, and it's been locked in the shelter ever since.'

'It's possible they're slow punctures. You may have ridden over something sharp this morning. What's certain, though, is you won't be going anywhere on that cycle today.'

'But I have to get home,' she protested. 'Gerald will be waiting lunch for me.'

'I've the jeep parked around the corner. I'll run you back to the bungalow.'

How long had he been parked there, she wondered? She was sure she hadn't heard a car arriving and it made her cautious. 'I'm lucky you turned up then, but why are you here?'

'I've come for Javinder. I'm taking him home as long as Dr Lane gives the all clear. When I visited him last night, he seemed well — well enough to leave.'

'I'm sure the doctor will agree. Javinder has made very good progress.'

'And that's largely down to you. Thank God you got him to the Infirmary in time, or there could have been a very different outcome. I never wanted him to go to the maiden, you know. I was pretty sure there'd be trouble, but the boy insisted.'

'Jocelyn was the heroine of the day,' she reminded him. 'She drove the pony and trap as fast as she could and in very difficult circumstances.'

'Jocelyn was wonderful, you're right, but you were splendid, too. Clear-headed and compassionate. Just the right qualities, I'd say, for a nurse.'

It was an attractive dream, but only a dream. She tried to smooth her crumpled dress into some kind of order and noticed a small rip in the skirt. She would mend it when she got home. And that's where she should be heading without further delay.

'Can we go now, do you think?'

'Just as soon as I've got Javinder in the car.' And before she could stop him, he'd picked up her bicycle and was heading towards the parked jeep. 'Come into the Infirmary with me,' he threw over his shoulder. 'It's far too hot to wait out here.'

Daisy was reluctant. For one thing, there was a pressing need for her to be home, but there was also a nagging doubt. She was uneasy that Grayson had seemed to materialise out of thin air, the very moment she'd fallen from her bike. But there was no walking back to the bungalow, not in this heat, and she could do nothing but follow him into the waiting room.

Dr Lane bustled in almost immediately. 'You've come for young Javinder? I'll have him ready in a jiffy.' He peered through his half-moon spectacles. 'Is that you, Daisy? Why are you still here? Well, since you are, you can boil up some *chai* for this poor man while he waits.'

'We have to be going, doctor,' Grayson said, much to her relief.

'I shall be several minutes. In the meantime, you can sit and drink.'

There was no escape and Daisy gave up the fight. 'You'd better come into the sitting room, Grayson. The stove is there.'

By the time she reached home, she reflected, Gerald would have eaten and returned to the cantonment, and before she saw her husband again, she would have to think up a convincing reason for her absence. He would be angry if he knew she'd spent time with Grayson Harte, and might accuse her again of setting tongues to wag.

The sitting room was smaller even than the waiting area, with a chipped sink at one end and an ancient primus.

'Shall I wait outside?' Grayson pulled a face. The two of them were wedged together with little room to breathe.

'There's no need,' she said briskly, trying to cover her discomfort at having him so close. 'The tea will be ready in minutes.'

He balanced himself on what had once been a brightly painted blue stool. 'How are you enjoying working here?'

'I like it.' Then enthusiasm overtook her awkwardness. 'I like it a lot.'

'I thought you might. I remember your description of your mother in the photograph. Nursing evidently runs in the family.'

'Maybe.' She was deliberately noncommittal.

'So might you one day do the training?'

'I'd enjoy that.' Her tone was wistful. 'But I don't think it's possible.'

'It wouldn't be easy,' he conceded. 'In all probability, you'd have to return to England. But Indian Army officers have a long furlough every three or four years. Something like eight months, I think. It might be possible for you to start your training then.'

She was fairly certain that Gerald would have no wish to spend such a magnificent leave waiting for her to return from hospital every day, but she wasn't about to share the thought.

Grayson was now launched into his own enthusiasm. 'If you decided to take the profession seriously, I'm sure you'd find Dr Lane encouraging. And getting qualified is certainly worth considering. It could stand you in good stead.'

Her questioning look made him explain. 'You might one day need an occupation.'

Why did he think that? She already had an occupation — as a wife. Was he concerned for her well-being, imagining a career would make her happy? Or was it something less charitable? Did he think she might one day be in need of money, might one day be alone again? She wondered if he'd heard that Gerald was in debt. Rumours were probably circulating in the bazaar right now, and it wouldn't be surprising if Gerald's name had been dropped into his ear. She had no illusions about her marriage, but if Grayson thought she would walk away at the first sign of difficulty, he was mistaken. The harshest of lives had taught her to persevere.

Daisy brushed his suggestion aside. 'Do ICS men have the same long holidays as the military?'

'Unfortunately not. Griffins, that's new members like me, have to wait eight years before we get the slightest sight of home.'

She handed him the least chipped mug she could find, and he sipped his tea slowly. 'Of course, if there's a war, that might change things.'

'You would have to return to England?'

'More than likely.'

'And what would happen to Javinder?' She'd grown fond of the young man she'd cared for.

'I can't be certain. All I know is that life here would change and change greatly. It doesn't feel like that now, I know. There's a strange sense of timelessness, as though this world will go on forever. But it won't. Your husband's regiment, for instance. Right now all over India the cavalry is mechanising. Soldiers are learning to drive tanks for the battles to come. In time, all their expertise with horses will fade into a folk memory.'

'That will be sad. But I've been gaining some expertise myself.'

'In horse riding?'

'Yes. Anish, Anish Rana is teaching me, and I'm doing well. Or so he says.'

Grayson's face went blank. Quite literally. All expression wiped clear. He knew Anish, she thought. According to Anish himself he must do, so why this strange reaction? Perhaps there had been some falling out between them. And Gerald must be involved, too. He'd warned her several times that Grayson meant trouble. Was it simply that Gerald was frightened his former school mate would reveal his true identity and Anish, as his friend, was similarly concerned? Or had something else happened? One thing was certain: she would never know. This was a man's world and a woman learnt only those things they chose to tell her.

'I wish you success,' Grayson was saying, at his blandest. 'Everyone rides, and you'll find it very useful, particularly when the cooler weather arrives. You'll be able to join in a lot more of the entertainments — paper chases, gymkhanas, that kind of thing.'

'They might be a step too far,' she laughed. 'And maybe I won't have much time for "entertainments". I might still be working here. There's been no further trouble, but the Infirmary has still been very busy.'

'No further trouble so far, but we should expect it. Life won't be quiet for long. Until independence is granted, if it ever is, there's likely to be nothing but trouble.'

'As bad as the riot last week? That was savage.'

'Quite possibly worse. Has your husband spoken to you? Arms have gone missing from the cantonment. Imagine that scene on the maiden, but with a legion of guns.'

Gerald had said nothing of guns being stolen. It was a frightening situation and he must have wished not to worry her.

'I don't like what's happening in Jasirapur,' Grayson went on. 'And I don't like the fact that you're living so far from the civil station in what could be difficult times.'

She batted away his fears. 'You mustn't worry. I'm really not that feeble.'

'On the contrary. I know you're not easily daunted, but none of us really understands what we're dealing with, and I don't want to see you hurt.'

'But you know the men involved?' She tried to sound upbeat. 'The ones who started the riot. I thought I recognised one of them during the fighting. Do you remember, when you helped me with Sanjay at the bazaar, there was a man—'

'Yes, I remember. He's one of the ringleaders and we have him under lock and key, but he's not alone. More and more agitators are coming into the area intent on confrontation. You could keep your eye out for another man you might recognise and let me know if you see him. One of the men from the *Viceroy*.'

She looked puzzled.

'One of the prisoners who knocked you down. You must remember. He was in the ship's gaol, being deported from England, but somehow he managed to escape with several others and went on a rampage.'

Daisy's face suddenly lost its colour. 'And he's still free?'

'He was recaptured on board ship, but then I'm afraid, escaped again. In Delhi, this time. Don't worry, though.' He was looking anxiously at her. 'He can't possibly harm you.'

She was sheet-white and, seeing it, he steered her to a chair.

'I'm so sorry, Daisy. I had no intention of scaring you.'

'You haven't.' Her voice was little more than a whisper.

'But then what — what did I say to upset you so badly?'

'You mentioned the boat, the accident. I was being foolish. A silly moment but it's over now.'

He looked directly into her face, his blue eyes searching. 'Why do I have the feeling that it isn't?'

She looked back at him and saw only kindness. 'It's nearly over.'

'What happened on board? I felt at the time there was something bad. Worse than just a tumble on the deck, but I didn't know you well enough to ask.' When she stayed silent, he said hopefully, 'Perhaps you can tell me now.'

Perhaps she could. Ever since it happened, she'd felt the need to tell somebody, somebody who would listen, somebody who would recognise her loss, recognise that there had been a baby once, in a way Gerald refused to.

'I lost my child,' she said.

'I'm so sorry. I had no idea. Well, if I'm honest, perhaps a small suspicion, but I thought . . .'

He was unwilling to spell out what he'd thought, so she did it for him. 'You knew I was unmarried, and you didn't wish to think badly of me.'

'It wasn't that black and white. It was more that you seemed so young, in many ways unworldly.'

'I was.' Unworldly was just another word for naive, she thought. And naivety had certainly marked her relations with

Gerald. The unaccustomed drink, the soft words, the promise to marry. She had been gullible and swallowed it all. 'It wasn't meant to happen, the baby I mean, it was an accident.'

'You're hardly alone in that,' he soothed. 'But Gerald — I hope he's been a comfort?'

'He . . . he's not been so badly affected as me. He never wanted to marry, you see.' She felt scorched by her own confession.

'I see.' And the dawning comprehension on his face told her that he did.

He reached out for her hand and took it in a strong clasp. 'I'll make sure the prisoner who escaped is behind bars very shortly. And that's a promise.' It was the best he could do for her, she saw, the only compensation he could offer.

She gave a weak smile. 'I'm sure you will.'

'And in the meantime, keep drinking the goji berries. You're still sleeping well?'

'I seem to be. Rajiv makes me the drink every night.'

'That's good.' He rose as Dr Lane poked his head around the door. 'I'll make sure I keep them coming.'

CHAPTER TWENTY-FOUR

That evening, Daisy sat in the unyielding cane chair, pretending to read. Gerald had left by the time she'd finally made it back to the bungalow and, when they met again at dinner, he'd shown little interest in her earlier absence. The bicycle was back on the veranda — Grayson had miraculously found a puncture kit in the jeep's glove box — and the flimsy story she'd concocted around a lack of tongas to drive her from the bazaar seemed to have satisfied her husband.

But *she* wasn't satisfied. The incident at the Infirmary was still puzzling. She was mystified that she'd managed to collect two punctures in a short ride to the hospital, and mystified too, at Grayson's appearance. It was providential that he'd turned up when he did. He'd come for Javinder, he said, and that was plausible enough, but he must have been close by for some time since she hadn't heard a car arrive. And then just when she needed rescue, the very moment she'd fallen from her bicycle, he was there right on cue. It seemed to fit too well the pattern Gerald had been at pains to point out and it was making her wary.

From their first meeting, she'd been charmed by Grayson but had never completely rid herself of distrust. He was vague and evasive and refused to answer her questions directly. The memory of the riot and his battered and blood-stained figure sitting beside her on the hospital bench was still vivid, but no matter how many times she'd gone over the events of that day in her mind, she could not fathom what Grayson had been doing at the parade. She'd been at a distance from the action but it seemed to her that, with Javinder alongside, he'd plunged into the crowd trying to reach the protesters. A District Officer was responsible for administering law in the villages, she knew, but how could he be involved in keeping order in Jasirapur, if that indeed was what he'd been doing?

No, she didn't completely trust him, and she should have been more reticent today. Instead, she'd related the most painful experience of her life: the crumbling of a dream, the loss of a small being for whom she'd already felt unconditional love. Why on earth had she told him? He was young, he was a man, and one not even distantly related to her, yet she'd felt compelled to unburden herself. And he hadn't disappointed. He had understood, understood even the things she couldn't say.

Despite that, Daisy kept away from the Infirmary the next day and for several days following. It was stupid, she knew, but she needed time before she made the journey again. She sent a note to Dr Lane apologising for her absence and assuring him that, by the end of the week, she would be back at the hospital. In the meantime, she continued to ride out with Anish. She'd grown to love the landscape they travelled through on their dawn rides and was always happy to lose herself in the sounds and smells of the Indian countryside.

Two days after the contretemps at the Infirmary, Anish arrived at the house very early, but she was already dressed and waiting for him. It was some time since they'd visited the river, but today they intended to attempt a return. He considered her a strong enough rider now, but if she began to feel at all weary, he warned, she was to say and they would turn the horses and head for home.

She walked out onto the veranda, impatient to be gone, and saw that Gerald, already in uniform and waiting for his transport, had advanced down the path a short way and was talking with Anish. The two of them had their heads close together in earnest conversation. Momentarily, she glimpsed Gerald's face as he raised it and, even from this distance, she could see the two deep lines raking his forehead. Beside him, Anish's gestures suggested an increasing frustration. She waited quietly on the veranda, unwilling to interrupt what she thought must be official business, but the men saw her almost immediately and broke off mid-sentence.

'How are you today?' Anish greeted her.

'Feeling fine, thank you.'

She tried not to mind that Gerald was ignoring her. A car had arrived at the end of the lane and her husband was already walking towards it without bidding her even a brief goodbye. Anish glanced at his friend's retreating back.

'Gerald is happy for you to go riding.'

It seemed a strange thing to say. Her husband had most days stood on the veranda, only too pleased to wave her off.

'I'm glad that something is making him happy.' She sounded bitter even though she'd not meant to.

'He has problems, Daisy, and they weigh heavily.' She knew what they were, of course. Gerald was still in debt and still married to the wrong person. 'So, are you ready for our expedition?'

'I'm looking forward to it.'

And she was. She felt confident now, confident enough to tackle the ride that had given her so much trouble previously. If she made it to the river in one piece, it would be a small triumph. Well within the hour, though, they had reached their destination. Without her realising, her horsemanship had improved hugely over the weeks and today she'd ridden far more swiftly than she'd ever thought possible.

For a while, they continued parallel to the river, hearing it lap gently against the muddy banks, and watching from the corner of their eyes several black and white skimmer birds, flying low over the brown water, their bright bills open to scoop up an unwary fish. Anish pointed ahead to a cluster of trees which lay round several deep bends.

'We'll make for those. They should give us some shade.'

The sound of laughter came to them, weaving a joyful path through the air. Around the last bend, a party of men and girls were camped by the river's edge. As Anish and Daisy passed, the group looked up and waved, their faces wide with smiles and their voices raised in fun. A blanket lay between them, plates of cold chicken and glasses of champagne spread across its surface.

Two of the girls were lying full length on the grass, their heads in the laps of men dressed in the uniform of army officers. Daisy was astonished by the informality of the scene; she had witnessed nothing like it since coming to India. The girls, she noticed, were extremely pretty — beautifully made up and fashionably dressed. No wonder the men looked happy to be with them.

'The fishing fleet has departed,' Anish remarked laconically as they rode on.

'I don't understand.'

'It's that time of the year. All the marriageable girls have gone back to England and when that happens, the rules relax. Plenty of picnics at dawn, dances in the moonlight, that kind of thing. Plenty of passion, too!'

She ignored this tantalising strand to work out who the women might be. 'I know I haven't socialised much since I arrived, but I've never seen those girls before.'

'That's hardly surprising. They keep a low profile in the cool season when everyone's daughter or sister or cousin pays us a visit. But once the ladies have left, these girls come out to play.'

'But who are they?'

'They're Eurasian. Not one thing or the other.'

'And what does that mean?'

'It means, Daisy, that they move in a parallel world. They may live alongside the British, but they don't belong with them. And they don't belong with Indians either. In fact, they're despised for being casteless.'

She was shocked at the disdain in his voice. 'But that's so sad. They are very lovely.'

'Lovely they may be, but a gentle warning. You shouldn't mix with them. They're considered your social inferior, and you need to keep a strict distance.'

He gave her a searching look, and she remembered the woman's crass comment at the Club all those weeks ago. A swift glance back at the girls told her that the lightest of their skins was little darker than her own. Anish's warning loomed unpleasantly, but she felt an impulse to defend the carefree young women they'd ridden past.

'If they *are* socially inferior, it doesn't seem to be a problem for the young men.'

He shrugged. 'The girls are young and good-looking, as you say. And they're fun. But what they aren't are future wives, believe me. Marriage with Anglo-Indians is frowned upon and any man who marries one can never hope to become an officer in the Indian Army, or the British Army for that matter. And if he's ICS, he'll never rise to the top of that particular tree.'

Daisy digested this in silence. One more, she thought, to add to the list of barriers that people erected to keep themselves safe.

By now, they had reached the shelter of the trees. Anish helped her to dismount and together they found a spot on the almost bare ground, smooth enough to provide a comfortable resting place. Once Daisy had settled herself against a tree trunk, Anish stretched out his long form along the edge of the riverbank, his hand dipping lazily into the slow-moving water. Rudolf and his comrade stood patiently beneath the trees a little way off and chewed at what was left of the grass. She looked across at them with affection.

'It will be a dismal day when the cavalry no longer rides horses.' Grayson's words were in her mind, but she spoke unthinkingly.

'Who told you that?'

'I heard a rumour. I'm not sure where,' she fudged.

'India is a very old country and hardly changes. Horses have lasted longer here than almost anywhere and you can see why. Where roads are bad, horses will always be the best means of getting about. But you're right about the army, things will be different. It will soon be goodbye to these beautiful creatures and welcome to armoured tanks.'

'Won't you find that hard, Anish? You must have been riding most of your life.'

'In fact, no. Before I joined the cavalry, I rode occasionally, but not very often. My mother hadn't money for a pony and I could ride only if my cousins visited.'

'Your cousins must have been rich enough to keep horses then.' She was intrigued.

'My mother's family, my uncle, was very wealthy though my mother was not. She was a widow, you see. My father died fighting on the Somme.' His expression had grown flint hard, all laughter fled.

'I'm sorry. I had no idea.'

'How could you?'

'But your uncle — he must have been a great support to his sister.'

Anish didn't speak for a long time and, when he did, his tone was severely clipped, as though he was almost biting off his tongue. 'Do you know how widows are treated here?'

She shook her head, but his voice told her it must be badly.

'A woman has no status of her own and, when her husband dies, she becomes nothing. Years ago a widow was required to throw herself on her husband's funeral pyre. Now, she dies a more lingering death. She is shunned by society and seen as a drain on her family. Even her shadow is considered bad luck.'

Daisy stared at him. 'But that's terrible. How can it be? Who says this should happen?'

He smiled thinly. 'You have a very English perspective, Daisy. Who says? India says. Hindu scripture says. It suggests that widows should spend the rest of their lives without worldly possessions. And that suits their families well, for then they have sole ownership of the dead man's assets and no responsibility for his widow.'

Daisy was finding it difficult to believe this was the truth. 'If that's so, how does a widow support herself? Can she work, can she remarry?'

'Neither. No one will employ her and there is no remarriage. The only recourse for such women is to beg outside the temples. And that makes sense, doesn't it? After all, being poor is their only reason for being alive. Their poverty becomes their whole world. They must sleep on the floor, eat only one meal a day, dress always in white and have their hair cut short. These things are punishments for losing a husband.'

'How truly dreadful!' She felt anger spurt, then a huge sorrow as she realised the full implications of what he'd told her. In an uncertain voice, she asked, 'And is that what happened to your mother?'

'My mother found her own escape. You must not imagine she died in penury. Far from it. But did she die in disgrace? Yes.'

'How is that possible?'

'Parvati Rana was very beautiful and a beautiful woman can always name her price.' He ignored Daisy's gasp. 'I can't rail at her choices. They kept me fed and clothed. And they gave me a mother. My father's family wanted to take me away, but she was tenacious and held fast to me. She made sure I was well educated and she used what influence she had to help me. I owe the fact that I'm a cavalry officer to one of her sponsors. He was married with his own family but I like to think that, in his way, he loved her. It was his money that made me who I am, so I can feel only gratitude to him. And, of course, to her.'

'I'm so sorry,' she repeated, and she meant it from the depths of her heart.

'There's no call for sadness. The old life has passed and, with it, old sorrows. My mother died several years ago and she had me to mourn her.'

'But your father . . .'

'I know little of him. Only that he died early and deserved to.' There was a new sourness in his voice. Daisy said nothing, waiting for him to explain. At length he said, 'He was wounded in France and taken to England to recuperate. Then he decided to fall in love with an Englishwoman — or what he called love.'

'And your parents' marriage . . . ?'

'It was arranged, as most Indian marriages are. It may not have been a happy one. I've no idea. Perhaps when Karan Rana was sent abroad to fight, he felt he'd earned the right to break free. Once the war was over, he was going to leave his wife and his child. And he would have done it, too, except the Somme intervened.'

'Did your mother tell you this?'

'She would never speak of him. I read it in a letter he'd sent from England. I didn't discover the truth until I was much older and no longer a child. For years, I'd considered my father a hero, a great man who fought for his country and for the Empire. But then I found that letter, and realised he was in fact a little man, a man capable of deserting his wife and child for a prostitute.'

'Perhaps she wasn't what you thought her.' Anish was making no allowance for the vagaries of love, Daisy thought.

'What else could she be?' he returned angrily. 'He was married with a small child and the woman must have known that. What else can you call it but prostitution? And to think that telegram almost destroyed me — the telegram to say that he'd died. Now, I'm glad he did. If he'd survived the war, I would have killed him myself. He threw my mother into darkness. No one was there to help her. Not the country he'd fought and died for, not the family he'd left behind. No one.'

CHAPTER TWENTY-FIVE

Daisy was shocked into silence. It was a dreadful story, and not just a story, for Anish was the living reminder of his mother's fate. She wondered if this was the first time he'd told his history to another person, and thought that it might be. It made her feel a true friend. She wanted to cheer him, to show her support, her sympathy, but she was wading in deep waters.

At last she said, 'If India gains her independence, do you think widows will be freed from such cruel expectations?'

'Unlikely. The two things are quite separate. We have a caste system that won't change easily. It's embedded in hundreds of years of tradition and that makes it very strong, stronger even than the one that operates among the British.'

She looked confused and, in a lightened mood, he said teasingly, 'Haven't you realised that you're part of a caste system?'

'I've never thought of military life in that way.' But perhaps she should have. It might have made sense of the petty discriminations she'd witnessed over the past few weeks.

'Our two peoples are more alike than you might think,' he went on. 'It's why we don't mock the British insistence on precedence. We understand hierarchy and ritual. Our rulers have always been accustomed to unquestioning obedience. The only difference is that our civilisation is far older than our overlords'. And far more complicated. Only the lowest caste, for instance, can be sweepers while a Brahmin, even if he's a simple gardener, will throw away his food if your shadow so much as falls on it.'

'It's as well we don't have a gardener then.'

He nodded. 'It's why you'll find that most table servants are Moslems.'

'But not Rajiv.'

'No,' he said thoughtfully, 'not Rajiv. But come, we should go. The sun is beginning to climb.' And he jumped smartly to his feet. 'Let me adjust your saddle before we leave. I thought the stirrups looked a little loose.'

Reluctantly, Daisy got to her feet. The river was beautiful and sitting by its slow, flowing waters, she'd been filled with a deep sense of peace, despite the harrowing nature of Anish's recital. But she followed him over to the horses and was soon in the saddle. Tugging on the reins, she was delighted when Rudolf turned obediently to face in the right direction.

Anish smiled approval. 'You see, we've made a horsewoman of you.'

He rode ahead, leaving her to follow in his wake. She hoped he knew where he was going, for they were not returning by the path they'd come by and there was no clear trail to see. They had turned inland from the riverbank and were riding through a forest of small bushes. Every so often, she lost sight of her companion, and a momentary panic would grip her. What if she were to be stranded in this place with no notion of how to get home? But then she would see Anish's back hove into view and know that he was not too far distant.

They rode in this way for a good twenty minutes, and Daisy was sufficiently relaxed to allow Anish to pass out of sight without feeling concern. She was pushing her way beneath several low hanging trees, which grew in a cluster among a sea of bushes, when she saw something lying in her path. She tried to steer Rudolf around it but, though in general compliant, this was an obstacle he'd taken in deep dislike. He snorted and shook his head. It was a large tree branch, she saw, twisted and gnarled, but the horse had decided it was a dangerous enemy and refused to move. She called ahead to Anish, but he did not hear.

Daisy dug her heels into the horse's flank as she'd been shown, but Rudolf stayed obstinately where he was. She dug harder and suddenly the horse lurched ahead, toppling her forward onto his neck. She clutched at his mane, trying to regain an upright position, but the saddle was slipping in a most worrying fashion and she found her right foot slide out of the stirrup. The whole saddle had tipped sideways and she was hanging on to the reins, with one foot dangling loose and the other caught awkwardly in the second stirrup, which had risen far too high. Having thoroughly frightened himself, Rudolf sprang into a gallop, travelling faster than Daisy had ever known. She cried out in terror, but horse and rider had veered violently to the right, leaving Anish to fade from earshot.

They were thundering over rough ground, Daisy clinging desperately to the leather edge of the saddle, her hold growing stickier and more insecure by the second. Her head was tilted downwards and she saw the earth rushing past in a blurred vision, felt her hands slipping, her body dropping perilously close to the earth, and could only close her eyes in silent prayer.

Then a shout from behind, and another horse was suddenly there at her side. One of the young officers she'd seen picnicking a short while ago was drawing abreast. He raised himself out of the saddle and leaned across to grab at the reins. The hard tug on Rudolf's mouth surprised him into slowing his frantic pace until finally he came to a halt, his eyes wild and his legs trembling. The young man jumped from his horse, and gently helped Daisy to the safety of solid ground.

'Hey there!' he yelled at the horseman in the distance, and this time Anish heard.

He turned and cantered back to them.

'Daisy, what happened to you?'

'I'm not sure.' Her face was flushed and she was shivering in the scorching air. 'The horse wouldn't move, so I dug him with my heels — as you taught me — and then suddenly he took off, and the saddle slipped, and I ended upside down.'

Her rescuer was calming Rudolf, who was still unhappy. 'No wonder the saddle slipped, look the leather has worn completely around the girths.'

'Where?' Anish demanded. He strode across and followed the young man's pointing finger. 'I didn't notice that. My God, Daisy, I'm so sorry.'

'It's fine. I'm fine. I'm afraid I'm a trifle accident-prone these days.' She tried to smile, but it wasn't a success.

'It's entirely my fault. I should have noticed the problem when I adjusted the stirrups, but I didn't see it.'

'The sun was too bright, I guess,' the young man offered, 'It plays tricks with the eyesight. And your horse doesn't look as if he likes the unpredictable. Probably better to keep to the known tracks. Anyway, no harm done. I've tightened the strap to where the leather is still intact.'

Anish thanked him, and then muttered as though he couldn't quite believe what had happened, 'I didn't hear her call.'

'Don't think about it!' The officer waved them a cheerful farewell. 'Just get her home. She's had quite a shock.'

* * *

Their return to the bungalow was swift and incident free, but Anish refused to leave until he'd seen her into a chair and placed a cold drink in her hand. She knew he was blaming himself for what had happened and, though she still felt shaky, she was anxious to reassure him.

'You really mustn't worry. I'm as fit as a flea.'

'But you might not have been.'

'This isn't the first accident I've had,' she reminded him. 'And I'm still in one piece.'

He didn't look convinced. He looked agitated, his fingers tugging at his usually immaculate hair. 'You've certainly had your fill of bad luck since you've been here. It's almost as though someone has cast a wicked spell. You see, you should have taken my advice and gone to Simla.'

'Then I'd probably have fallen off the mountainside. And I'm glad I didn't go. I'm very happy to be in Jasirapur.' When he looked doubtful, she said, 'Really, Anish, I am. Learning to ride has been — well, liberating — and since I started to work at the Infirmary, my days have been full.'

'You've actually started to work at the hospital? I had no idea.'

'No one has.' That wasn't quite true, but she didn't want to bring Grayson Harte's name into the conversation.

'And does Gerald know?'

'Not yet. I'll tell him, of course. At the right moment.'

He pulled his mouth down in a wry grimace. 'I'll leave that one to you!'

* * *

For a long while after he left, Daisy sat looking blankly through the window without seeing anything of the wilderness outside. Until Rudolf had bolted, she'd been enjoying the ride more than any other she'd taken. She was used to Anish talking to her as one friend to another, but it was rare for him to touch on the personal. Today had been different. She'd learned something of his past, and felt it helped her understand better the complex person she'd always suspected lay within. The day had been a very happy one until the accident. And the accident had upset her more than she realised. The worn girths were a bad oversight, but perhaps the problem was not that uncommon and ordinarily would not have led to disaster. It was the fact that she was an inexperienced rider and had no idea how to handle a terrified horse.

Nobody was to blame for the accident. How could they be? The cantonment was heavily guarded, and it was impossible that anyone could have gained entry and tampered with Rudolf's saddle. Today had been bad luck. That had to be the case. And if today were bad luck, then so were all the other incidents that had dogged her since she'd come to India. The snake had ventured in from the garden to find a cool bathroom, the block of masonry had fallen but from a ruin that was already crumbling. The unknown trespasser that first night and later the locked door were as easily explained: she'd been badly affected by the unfamiliar heat and had woken up befuddled and unaware of where she was.

Yet her misgivings persisted, and she couldn't share them. If she went to Gerald, he would think she'd run mad. He would say the sun had made her irrational, and accuse her of allowing her imagination too much licence. And he would be right. It was this house as much as anything — unhappy and isolated, cut off even from what passed for life in the cantonment — that encouraged false fancies and sent her mind spinning into the darkest of shadows.

But try as she might, she could not prevent herself hearing the small, nagging voice which whispered that her doubts were justified. She had joked to Anish that she was accident-prone, but the accidents were becoming a little too frequent. And a little too dangerous. Previously, she'd felt their threat and been scared enough, it was true. But today had been different. Today, she had come within an inch of being killed. If that young officer had not finished his picnic early, if he'd not heard her calls for help and she'd not had the strength to hang on long enough for him to reach her . . . she would surely be dead.

How impossible to believe, though, that someone was deliberately seeking her out, that she was somebody's chosen target. Who would want to hurt her, and why? She was a nonentity, an unimportant stranger who knew nothing of local affairs and who knew nobody of any importance.

Her bewilderment strengthened an already deep sense of solitude and amplified her disquiet. Even as she sat thinking, the tentacles of fear spread and multiplied in the deathly quiet of the house. She was alone, and thousands of miles from home. Very much alone. She was married, but to a man who showed little interest in her. Anish was a kind companion, but his life lay elsewhere and his friendship would be fleeting. And Grayson, was he friend or foe? She couldn't decide.

CHAPTER TWENTY-SIX

Gerald had given up any pretence of dressing for the evening meal and considered a quick sluice of hands and face sufficient preparation for eating with his wife. He rarely had much to say and it was most often left to Daisy to fill the awkward quiet that hung over the dining table. Tonight he ate swiftly and in a silence so determined that she made no effort to talk. In any case, what could she say? That she had come close to death today and that his friend blamed himself for her terrifying experience. The accident was something she couldn't tell Gerald. Something else she dare not say. He might forbid her to ride again and she'd no wish for another deceit to hover between them. She crossed her fingers that Anish would make no mention of it. Probably not, since he'd been mortified by what had happened.

To her watching eye, Gerald seemed more preoccupied than ever. In the brief conversations she'd had with him recently, he'd never spoken of the guns which had been stolen from the regiment and she wondered whether he was worrying over the lack of security at the camp. Had he been personally responsible for the firearms and was he now in trouble over their disappearance? He wouldn't tell her even if he were, and the thought that they shared so little left a new emptiness in her heart.

As soon as he'd eaten his last mouthful, he got up from the table and went over to his desk. Daisy had kept her distance from it since the day she'd read Joseph Minns' letter, fearing what she might find if she looked too hard. It was a fair assumption that somewhere in its contents was a demand for money. The pile of papers on the desk never seemed to decrease, but it didn't stop Gerald from a nightly sifting. Maybe he thought that by regularly moving them from top to bottom, side to side, they would miraculously disappear.

She wished he'd confide in her and speak of his difficulties, but it was unlikely he ever would. For a short while their future had looked more promising, but as the weeks had slipped by, she'd stopped expecting love from him or anything close to love, and been ready to settle for companionship and a husband who might one day, perhaps, share her bed. She knew now that she would have neither. They were doomed to remain mere acquaintances, sharing a house but not a life. She was powerless to influence his feelings towards her, and she realised with a nasty surprise that she no longer cared to try. How could she have fallen out of love so quickly with a man who'd been for her the very pinnacle of all things wonderful? Perhaps that was why. She had given him almost god-like qualities, and then found him a fallible man. Her fall into reality had been sharp and painful.

She was the wife Gerald did not want. How ironic it was then that he shared a whole history with her, a history that neither could talk of. Both had started their lives in the same shabby corner of London, both had struggled to free themselves from the narrowness of that world, and both fought and overcome the most difficult of barriers to do so. Yet they were as much divided by their history as they were allied. He had parents who loved him, loved him enough to risk beggaring themselves so that their son could have the advantages they never had. She wondered what that must feel like.

Gerald had turned his back on his family and made himself an orphan. She had not been given the choice.

Tonight she felt weary, fatigued from the long ride and severe fright and, taking her place in one of the wicker chairs, she hardly noticed the broken canes prodding into her back or the cushion lumpy beneath her. Mechanically, she began to turn the pages of her book, page after page, but nothing she saw made sense. Words jostled, sentences danced, moving black shapes formed and reformed without meaning. When Rajiv brought her the glass of goji juice, she took it listlessly. She really wouldn't need this tonight. Despite the suffocating closeness, she would sleep easily and be ready for the Infirmary tomorrow. It was good to be going back, good to be losing herself in work.

She sensed Gerald had turned from the desk and was watching her. 'You should enjoy the juice,' he said. 'We've a mountain of berries — your friend delivered another basket this morning — and tonight Rajiv has made your drink with sugar. You'll like it.'

'Why sugar?'

'I asked him to. You look very tired and sugar will give you energy.'

She would need to feel a good deal livelier for the hospital tomorrow, Daisy supposed, and it was a kind gesture on Gerald's part. She took a sip. It was very sweet and she wanted to leave the glass untouched, but he was still watching her and since she could not bear to quarrel tonight of all nights, she gulped down the drink. Then went to clean her teeth to get rid of the sticky residue which clung to her mouth. Bidding Gerald a brief goodnight, she left him still poring over his papers and slipped into bed. She was asleep before she had pulled the sheet over her knees.

* * *

She hardly knew that she'd woken. Her head didn't feel her own and her eyes remained half-closed. There was a chainsaw slicing through part of her brain and a deep, dark throb in the back of her neck. She tried to open her eyes properly, but her vision was badly clouded. For a moment, she thought herself back in the cheerless dormitory of Eden House, but it was too bright and there were no snuffling children on either side. It was night, though. That, at least, she could make out; the intense light of a full moon was flooding the room and throwing shadows against the whitewashed walls. Not the orphanage then, but her Indian bedroom. Her mouth was parched and sore, and she was desperate for water. She must get up, get to the glass jug that sat atop the chest of drawers. She dragged herself into a sitting position, her head feeling as though it might explode at any moment.

The bungalow rested in silence. She must have woken because she felt so ill. Either that, or Gerald was moving around in his bedroom unable to sleep, agitated perhaps by the worries of the day. She swung her legs out of the bed, and stopped — there was a noise after all. Was that furniture he was moving? She wondered what he could be doing at this hour and supposed she should find out. Her legs felt for the floor and she tried to stand. The room swam dizzily to one side, and then teetered to the other, while her legs folded neatly beneath her. She literally could not stand. Lying sprawled on the rush matting, she scrabbled against the bed frame, trying to get a purchase. What was happening to her?

Somehow she managed to get to her knees and, for what seemed an age, knelt there as though she were a penitent at prayer. Her vision was dreadfully distorted. Furniture loomed at her, then retreated, the sheet blurred into a white snowfall, then turned grey. She was sick, very sick. The drill which had been piercing the back of her head went into overdrive. That must have been the noise she'd heard. The noise was coming from inside her head! With a mighty effort, she grabbed at the mattress and hoisted herself half into bed. She lay there, eyes closed, drowning in a whirlpool of spin and confusion, sinking, sinking.

* * *

When Daisy woke again, bright sunlight was streaming through the plaited blinds and into every crevice of the room, the heat a stifling blanket bearing down on her head. The house had again retreated into stillness except for the call of the hoopoe birds in the garden, their art deco plumage puffed with pleasure. Memory flooded back. She had tried to reach the water, tried to reach the door and then collapsed, her legs mere cushions of air, as insubstantial as a straw doll's. Cautiously, she tried to sit up, clasping the iron bed frame as support, and feeling with her feet for her slippers.

Somehow she managed to pull herself upright. Her entire body felt unwell, aching and shivering. She must be sickening for something. It couldn't be anything she'd caught at the Infirmary since she'd not been there for nearly a week. Perhaps it was something she'd eaten. So far, she had escaped the stomach problems she'd been promised but she ate only Rajiv's food, and that had never made her sick before. Was it something she'd drunk? Perhaps the water had not been boiled sufficiently well.

Or . . . was it the goji juice? It had been so sweet she'd not been able to taste it properly. What if the berries had been overripe or not ripe enough? Or what if . . . no, she wouldn't think it. But what if they'd been tampered with? The berries had come from Grayson and he'd been sending them ever since the day of the riot. She'd felt grateful for his concern, but now for the first time began to wonder just why he would send them. Rajiv must be able to buy berries from the market, so why had Grayson taken it on himself to deliver them personally to her door?

In the past, they'd appeared to do her good, and they'd certainly never had such a dreadful effect. But, what if last night she'd drunk something other than pure goji juice, what if there had been something nestling among those innocent berries, something that was not goji but could easily lie hidden in their midst? Would Rajiv have noticed? Probably not. And there were plenty of poisonous substances that could go undetected, plenty growing in this very garden. Oleander seeds, for instance. She had been warned by Anish never to pick them, never even to touch them. If they were the culprit, it was unlikely they could have accidentally become mixed with harmless fruit. And that meant that last night someone had attempted to drug her, and succeeded in making her very sick. But who and why?

She stayed dozing in the chair for much of the morning, too unwell to go to the Infirmary. Gerald had left a note to say he was not returning until evening, and a blank day stretched before her. Daisy felt too ill to care. When Rajiv brought her lunch, she could only pick at it a while before returning limply to her chair. Her eyes had once more begun to close when she heard Anish's voice at the door.

'I thought I'd call to see how well you're recovering.' He meant from yesterday's ride, of course.

'I'm feeling a good deal better,' she lied. 'Just a little sore from bumps and bruises.' She would say nothing of the night's events. Anish was already suspicious of Grayson Harte and she had no wish to cause further trouble.

'You'll be glad to hear I've had Rudolf's tack completely changed so whenever you feel fit enough to ride again, let me know.'

'That's kind of you — but if we could leave it for a few days?'

'Of course. I can see you're still shaken up. You haven't gone to the Infirmary.'

'Not today, I'm afraid, though I was due to go. I feel bad about it. I haven't been able to get a message to them.'

'Can I help?'

'Would you mind very much calling in on your way back to camp and letting them know why I haven't put in an appearance?'

'Consider it done. Dr Lane will understand, I'm sure. You're a volunteer after all. I imagine the work is pretty tiring and you need to be on top form.'

He settled himself opposite her and stretched out his legs. She noticed his boots were so highly polished that she could see her reflection in them. 'I understand you need something to keep you busy,' he went on, 'but what made you choose to work at the hospital?'

'I don't rightly know. It seemed a useful thing to do, particularly as they're very short staffed at the moment. I thought I could help. My mother was a nurse — perhaps that's what gave me the idea.'

'It must be satisfying to follow in her footsteps. Is she still nursing?'

Daisy's face clouded. 'She died when I was a few years old.'

'I'm sorry. You never said. It seems we share the same family story.'

'Not exactly. I had no family at all. I was brought up in an orphanage.'

That made him sit up. He leaned towards her, a frown creasing his forehead. 'I had no idea. It couldn't have been much fun.'

Her head had again begun its incessant throb but she tried to answer truthfully. 'It wasn't. I didn't have the easiest of starts, it's true, but like you I've managed to survive. My mother was a disgraced woman, too, as it happens. Not a widow but a woman without a husband. And the orphanage had clear rules about such things. Children were tolerated if they'd lost both their parents, but if they'd never had them, they were treated miserably.'

'It sounds an even less happy life than mine.'

'I can't really complain. I was lucky to be befriended by one of the patrons. Miss Maddox took me into her household and showed me a great deal of kindness. It was more than I deserved.'

'You were her adopted daughter?'

Daisy felt herself growing hot and not just from whatever poison she'd swallowed. It took her a while before she answered. 'Nothing like that. I worked as her servant.' It was an admission she had never made to anyone since leaving service. But she trusted Anish and now she had begun, she might as well tell the whole truth in all its harshness. 'I started as a kitchen maid — that's the lowliest of positions — but then I became a downstairs maid, and finally personal assistant to Miss Maddox herself.'

Anish's eyebrows knit together. 'I thought Gerald told me he met you in a shop.'

'He did. Miss Maddox had to leave London and go to her sister, who was very sick. There was no room for me at the new house and I had to find another job. She was so good to me. She knew I couldn't bear to go into service with anyone else, so she spoke to the owners of a department store that she knew — in the West End.' There was still pride at the thought. 'They took me on. In the restaurant to begin with, but then I was promoted to work in the perfumery. That's where I met Gerald.'

Anish stood up and began to walk back and forth across the rush matting. It was clear he was thinking over what she'd said, and it was disturbing him. Eventually, he stopped in front of her. 'Does Gerald know? I mean about the orphanage, and being in service.'

'No,' she said in a quiet voice. 'We've never talked about our families and he thinks I've always worked at Bridges.' It was an admission she didn't like to make. If Gerald had falsified his background, was she really any better? Hers was a sin of omission but she, too, had been trying to cover her tracks, pretend she was other than she really was.

'I'm sure you don't want my advice, but if you were to ask me I would say keep it that way. Never tell him. If you did, you'd gain very little and you might lose a lot. He can be extremely touchy.'

'About servants?'

'About where people come from. He likes to fit in. I think it's been a struggle for him.' That chimed with everything she suspected.

'You notice a lot, Anish.'

'It's simply that I know him well. I watch him watching others and always trying not to make a mistake. He's not at ease.' Whereas you are, she thought.

There was a pause before he said, 'You've had an eventful life. It must make coping with the army, with army wives, quite difficult.'

He was being kind, she knew, picking his words carefully.

'A little. It's rather like being dropped into the sea without a lifebelt. But so far I haven't drowned.'

He sat down again and fixed her with a warm smile. 'You've done amazingly well. And I can appreciate just how well. Like you, I've travelled a long way, though I've chosen to forget the past.'

'I wouldn't want to do that.' Her voice was firm. That would deny everything that had made you the person you were, she thought.

'Do you think much about your early life?'

'I didn't. At least not until a few months ago. I think I was too busy just getting through each day.'

'So, what has changed for you?'

'India maybe. I've thought far more about the past since I've been here.'

'How strange that my country has stirred memories for you.'

He rose to leave and she got up from her chair, her legs still unsteady, and walked with him out onto the veranda.

'Not so strange. It's happened slowly.' He looked at her questioningly and she tried to explain. 'It must have been my visit to the temple that started it. I saw a necklace there, carved on a stone goddess. There was a pendant hanging from the necklace and I remembered seeing my mother wearing a brooch just like it in the only photograph I have. It made me think about her for the first time — I mean, really think about her.'

'And did it make you think of your father, too?'

'I'm afraid not. To be honest, there's little to think of. I don't even know his name, and I've no idea how I'd begin to find out. I'm not even sure I'd want to.'

He nodded and took her hand in farewell. 'Your instinct is telling you right, I'm sure. It's better to leave the past undisturbed.'

CHAPTER TWENTY-SEVEN

She watched him walk down the veranda steps towards the tree where his horse was sheltering. He threw himself into the saddle and, shading her eyes, Daisy followed rider and horse to the end of the path where they wheeled left onto the track that led to the main thoroughfare. A last wave and Anish was gone. She turned to walk back into the house, but almost on cue an engine spluttered into life nearby.

Surprised by the sound, she retraced her steps onto the veranda and peered into the distance. That was odd. Except for vehicles commandeered from the regiment, she had never seen a car in the vicinity. The noise had come from the right and that was even odder. She'd thought the track petered out just beyond the bungalow and had never ventured along it, but it was certainly a car that she saw driving past the end of the garden, and it had come from that direction.

She squinted across the spread of dry grass, still broiling from the midday sun, and saw a metallic roof shooting sparks of light into the bushes that bordered the lane. It looked like an ICS car, like the jeep Grayson Harte used in Jasirapur, but it couldn't be. Or could it?

Was Gerald right after all, and the man had some kind of obsession with her and was conniving these so-called accidents in order to see her, to be close to her, to act as her saviour? Had he come to commiserate over her illness, but seen Anish's horse grazing in the garden and thought better of it? If so, he must know her drink had been tampered with, know that the goji berries had been mixed with less benign fruit. She felt wretched in suspecting him of such a dreadful deed, but what other explanation could there be for his presence in the middle of nowhere?

Retracing her steps into the house, she fell back into her chair, exhausted and feeling stupidly weak. A small army of flying insects had mustered on the ceiling, and she fixed her eyes on them, trying to think her way through a miasma that was gathering pace. She hadn't told Anish about the poisoned juice, and she couldn't tell Gerald either. He was liable to accuse Grayson outright, and she didn't want to see the man smeared, his career in India compromised before it had truly begun.

Whatever he might have done, she couldn't stop herself liking him. He'd shown her kindness on board ship when she'd needed kindness most. And shown her the same warm concern each time they'd met; encouraged her even to confide her most private sorrow. Daisy hoped very much that her imaginings were wrong and she'd be careful to say nothing to anyone. But there was one thing she would do — she would refuse to drink any more goji juice.

As always around nine o'clock that night, Rajiv handed her the glass and she thanked him for it. But she didn't drink. Instead, she said to Gerald who was playing an irritable game of patience at the table, 'I'm very tired. I think I'll go to bed and have my juice there.'

He nodded absently and she slipped from the room unnoticed. Once in her bedroom, she raised the *tatty* very slightly and poured the liquid out of the window. It settled into a small pool on the veranda but then slowly disappeared down the cracks of the wooden planks. She felt immediate relief. She must do that every night.

* * *

For the next three evenings, Daisy did just that, trickling the liquid harmlessly down between the veranda's boards. As a consequence, she slept very badly in the closed room, unable to find even one cool spot amid the burning sheets. Whenever she fell into an uneasy doze, the noises of an Indian night — jackals, dogs, the harsh croaking of frogs — brought her back to full consciousness. But it was better to lie wearily awake, she thought, than pass the night in a poisoned coma.

She saw herself looking more haggard as each day passed, but Gerald seemed not to notice. Indeed, he was hardly ever at home, seeming to spend more and more time at the cantonment. When he did stay for lunch or arrived back for the evening, he hardly spoke. It was almost too hot to speak, Daisy thought. The temperature was still mounting, and by the end of each day the house glowered like a stoked furnace.

'The monsoon will soon be here,' he said one night. 'You'll feel a lot better when it comes — we all will.' Perhaps, after all, he had noticed how ragged she looked. 'The wives will soon be back, too,' he went on, 'and you'll have four months of fun ahead. Parties and dances galore. There'll be horse shows, race weeks — gymkhanas. Keep up the riding, and you'll be ready for them.'

'At the moment, I'm finding it too warm to ride,' she prevaricated, 'even very early in the morning.'

She hadn't gone out on Rudolf since the accident, though she'd resumed her work at the Infirmary. She supposed she could have sent a message to Anish saying she would like to ride, but something always held her back. She wouldn't now be the proficient horsewoman he'd prophesied and the gymkhanas would be given a miss, she thought wryly. In fact, she would have liked to give the entire social calendar a miss. Gerald's promise of a butterfly existence filled her with misgivings. She hated the thought that very soon she would be surrounded by the women she'd met that night at the Club.

She mustn't forget, though, that Jocelyn would be returning with them. That, at least, was a comfort. The girl would be in Jasirapur for only a few weeks, but Daisy was already looking forward to seeing her. For the first time in her life, she had friends. Anish and Jocelyn. She'd always pushed people away, wary they might discover the real Daisy, but Jocelyn had been irrepressible, and she was glad of it. When the girl returned, it would be cool. At last. Cool enough, she hoped, to cope better with the wives. Cool enough to brave even a Rosemary Laughton.

'Like I mentioned.' Gerald pushed aside his plate, his meal half-eaten. It was almost too hot to swallow. 'The heat will break soon, but the locals are celebrating already. There's a big festival happening on Friday. It's called Teej, and it's quite a spectacle. It's a religious thing, but still fun. Like a carnival really — huge crowds enjoying themselves.'

'We should go.' The festival sounded exciting and she spoke without thinking. But he didn't immediately pour cold water on the notion as she'd expected.

'It's a good idea.' He nodded to himself. 'Yes, we should go. You'd enjoy it.'

'But can we go together?'

'Some of the troops will be on standby in case of any trouble — I can't imagine there will be. But I'll make sure I get time off, and rustle up some transport.'

His words surprised Daisy, since earlier promises had come to nothing. There had been no second drive to the river, no willingness even to spend more than an hour in her company. Too little, too late, came to mind, but she was grateful he was making even a small effort.

* * *

She woke the next morning to a room that was unusually dark. Snatching up her watch, Daisy brought it close to her face and saw that it was early morning despite the absence of light. She went to the window and lifted the blind. The sun had gone, disappeared behind a mountain of grey cloud, and there was a stiff breeze whiffling through the long alfalfa grass. It was far from cool, however. If anything, the heat was more oppressive, spiralling itself downwards from a sky that seemed to sit just above her head.

She had barely taken a mouthful of the small breakfast left for her, when she heard a tap on the window. Then another tap. And another. Large, hard drops of water. It was rain! She ran out onto the veranda, hardly able to believe what she was seeing. But sure enough, water was tumbling from the skies. Clambering down the wooden steps, she dashed into the mass of grass, unmindful of what might be lying there, and pirouetted round and round in ever widening circles. She danced wildly on the spot, smiling and laughing and giving out small whoops, holding her face up to feel the full power of the rain drenching her skin. Then, as though a hand above had switched off a tap, the rain stopped and she was left dripping in the midst of a sodden garden. The skies began to clear almost instantly but in an atmosphere that was muggier than ever.

She didn't understand. She'd read that when the monsoon came, it went on for hours, for days, for weeks.

'It's the *chota bursat*,' Dr Lane explained, when she reached the Infirmary. 'The little rains. They arrive ahead of the real monsoon but they fall for only a few hours.'

'It was only a few minutes, I think. But it was wonderful while it lasted. For once my skin stopped burning.'

'It's good that you made the most of it — it will be hotter now. You should stay home for a few days, Daisy. This week isn't too busy. Two more patients left before you arrived.'

She started to protest but Dr Lane was adamant. 'The heat will be worse than ever until the monsoon breaks. Take my advice — stay home and listen for the honk of wild geese. They'll be coming from Siberia. A kind of advance guard for the cool weather.'

He was right. The thermometer climbed rapidly during the morning and, once again, the clouds piled high, dark and threatening. Daisy left the Infirmary to find a sky filled with a thunderous beauty, a pyramid of clouds banked one on top of another, and air she could almost touch, dank and heavy, a grey blanket of rolling warmth. By the time she pedalled up the pathway to the bungalow, she was once more exhausted.

If she'd thought herself uncomfortable on previous occasions, it was nothing to the wretched time she had that night: tossing and turning constantly, her body sweating, her skin itching from the misery of prickly heat. Once or twice she got up and walked around the bedroom, thinking she might cool herself by doing so. But nothing worked. She lay on top of the unmade twin and waited for dawn. Everything around was still. Even the dogs had fallen silent. Every living creature seemed to be waiting in deathly quiet for the crash that would signal the monsoon proper.

She'd fallen into an uneasy doze when she heard a dragging sound. The same dragging sound she'd heard before. So the noise hadn't been in her head after all. It had been real, it had existed. What was it? Daisy padded quietly to the door and opened it the smallest chink. A shock was waiting for her. She almost slammed the door in fear, but something kept her where she was, kept her from crying out.

Standing within touching distance was a stranger, an Indian. He was looking ahead and didn't notice the slight opening of the door. And he was not that strange. He was the very same man she'd seen in the garden the first night she'd slept at the bungalow. Daisy was sure of it. He had to be a friend of Rajiv's, but what was he doing in her house in the early hours of the morning? And why had Rajiv denied that he knew the man?

All her old suspicions came alive. Keeping her hand as firmly as she could on the doorknob, she put her eye to the gap between the door and the frame. The man was walking away towards the side door. That would make sense, that was the way to Rajiv's quarters. She dare not open the door wider in case he turned and saw her but, as she watched, he disappeared. She was sure he'd not even reached the side entrance, but he must have done, else how could he have simply disappeared? She held her breath for a moment, then slowly opened the door a fraction wider. There was nothing to see. A little wider, and still she could see nothing and no one. Taking courage, she walked out into the passage and through into the sitting room. It was empty.

Padding back along the passage, she made for Gerald's room. She must wake him and tell him what had happened. He needed to know they were playing host to strangers. But there was no sign of him. Had Gerald been woken by the same noise and followed the Indian to Rajiv's quarters to find out what was going on? If so, he would be back very soon. But the side door hadn't opened, Daisy was sure and, when she retraced her steps, she saw it had been locked from the inside. So there *were* keys in the house after all, and no one could have passed that way. But then, where had the man gone? And where was Gerald?

CHAPTER TWENTY-EIGHT

She was not going to find out in the middle of the night. There was nothing she could do except wait for morning and hope Gerald would be back to solve the puzzle. But when she rose the next day, hot and unrefreshed, it was to find he was still absent. She went out onto the veranda and scanned the empty garden.

Noiselessly, Rajiv appeared at her side. 'Sahib Gerald at camp,' he said indifferently.

'When did the sahib leave?'

Rajiv shrugged his shoulders. Either he didn't know, or wasn't interested enough to tell her. The image of the unknown Indian came unbidden into her mind, and she was tempted to ask the servant about his friend and at least clear a little of last night's mystery. But Daisy knew she would get nothing from him. Instead, she reeled off a list of items that were needed from the market. They would keep him busy and out of the house for an hour at least.

A plan had begun to form. She would go to his quarters — never mind what Gerald said — go there and try to discover just what was going on. Whatever it was, it was suspicious, and Rajiv was involved. She would get the proof against him that she'd once wanted and, when Gerald eventually returned, she could surprise him with her resourcefulness. Daisy looked forward to that moment.

She saw Rajiv trundle his old bike along the path and out of the garden, a large basket tied to the handlebars, but made herself wait. It felt a very long ten minutes but, once she was sure he wouldn't return to the house on whatever pretext, she left the veranda and took up a position just outside her bedroom. Before she trespassed in Rajiv's quarters, Daisy wanted to be sure she'd got things right. She stood in the exact spot the man had stood, a few inches from her bedroom door and facing away towards the side entrance. There was nowhere else he could have gone except through that door, but how had it locked itself after he'd passed? It was preposterous, yet somehow it had happened.

She started towards the door leading to Rajiv's accommodation, but almost tripped on a piece of rush matting that had slightly rucked. Another accident waiting to happen, she thought tiredly, and bent to prod the matting into place. It remained annoyingly bunched, and she had to kneel to push it back more forcefully. The matting had been cut into a square, hardly perceptible in the overall spread, but at close quarters its outline was clear. Perhaps there had been a misjudgement when the rush matting had first been laid and this was an infill putting right the mistake. Something about it, though, was too neat, too symmetrical.

Daisy stopped pushing and, instead, flicked at the recalcitrant piece of flooring. It came up easily and when she flicked some more, the rest of the square peeled back and revealed an exactly matching wooden square with an iron ring sitting in its centre. She was stunned. Was there a cellar she'd been unaware of? Was this where the man had disappeared?

Her heart was beating rapidly and she was sweating profusely, as much from excitement as from the airless room. She wiped her hands dry on her dress, thankful that this morning she'd chosen to wear an old cotton brought from England, since it looked likely to get very dirty. She tugged at the ring and the square of wood came up easily. The trapdoor, for that was what it was, was evidently in regular use. The Indian had been here before. The talk about ghosts when she'd first seen him in the garden had been to confuse her, to discourage her from asking more questions. And it had been Rajiv who'd been behind the story.

A narrow ladder stretched down into darkness. She would need a light if she were to venture into that black void and, scrambling to her feet, she hurried back to her bedroom. The kerosene lamp would have to do. It gave only a half-hearted glow, but it was sufficient for her to find her way down the ladder, step by step, to the solid floor beneath. Holding the lamp as high as she could, she swung the light in an arc. Even by its muted glimmer, she could see that she was in an enormous space, equivalent, she calculated, to the entire floor area of the bungalow. She must be below ground level for the air was remarkably cool.

But why had the Indian been here? As far as Daisy could see, there was no reason. It was an empty space, leading nowhere. Guiltily, she realised that she'd been half-hoping for a tunnel and scolded herself for her childishness. Edging forward, she held the lamp high and to the front of her. Its swinging beam flashed from wall to wall. They had been fashioned from mud and straw, she saw, and left roughly finished, unlike the whitewash of the rest of the house.

Halfway along one side, a dark shape loomed into sight. It appeared to be growing out of the floor of beaten earth. She went slowly towards it and, once it was fully within the lamp's beam, saw with relief that it was nothing more than a stack of boxes: large, rough-looking crates, coffin shaped, and piled one on top of each other. Behind the first stack was another, and behind that, another still.

The boxes were made from coarse plywood and she could see marks stencilled on their sides, though nothing she could make sense of. She tried to lift the cover of the box nearest her, but it was nailed fast. The top box of the second stack was similarly hammered down but, passing on to the third, she managed to dislodge one of the wooden covers.

Very carefully, she settled the lamp on the uneven floor — it would be disastrous if she lost the light — and manoeuvred the lid to one side. Her hand trailed inside the box, discovering it was filled with straw. It looked to be a disappointing end to her adventure.

Standing on tiptoe, she plunged her hand further into the box and, this time, her fingers touched metal. Cold, heavy, sharp-edged. She had to use both hands to pull the object clear and, retrieving the lamp from its resting place, Daisy held the wavering light over her discovery. A short, sharp gasp sounded in the stillness. She had found a rifle!

Frantically, she delved into the case again and brought out another gun, and then another. The crate was filled with firearms and the remaining crates, identical in size and lettering, must contain the same. Suddenly, the adventure died. Suddenly, it all made sense, horrible, gut-wrenching sense. These were the missing arms, the guns from the regiment. It had to be them, and they were here in this house. They must have been stolen and hidden by Rajiv and his accomplice. She'd been right about the servant, but that seemed unimportant now. It was clear Rajiv intended to make money by selling arms, and almost certainly to the protesters she had seen. This was what Grayson had feared.

Daisy felt herself paralysed by the dreadful knowledge and had to pinch herself hard. The first thing to do was to get out of this cellar. Rajiv would be back very soon and he mustn't discover her here. He mustn't know that he'd been found out. She would get word to Gerald — he would know how to handle things.

Moving with a new decisiveness, she packed the guns back into the straw, trying to push them as far down as she could, and then replaced the crate's covering in the same position she'd found it. She must leave no trace of herself, no sign that she'd been here, and scurried up the ladder as swiftly as she could. Only just in time. As she lowered the trapdoor and replaced the matting, she heard the creak of Rajiv's bicycle being wheeled to the kitchen. Had she thought of everything? Through the panic, she remembered. The lamp — the lamp must be returned or there would be questions. Emerging from her bedroom, she was just in time. Rajiv was gliding towards her from the side entrance.

'How was the market. Did you get everything?'

She tried to speak as evenly as she could, though her breathlessness made it difficult. Was it her imagination or was he looking at her oddly?

'No fresh dates. Water melons coming later.' His tone was brusque, uncongenial as always. He couldn't suspect anything, but her heart was still beating far too fast and she was sweating profusely. No wonder he looked at her askance. The sooner Gerald got back, the better.

When Rajiv had disappeared into the kitchen, Daisy sat down and tried to think. Rajiv had been her tormentor, that was certain, and now she knew why. He had been disagreeable from the first. He'd not wanted her here, but not because of his intense loyalty to Gerald as she'd thought, but because her presence in the bungalow could tear his plans to shreds.

It must have come as a severe blow to him when Gerald announced that a memsahib was coming from England and would be around the house day and night. Perhaps he'd been planning to move the stolen guns when Gerald was at work, maybe even sell them from the bungalow. The house was isolated enough. But her arrival on the scene had put paid to that idea, and he'd been forced into working by night. They were the sounds she'd heard: weapons being shifted in and out of the cellar. Thinking back, Daisy could see there had been a regular pattern to the noises. Twice a week, guns had arrived and guns had been despatched.

She had been a problem for Rajiv from the start, a nuisance that had to be got rid of. And he'd done his best. He'd tried to scare her, hoping perhaps that if he made her fearful enough, she would go to Simla with the other women. He'd been the one to pretend a ghost, the one to lock her door, the one who'd encouraged the snake into the bathroom and then deliberately ignored her calls for help. But his ploy hadn't worked. She hadn't packed her case as she should have done and the attacks had escalated.

His final attempt had been to tamper with her juice, no doubt mixing oleander seeds with the goji berries. Who, after all, could have a better opportunity? How easy it must have been. Oleanders grew everywhere in the garden and she'd discovered from Dr Lane's medical dictionaries that just a few could cause headache and nausea and even induce a coma.

Rajiv was thoroughly wicked. She wondered how Gerald would take the news that his loyal servant had plotted against his wife, even tried to kill her — she'd come close to tragedy several times. He wasn't just wicked, though. He was clever as well, to have pursued such a successful vendetta. Her thoughts slammed to an abrupt halt. Could he be that clever? She'd suffered 'accidents' while she was not at home. It seemed unlikely that Rajiv could be everywhere.

Earlier, she'd dismissed the idea of an accomplice, someone working with him to frighten her away, but now she had a face to conjure with — the Indian she'd seen last night. He could easily have followed her to the temple. He could have found his way to the top of that crumbling edifice and levered a stone into freefall. But could he have tampered with the saddle in the regimental stables? He would have found it next to impossible to gain entry to the cantonment. Every gate to the camp was guarded and, unless he had a valid reason for being there, he'd be turned away. Was there someone else then, beyond Rajiv and his friend, someone she didn't know of? A man who could move easily around the locality, whose time was his own, and whose presence would not be questioned.

She knew no one. Or did she? Grayson's was the name that came to mind. He fitted her description perfectly. But it couldn't be him. Wasn't he committed to stopping the protesters, not aiding them? In the aftermath of the riot, she'd seen him striding through the crowd to apprehend them. Or had it been to protect, to hurry them away out of reach of the police? There was no way of knowing. And nothing to say why he'd been at the maiden. The police and the army were there to restore order, so why would Grayson be needed? He'd never explained his presence that day, never told her, in fact, what he was doing in Jasirapur.

Had he become a rogue officer, she wondered, and somehow got himself involved with criminal elements? He'd come to India to work in the Civil Service, a respected member of 'The Incorruptibles' as she'd heard them called. But what if the work had badly disappointed? In the past, he'd turned down the opportunity to join the army, and he hadn't settled to the sugar business either, so might he have quickly grown discontented with the ICS? He'd always struck her as a man looking for adventure, and the mundane duties of a District Officer did not fit the image she had of him.

Daisy's mind hazed. She liked Grayson, she liked him a lot, but he had never completely gained her trust. That didn't mean, of course, that he was guilty of this most shocking crime and she hated to think ill of him. Yet, she couldn't lose her suspicions. It was foolish, though, to be caught in this endless circle of speculation. Pointless, too. She must wait for Gerald to come home and, in the meantime, she would think no more.

CHAPTER TWENTY-NINE

'Hello there!'

Daisy jumped at the voice, startled by the sudden noise that she almost bounced to her feet. Despite her best efforts, her mind had been elsewhere, lost in its own labyrinth. Anish had ridden up to the house, mounted the veranda steps and walked halfway across the sitting room before she heard a sound.

She stood facing him, her hand clutching at her chair. The sight of his familiar face had blown her vow of calmness to the winds.

'Thank goodness, Anish, thank goodness you're here!'

He blinked, taken aback it seemed by her intensity, but in his usual smooth fashion said, 'I came in the hope of persuading you back onto a horse — tomorrow, perhaps? It's been a while since we rode and you're at risk of growing rusty.'

When she didn't reply, he walked further into the room, his eyes fixed on her face. 'My poor girl, you look quite ill.'

She ignored this and tugged urgently at his sleeve. 'You must help me.'

'I'm at your service, Daisy,' he said gallantly, and gently released her fingers, 'but what has made you so upset?'

‘I’m sorry, I’m not making much sense, I know. This morning has been . . . I can’t believe . . .’ She broke off and held up her hand in a cautioning gesture. ‘We should walk in the garden.’

‘This is all very cloak and dagger,’ he joked, but he followed her obediently down the steps and into the wilderness.

They strode a short way along the path before he put out a hand to stop her. ‘If you don’t mind, we’ll stay here. I’ve no wish to meet an irritated snake.’

‘I’m sorry to drag you from the house, but we mustn’t be overheard.’ The seriousness of her tone made him look at her in surprise.

‘So what has happened this morning to put you so on edge? Unless you tell me, I can’t offer much assistance.’

Daisy hardly knew where to begin. ‘I saw someone last night. It was the Indian I’d seen before in the garden, but last night he was outside my bedroom door.’

‘Good gracious. What was the man doing there? Did Gerald see him?’

‘Gerald wasn’t here. I don’t know where he was, and I don’t know — didn’t know,’ she corrected herself, ‘why the man was in the house. He seemed to disappear into thin air before I could think and I had no idea what to do. It was the middle of the night and I was alone, so I went back to bed.’

‘Very sensible. Then you woke up this morning and found that it was all an unpleasant dream?’

‘It wasn’t a dream.’

‘But, surely it must have been,’ he coaxed. ‘I have to tell you, Daisy, that even in India a stray man roaming through one’s house at night is unusual. And don’t forget, you were the only person to see this chap. I imagine you’re sleeping badly. We all are. It’s likely that in your sleep you saw yourself getting out of bed, opening the door, and finding the man outside. But, really, he was just part of your dream.’

‘He was real,’ she said flatly, ‘and I have proof.’

For the first time, Anish looked interested. ‘Proof that an unknown Indian was wandering your home in the middle of the night?’

'Proof of where he went. He didn't leave the house, at least not while I was watching. I couldn't work it out at the time, but now I know. He disappeared down into the cellar. Did you know there was a cellar in the bungalow?'

He shook his head, mystified.

'Well, there is. And in that cellar there are guns, Anish. Hundreds of them. And I think they've come from the regiment's armoury.'

He said nothing, and she wondered if he'd heard her. 'There have been weapons stolen, haven't there?' she prompted.

'Yes, but—'

'They're here, beneath our feet. Or at least they would be if we were standing in the house.'

'But how, why? It makes no sense.'

'That's what I've been trying to work out. I'm almost sure that Rajiv is responsible and that the Indian I saw is his accomplice. I think they've stolen the guns — though I don't know how — but it's clear they mean to make money by selling them. I imagine there are plenty of agitators who will pay well.'

'Do you mind if I say that the whole thing sounds crazy?'

'I know it does, but I'm telling the truth. Really, I am. And the regiment needs to know immediately. I was waiting for Gerald, but he still isn't back. That's why I'm so glad to see you. It's vital the authorities know before Rajiv guesses his crime has been discovered. Would you ride to the camp straightaway and tell them to come quickly?'

'And what if I bring a senior officer back with me and there are no guns in the cellar?'

'There will be,' she said grimly, 'I'm not moving from here until the Colonel comes to see for himself.'

Anish did not appear to share her urgency, and she was forced to prompt him again, 'Will you go now?'

'Of course I will, but—' He broke off, seeming to be deep in thought.

'But?'

'What if it's not just Rajiv and his friend involved? It must take more than two to move such huge loads in and out of the cellar, even supposing they were able to transport them here in the first place.'

He didn't believe her, Daisy thought hopelessly. He wasn't going to do anything. She would have to take him to the cellar to see for himself. But then Rajiv would know he'd been discovered and make his escape.

'There could be a gang, I grant you, though I've only ever seen the one man. But however many there are, it's surely better to arrest the two we know before they can leave. Then if there are more—'

'That's the problem.'

'What do you mean?'

He didn't answer her directly, but said, 'Perhaps it would be better simply to move the guns.'

She was puzzled. 'Move the guns? Why would we move the guns?'

'It might save a reputation or two.'

She was even more puzzled. Was he wanting to help the officers who'd been in charge of the armoury? 'You think we should take the guns back to the regiment?'

'Not exactly. We can't restore them. If guns that have been lost were suddenly to reappear, questions would be asked. No, I was thinking of losing them completely as though they'd never been here.'

'But then Rajiv would not be punished.'

'I wasn't thinking of Rajiv.'

'And neither would the other man or any of their gang.'

'Think, Daisy, who else could be implicated?'

His face was kind and concerned, but she couldn't see what he was driving at. 'Where, for instance, was Gerald last night? You said he wasn't here. Do you know where he was?'

'Gerald?' she faltered.

Where *had* he been last night when she'd looked for him? And where on the other night she couldn't find him? At the time, she'd assumed he was visiting Jocelyn, but that had proved false. In any case, the girl had left weeks ago, so what about last night? The question had become all- important, yet she fought against the obvious answer.

'You can't think he's involved,' she protested, but her voice held the first glimmers of doubt.

Even as she spoke, she was reminded of Gerald's recent volatility. If he were involved in a criminal business, the stress he must feel would go a long way to explaining his rapid changes of mood over the past weeks.

'I hope not. Sincerely, I hope not. But have you never wondered why he chooses to live in such an isolated place? Why he employs only one servant? It's been a talking point in the regiment for some time, and I must admit I've always thought it odd.'

'But he's an honourable man. He would never do such a thing. It would mean jeopardising the career he loves. He'd be ruined if he were discovered. Why would he risk that?'

Anish's eyebrows rose slightly. He didn't need to remind her. Gerald was in debt, badly in debt. Was this how he'd decided to solve his problem? He'd had merchants chasing him for the money he owed, and then suddenly they were no longer on his tail. She'd never asked him how he'd repaid those men, and he had never explained. Could it possibly have come from selling stolen guns?

Her mind was finding it difficult to take in the enormity of what was happening. Beads of perspiration dotted her face and trickled down between her breasts. Gerald! It wasn't possible. But it wasn't impossible either. If you were thinking at all sensibly, was it likely that he would be ignorant of a cellar beneath the house he'd lived in for months, or ignorant of the activities of the one servant he employed? If Gerald were involved in the whole dreadful business, it would explain why he'd been so insistent that she went to Simla. He'd wanted her out of the house as much as Rajiv.

He had wanted her out of the house . . . he was an accomplice too. He was behind the so-called accidents she'd suffered. Daisy covered her eyes with her hands. She'd had few illusions left about her marriage, but the very last of them had just crashed to the ground. Her husband had planned to harm her. It was as monstrous as that.

She felt Anish looking at her, saw his eyes infused with sympathy. She had to say something. 'If Gerald knows of the guns, he must have been responsible for the bad things that have happened to me,' she stammered. 'He's been plotting against me.'

'That's quite a leap. I'm sure Gerald could never wish to harm you,' Anish said softly. 'And when you say bad things, what do you mean?'

'A lot of so-called accidents which weren't accidents at all. One night, I was made a prisoner in my own room, then a dangerous snake was let loose in the bathroom and at the temple — the day I met you on the road — a slab of stone fell from the roof and narrowly missed me.'

'I can see how frightened you must have been, Daisy, but every one of those could easily have been the accidents you supposed. And if they weren't, if they were deliberate, then what's to say that it was only Rajiv who was behind them?'

'He couldn't have been responsible for the accident I had riding with you. That had to be someone with permission to be in the cantonment.'

'I can set your mind at rest there. That really was an accident. The girths were badly worn and I was negligent in not noticing.' He took her hand and pressed it tightly. 'You're very upset and leaping to conclusions. A moment ago, you thought Gerald an honourable man and you must have believed that or you'd never have married him. So, let's think sensibly. It would seem Gerald has made a bad mistake, but at heart he's sound, and we can help him, you and I together. If we don't, he'll be court martialled and disgraced. And not just in a military court, but in the world outside. He'll be judged a criminal and go to prison. Neither of us would want that, would we?'

'No, of course not,' she mumbled. 'But to risk his whole career in this way . . .'

He let go of her hand and walked a few paces into the garden, then turned back towards her. 'Do you remember asking me how common debt was among young officers? Gerald has been extremely stupid and dug himself a deep pit. He may have been so desperate for money that he believed this was the only way out of the mess.' Anish pulled down the corners of his mouth in a grimace. 'I guess that's what comes of being doted on. I believe he's the only child of an elderly father.'

She was astonished he knew so much about her husband. She'd imagined Gerald had stayed as silent to the world as he had to her and, though the situation they faced was critical, she wanted to hear more. 'Has he talked to you about his father?'

'Very little. All I know is that his family doesn't fit the usual mould for an officer in the Indian Army.'

No, she thought, the family didn't fit at all. Not if she'd guessed right. It might be time to be honest. 'I found a letter . . . I think it came from Gerald's father.' She wouldn't mention that Gerald had told her that his parents were both dead. She couldn't bring herself to be that honest. 'The letter was signed Joseph Minns. I believe Minns is Gerald's real name, and Mr Minns senior was once a master tailor in the East End of London.'

Anish let out a small whistle. 'You have been busy!' His shoulders hunched in thought. 'If what you say is true, I'm not surprised he kept quiet about his family. It's evident he's been trying to be what he isn't, and that's led him into this foolishness.'

Daisy would have called it more than foolishness, but she knew Anish wanted to help his friend and perhaps, too, he was trying to soften the blow for her.

'If he's in trouble, we must help him,' he repeated. 'And that means getting rid of the evidence.'

'But how on earth are we to move those guns by ourselves? And where to?'

'It won't be easy, I admit, but in the next few days, I'll come up with a plan, I promise. In the meantime, say nothing to anyone. And that includes Gerald. We can't be completely sure after all that he *is* behind the thefts.'

Daisy had begun to think the evidence too strong to doubt, but she willed herself to cling to this smallest of hopes. 'How will you find out?'

'I'll ask him — as discreetly as I can. I'm his friend and I know he'll tell me if he's in trouble. Then together we can work out what to do. We'll have to pay Rajiv to keep silent, but that shouldn't be a problem. Meanwhile, I'll say nothing of your involvement.'

'But if I hadn't told you, why would you have become suspicious?'

'Rajiv. I shall say that Rajiv let slip something he shouldn't and I put two and two together. How does that sound?' He smiled engagingly.

'I think it might work. But what should *I* do?'

'Nothing. At least nothing out of the ordinary. When I've spoken to Gerald, I'll let you know as soon as I have a plan. It might take a few days, but if you don't hear for a while, stay calm and try not to worry. All will be well — trust me.'

CHAPTER THIRTY

Over the next few days, Daisy tried to follow his advice. But. though she presented a calm face to the world, she felt sick with anxiety. Banished from the Infirmary, she had nothing to distract her from the endless, unanswered questions. What if Anish were wrong, she fretted, and Gerald had nothing to do with the crime? Anish's suspicions would break apart the one true friendship her husband possessed. What if Gerald *were* as guilty as they believed, but Anish was unable to persuade him the game he'd been playing was over? Then, they would be faced with a dreadful choice. And even if Anish had been successful — how could two men — four, if you counted Rajiv and his accomplice — cause crate after crate of guns to disappear without anyone noticing?

Gerald seemed oblivious that she knew anything of the deadly cargo lying beneath their feet: Anish had kept his promise to say nothing of her involvement. Her husband was on edge, it was true, but his nervousness did not appear to include her. If anything, he was more attentive, spending more time at home and showing her a degree of kindness that was unusual. The day after Anish's visit, Gerald had returned with a large basket of fresh fruits, ones he knew to be her favourites, and tonight he'd ordered Rajiv to mark the Teej festival with a special dessert — the little baskets woven from transparent toffee and filled with cream and tinned peaches that she had so enjoyed at the Club dinner.

She discerned Anish's hand behind the subtle change in her husband. By now, he must have confronted Gerald with what he'd done and, as well as planning a rescue, made him feel guilty for the distress he'd caused his wife.

That was only right; Gerald should feel guilty. It might have been Rajiv who'd plotted to harm her, but it was her husband who had turned a blind eye. And even if he'd known nothing of his servant's activities, which Daisy could hardly credit, he'd brought her to this house where he must have realised she would face danger. She tried not to dwell on what had happened, tried to be grateful for the small gestures of reconciliation, but her heart remained stubbornly cold.

'I've organised transport,' Gerald said with a cheerfulness that didn't quite ring true. They were finishing the last delicious toffee basket. 'The car will be here in an hour, but once we get into the town, we'll have to go on foot. Everyone follows the procession and walks to the river.'

The thought of taking part in Teej, with her husband alongside, had delighted her when Gerald had first mentioned it. But now, attending a noisy, crowded festival was the last thing she wanted. Still, she was supposed to act as normally as possible, and refusing to go would prompt questions she couldn't answer.

If only she could hear from Anish. He'd told her to trust him and she did. If there was anyone who could sort out the trouble they were in, it was Anish. He'd warned her it would take time and she had tried to be patient, but three days on Daisy was beginning to despair. It was just possible she would see him at the festival and, under cover of the boisterous celebrations, might learn what progress he'd made. The hope buoyed what little was left of her spirits.

* * *

The weather that day had threatened more than ever, the blackest of clouds forming fortresses in the sky and the air clogged and unmoving. A sundress was all she needed on this hottest of nights, and it took only a few minutes to change into the lightest of the *durzi's* creations. The car was already waiting when she walked down the veranda steps and sensed Rajiv's eyes following them into the vehicle and away from the house. Since the dreadful morning she'd made her discovery, Daisy had been more than ever alert to the servant's demeanour, but it never wavered and it was impossible to guess whether he knew he was suspected. He hadn't fled the scene of his crimes, so it was reasonable to assume he wasn't expecting punishment.

The car drove them swiftly to the centre of the town, winding its way through narrow alleys that smelt of smoke and dust and frying gram. The clouds had cleared temporarily and an enormous moon filled the sky, while fireflies fluttered in its light. Nearing the main square, their driver began to edge his way beside a trickle of people, smooth-skinned and graceful, with garlands of marigolds and sweet-smelling jasmine hanging from their necks. The trickle soon became a flood as more and more poured into the main square on their way to the river, their path lit by the moon and a sprinkling of fire torches.

'It's best we get down here.' They had stopped in the centre of the square and Gerald was opening her door. 'The procession will be close by, and we can follow it on its way to the river.'

He was right. They had gone only a few streets when the noise of beaten gongs, the sounds of people shouting and singing became so loud they could barely hear themselves speak. Daisy held tightly to her husband's arm, fearing to be swept away on the tide of people. It was a bittersweet moment. This was how she'd imagined their life, sharing a fascinating new world together, sharing a happiness that would grow. If only, she thought. But it was no good thinking of what might have been. A very different future awaited them.

Turning a corner, Daisy had her first sight of the procession, causing her to stare in wonder. Float after float, decorated with flowers, with pictures and images of gods and goddesses, were making unsteady progress along a wide, beaten mud road. Several of the images stretched many feet high, swaying on the poles of devotees, some leaning towards their followers with huge, staring eyes. Many of the goddesses were beautiful, but others terrible; all were made from wire and straw and clay, and elaborately modelled.

She walked on beside Gerald, jostled on either side by the crowd, a huge, expectant throng intent on enjoyment. It was as though they were attending a carnival and not a solemn ceremony. Infectious gaiety and religious devotion should surely not mix but, in some strange way, they did. How far this evening was, Daisy thought, from those bleak, grey mornings in the orphanage chapel, when as a child she'd been forced to kneel for hours on cold and unforgiving stone, while a preacher lectured his small audience on their shortcomings. The children had heard little and understood less.

The temple on her right could not have been more different. Lights were waving, music playing, gongs clanging, bells ringing, as the priest intoned his text. Each deity, she noticed, had his or her own niche in the temple forecourt and was surrounded by offerings of flowers. Followers were walking in circles, offering more flowers, more gifts, to their own particular god before they, too, joined in the river celebration.

Caught up in the magnificence of the evening, Daisy almost forgot her troubles. She melted into the good-natured crowd, soaking up the colour, the noise, the smell, the sheer bravado of the moment. Women in saris of scarlet and gold silk, saris of silver threaded cloth and brilliant blue brocade, clustered all around her. Heavy gold chains hung from their necks, golden earrings dangled from their ears. They wore jewelled rings on their fingers and toes, and bangles on their wrists and ankles. Even above the din of the procession, she could hear the jingle of the women as they pressed close to her.

She felt Gerald's touch on her arm. She was in love with this dark, jewelled night and only slowly became aware of his presence. She saw that he was holding a small sheet of paper.

'This message has just arrived.' She'd seen no messenger, but then she'd been far away in a world of her own. 'I'm sorry, but I'm going to have to go. It seems I'm needed back at camp. Some paperwork has gone missing. It won't be for long, I'm sure. Will you be all right on your own?'

It seemed odd that Gerald would contemplate leaving her here alone but, of course, she would be all right. What harm could come to her among this warm, loving crowd?

'I'll be fine,' she said, feeling a little guilty that she would.

'Good. I know you'll enjoy the ceremony. If I don't return before it's over, walk back to the square. I'll be there with the car waiting for you. Most of these people will be going in that direction so you won't get lost.'

'Don't worry, Gerald. I'll be there.'

In barely a second, he'd disappeared into the surging mass of people who had been walking behind them. Only after he'd left, did she wonder why he'd been called back to the cantonment for something so trivial as missing paperwork. It seemed unreasonable on a night like this and, for a moment, a cold dread gripped her. Was it possible that he'd been found out before his mistakes could be made good? But absent papers were unlikely to lead to guns in the cellar, she reasoned.

Was it rather that Gerald's problem, as she thought of it, was about to be solved? Tonight might be an ideal opportunity to move those guns. It was strange that she'd heard nothing from Anish, but she supposed he might have been too busy making arrangements to call on her. She must put it out of her mind. Whatever Gerald's reason for leaving the festival, she was happy to be alone. Happy to immerse herself so completely in the magic of the night.

When she finally reached the riverbank, the place was alive with people and with deities. The moon had once more disappeared behind lowering cloud but, beneath a dark sky, punctured by the flame of torches, the scene unfolded itself in all its glittering splendour. Daisy was enthralled. There were steps down to the river and people had taken up every square inch of them. The crowd was so dense that many had toppled into the river itself, but she managed to squeeze her way through and somehow room was made for her on the highest step. She had a grandstand view.

One by one, the images were carried down to the waters and floated by young men swimming out into the river. Torchlight glinted across the crowns of each god and goddess, glanced off their headdresses, then found its way downwards to their ornamented belts and weapons. As every image floated out into the night, gongs sounded and worshippers rang little brass bells. It was a cacophony of sound and colour and sweet-smelling incense.

Daisy must have sat there for over an hour until her body was stiff from the cold stone. When the last goddess had been sent on her way, the crowds began to drift from the riverbank and walk back towards the town. She started back too. Gerald had been gone for several hours and she wondered where he'd been. At the cantonment, as he'd said, or at the bungalow shifting weapons? She hoped it was the latter and that Anish's plan would work. If it did, and he managed to keep Gerald from disgrace, she supposed their marriage would go on as before. Except there wasn't really a before.

Ever since she'd arrived in India, she'd been falling out of love. It was hard to accept, but it was the truth. She'd been in love with an illusion, one that had started to crumble from the moment Gerald left his bride to be met by a friend and, instead, drank himself insensible. All the weeks since, weeks of trying to do the right thing, had been torture. And no doubt they'd been torture for him, too. But since her discovery of the stolen arms, whatever feelings she'd held on to, had gone. Now that she suspected her husband had known, even perhaps approved, the attempts to scare and to hurt her, Daisy could not forget. She would forgive, she had to forgive, but she couldn't forget, and it would always be there between them. Their future was as dark as this still, hot night.

The mass of people was gradually thinning, individuals and groups peeling off to the left and right, making for their homes along narrow alleyways, but a sizeable crowd was still snaking its way towards the square and Daisy followed them. Or so she thought. But then they, too, began to fade away into smaller and different streets, and she had still not arrived at her destination.

Without light from moon or torches, it was difficult to get a sense of direction. She was certain it hadn't taken her this amount of time to walk from the square to the river, but she'd been so entranced by her first sight of the pageant that she'd paid little attention to the route she was taking. Now, she was at a crossroads she could not remember, and she stopped for a while to get her bearings. Several family groups passed her, heading straight ahead. Should she follow them and hope to hit the square, or should she perhaps take another of these streets? The one on the right seemed broader. That was more likely to lead her where she wanted to go.

She started to walk down the road she'd chosen, but had gone only yards when she heard a voice calling. Calling her name. She swung round and saw the figure of Grayson Harte at some distance, waving vigorously at her. He wanted her to stop, wanted to catch up with her. But she didn't want his company. In her mind, an undefined suspicion still hung over him and she could not rid herself of the feeling. If Gerald could be involved in such a crime, why not him? Why not both of them together? They'd known each other since they were boys at school and who was to say for sure they were the enemies Grayson had suggested? She had only his word for it. Gerald's, too. Her husband was adept at deceit and could easily have pretended a dislike he didn't feel. It was fanciful, horrible even, but Daisy was no longer certain whom she could trust.

Hurrying forward, she saw he was beginning to gain on her. She broke into a trot and then a run, overtaken by panic. Without thinking, she plunged into a maze of narrow, ill-smelling streets, running on until her breath was coming short and a sharp pain tore into her side. Gasping for air, she stumbled to a stop. At least, she had lost Grayson Harte, but where on earth was she?

CHAPTER THIRTY-ONE

The crowds had melted away, and not a single soul was visible. Her nerves on edge, she turned to retrace her steps. The air seemed unnaturally still. Not a sound came to her. It was as though everyone had fallen off the edge of the world and left her here alone. She mustn't be alarmed, she told herself, she must simply return the way she had come.

The sky had darkened even further since she'd left the river, and now the blackest of clouds had formed a column of threat that seemed to stretch upwards into infinite space. An unbearable feeling of pressure bore down on her, and her head began to ache. She needed to get home, needed to lie down on her hard, narrow bed. It had never seemed more inviting. She wondered whether Gerald was still waiting by the car, or whether he'd grown worried and was even now scouring the streets looking for her. If so, they must soon find each other, for the town was not large.

Out of nowhere, a hot wind arose, pasting the skirt of her dress tight against her legs and swirling violent clouds of dust in her face. Along the street, unbattened wooden shutters began a loud clatter. But their noise was as nothing. A deafening crash overhead made Daisy freeze where she stood. It was as though a bomb had gone off a hundred feet above.

Suddenly the black sky broke apart, disintegrating into a vast avalanche of water.

Within seconds, she was soaked to the skin, the power of its onslaught nearly forcing her to her knees. Staggering upright, she tried to walk forward, but everywhere water gushed uncontrollably. The smell of the land soaking up its first real rain was pungent. Cracked earth, hard as concrete, that over the months had formed itself into a dull ochre mosaic, began to soften rapidly and in no time she found her feet glued in mud. She must find shelter.

Through the sheeting rain, she saw the faintest outline of a large house, an old merchant's home, she thought, once rich enough to boast a crumbling stone portico. Blindly, she stumbled through the deluge and found a temporary refuge beneath its roof. But water was thundering on either side of her, cascading from the stonework above her head, and it would be only a matter of time before her shelter vanished. The water was already inches high.

Shivering, she crouched as far back against the crumbling stone as she could. Flashes of lightning were streaking overhead. One huge strike of jagged crystal zipped through the blackness, tearing the sky almost in two, and by its neon light she saw a figure standing a few feet from her. She had no idea how he'd come to be there, and no intention of waiting to find out. She had taken one step out of the porch when, with startling speed, a hand came from behind and clamped a sickly-smelling pad over her mouth. Daisy felt her legs buckle, and then she knew no more.

* * *

She was emerging from a tunnel. There was a suffocating darkness and she could see and hear nothing, except for a far-off echo thrumming in her ears. That was her breath, she realised, coming in short, sharp gasps. Now the tunnel was expanding and the darkness was not so opaque. There seemed to be the slightest chink of light, away in the distance.

She opened her eyes a fraction and pain arrowed through her head. Her eyelids shut fast and she drifted back into a black haze.

Minutes ticked by, and gradually her body began to come back to life. Her head was heavy and throbbing and seemed detached from the rest of her limbs. She stretched out her fingers and beneath their tips felt a rough blanket, spread over the hard, mud floor on which she lay. When she tried to open her eyes again, she thought she could see brown — brown walls, walls made of mud. Cautiously. she turned her head, and the shape of a door cut into the furthest wall swam into her vision. She felt wretchedly sick. Her eyes closed once more and she lay unmoving, curled in a tight ball of misery.

It was a long while before she felt strong enough to try again to make sense of where she was. Very slowly, she allowed her gaze to wander around the room. This time she managed to focus on the one source of light, a thin bead of brightness at the top of the door. It showed her that the room she lay in was very small, hardly larger than a cupboard. Wherever was she, and how had she come here?

Daisy tried to remember back to her last waking moments. A motley of colour and noise filled her head, a confused jumble of gongs and goddesses, people and shouting, a river, water. Water — that was it. She'd been sheltering from water, from rain. And what rain! She had seen nothing like it in her entire life. It was night, and she'd been sheltering beneath a stone porch; it was old stone, ornamented. A tracery of flowers and birds was cut into its hard surface, she'd noticed. All around the road was flooded, rivers of water flowing over her shoes and wetting her ankles. But where was this porch, and why was she taking shelter there? Her head felt as though it had been battered by a hundred cudgels, and she strained to remember.

She'd arrived there breathless. She'd been running, running away but, away from what, from whom? The answer came to her slowly. She'd been running from Grayson Harte. How curious. But then she remembered how she'd flown into an irrational panic when she'd heard him calling her. She'd been desperate to get back to the square and to Gerald and the waiting car, desperate to get back to safety, but she'd run the wrong way.

Had Grayson caught up with her? Someone had. They had made her a prisoner. She became aware then of how badly her arms were hurting. They had been pulled awkwardly behind her back, and her wrists were sore. Sunk in a coma, she'd been too dazed to realise, but she was bound with a rope and, when she tried to flex her legs, she found that they, too, were hobbled.

Surely, this couldn't be happening. It was a nightmare she was living through and not real life. But when she managed to focus hazily a few inches from her face, she saw a piece of white cloth, a pad, the pad that had sent her into oblivion. This was no nightmare. This had happened, and now she could see the scene clearly: the lightning strike overhead, the figure of a man, a rough hand covering her mouth and something sweet in the air. Chloroform. It was little wonder she felt so ill: she had been drugged. Again.

A slight noise caught her attention and she looked towards the door. Now she could see there was a slit about two-thirds of the way up, and a face had pressed itself against the wood. An eye was watching her. The bolts on the door were slid back, and a vaguely familiar figure walked towards her and jerked her roughly to her feet. It was the Indian she'd seen in the garden, the Indian who had been outside her bedroom door. He bent down to untie her ankles and for a moment she thought wildly of kicking herself free of his hold when once the rope was slack. But through the open doorway Daisy had glimpsed other men, other figures moving around, and she knew there was no chance of escape.

He pushed her forward and she nearly fell, her legs forgetting how to walk after the long confinement. Another push in the back, and she was out of the door and into an enormous space. It looked like a deserted warehouse and was completely empty, except for several dirty plastic chairs and the group of men, none of whom she'd seen before. She counted them as she stumbled forward, one, two — six in total, but Rajiv was not one of them. At the very end of the warehouse, and what seemed a mile away, a door to the outside world stood very slightly ajar, a door she had no realistic chance of reaching.

The man pushed her down onto one of the plastic chairs which had been placed, deliberately it seemed, with its back to the open doorway. Her arms, still bound, were wrenched over the back of the chair and her ankles tied with rope to its front legs. Her body was screaming with pain, but she bit her lip, refusing to betray weakness. Weakness would not help her cause.

No sound had reached her in her prison cell, but here the rain beat a relentless tattoo on the iron roof. Over its staccato, she heard a deeper roar. Then it came to her — it was the sound of the river. No longer the gentle water of a few hours ago but a raging torrent. She was back by the riverside again. But why had she been brought here? Why was she a prisoner and who were these people? They were dressed in peasant clothes, dirty, slightly ragged, but there was nothing to distinguish them from the hundreds who toiled in the fields every day.

If they spoke even a little English, Daisy thought, it might be worth trying to talk to them, convince them they'd made a dreadful blunder. It was likely they were hoping to be paid a ransom — what other reason could there be for her captivity? — but they could not have chosen a worse victim. Her stomach clenched. When they discovered there was no money to be had, would they turn on her? She searched their faces for some sign of humanity, but the harshness of the overhead neon, striping the immense, empty space, blanked all expression.

The man who had fetched her from the small dungeon took up his station to one side of her. He spat noisily on the earth floor, and then relaxed into immobility. He seemed to be waiting, the others, too. They had ceased shuffling back and forth and were standing silent and still. Her ears had become better attuned now, and she heard his footsteps before the man came into view. It was a sure tread and drawing nearer. She felt the Indian at her side stiffen, almost to attention. She turned her head slightly and saw a familiar figure, a familiar face. Anish!

'Thank God, it's you!' She was almost crying with relief. 'Tell them, Anish, tell them they've made a terrible mistake. Please.'

CHAPTER THIRTY-TWO

Anish said nothing, but picked up another of the plastic chairs and sat down facing her. She was confounded. Why wasn't he setting her free? Her mind went into overdrive. He had to negotiate, that was it. He'd been brought here to negotiate her release. They were kidnappers, as she'd thought, and Anish was the go-between. She tried to control the tumble of thoughts, but his first words shook her into a vortex of disbelief. And utter, wrenching nausea.

'Why didn't you go to Simla, Daisy? I told you to go. Gerald told you to go. If you'd only followed our advice, this would all have been over by the time you got back.'

'This?' she croaked, struggling to understand.

He waved his hands at the men standing silent and watchful. 'You've become a worry to my henchmen.'

'You know these men! Who are they? And why have they imprisoned me?' Her voice broke on a half-sob.

'I'm sorry you find yourself in this predicament, but you have only yourself to blame. You're here because you know too much. And these gentlemen are very aware of that. You could hang each and every one of them.'

'These men are your friends?' Through a mist of bewilderment, she tried to grasp at any kind of certainty.

'That may be stretching things a little. But they *are* my companions. Companions in arms, shall we say.' Anish sat back in his chair and contemplated her.

'So you . . . it was you who stole the guns?' There was a long pause while she tried to absorb this dreadful knowledge. 'That's why you wouldn't go to the Colonel when I told you what I'd discovered.'

'How very astute.' She flinched at his mocking tone.

'But how? It's not possible you could have stolen them.' She knew his pride in his regiment, his loyalty to his comrades.

He took her words literally. 'You're right, it isn't possible. An Indian officer has no access to the armoury — another of those petty discriminations we discussed. But if *I* have no access, I have a friend who does.'

'Gerald?' But she already knew the answer. It explained in an instant why his conversations with Anish were so often halted the minute they caught sight of her.

'Indeed, Gerald. He was the man I needed. And he needed me. He's been busy for years constructing a daydream. His only problem was that he hadn't the money to sustain it. That made him a desperate man, a man willing to do anything.'

'So Gerald is a thief and a traitor.' She felt scorn rising within her, acrid and unstoppable.

'I fear so. But don't judge him too harshly. He's an accidental villain. At the outset he intended only to facilitate one consignment—'

'"Facilitate"? Don't you mean, steal?'

'If you like. As I say, our bargain was for just one consignment, but when that didn't quite pay his debts, he agreed to another. And then, of course, another. Poor Gerald. His fantasy trapped him on a treadmill he couldn't get off.'

'And now? How many more thefts will he facilitate? And where is he? Surely he should be here, gloating in triumph.'

She spoke bravely, but she knew her words were hollow. Anish had dealt her a mortal blow and her courage was failing. When she'd first seen his calm, kindly face, her spirits had leapt. She'd brimmed with relief. He was a true friend and he would rescue her. But in seconds, the benign vision she'd always carried of him had splintered into a thousand small pieces. It was too hard, too much to bear.

'Gerald is taking cover, I imagine. He can be a trifle squeamish, but it's of no matter. He has done his job, and we no longer need him.'

'We?'

Anish rose from his chair and paced back and forth, his wet footprints tracing a pattern on the hard, mud floor. 'These men are patriots, and so am I. We care about the future of our country. You and I have often spoken of it.'

'So your thefts have not been for money?'

His expression registered distaste. 'That's something I leave to Gerald. I believe my motive a purer one. A free India.'

Daisy looked at him then, really looked at him. Perhaps for the first time. Why had she never seen that messianic glow which lit his face, the zeal which lurked behind the soft, brown eyes?

'Can we not forget the guns?' She tried to reason with him, to speak words that might persuade him into freeing her. 'You don't need them. India will soon have its independence. Everyone says so.'

'Everyone says so,' he mocked again. 'And everyone has been saying so for centuries. It won't happen. Our overlords may give a little here, a little there, but they will never leave this country. It's far too valuable to them. And our politicians won't make them. Congress talks and talks but nothing happens.'

He stopped in front of her then and bending down, took hold of her shoulders in a firm grip. 'The only sure way to free India of British rule is to fight. And that is what we're doing. Without force, the British will never leave. They will talk, they will make small concessions, but they'll not give up power. They'll employ every trick to avoid such a thing. For all their fine words, they will deceive, as they always have.'

'And you think you can take on the might of the British Army with *these* people?' Her eyes flicked across the men gathered behind Anish and her expression was contemptuous. It was Daisy's turn to mock, and in response his face darkened angrily.

But when he spoke, his voice was determinedly even. He was not to be goaded. 'Never think that we are alone. The British may divide and rule, but there are groups like ours all over the country. Dozens in Rajputana alone. And not just Hindus. Moslems too, militant groups on all sides. And all are arming. There's been too much talking — action is what we need. The British will be made to leave, and this is the moment we do it. Everything points to that.'

'You think they won't fight back? You said yourself they always have.'

'Right now, they're looking elsewhere. Their own country is menaced and soon they'll be immersed in a war with the most powerful military force in the world. They'll have too many pressing worries near to home, and they'll take their eye off the ball — isn't that the right phrase? That's when we strike. And when the Japanese come, and come they will, the British will be too slow to respond, even if they find sufficient troops to defend India, which I doubt. The jewel in the imperial crown will be lost forever.'

'What makes you think the Japanese will be interested in a free India?'

Daisy had no notion of the politics of the situation, and no doubt she sounded witless. But she didn't care. A vague idea hovered in the back of her mind that the longer she could keep Anish talking, the longer there would be for someone to find her. But who, in truth, was going to find her? Who was even looking? She'd been deserted by the man she'd married and now deserted by the man she'd thought her friend.

'Japan will help to liberate us.' His tone admitted no argument. 'But, in the meantime, we must do our best to convince our lords and masters they are no longer welcome. And that, I fear, applies to you, too.'

It was hopeless, she knew, but she had to keep him talking, spin out the minutes as long as she could. 'What made you and Gerald think of stealing from the armoury?'

Anish fell for the bait. 'It was my idea,' he said grandly. 'Gerald was simply useful. I found out quite by chance that your house had a cellar. It's the only building in the entire area that has any kind of underground storage. Years ago, it belonged to the chief railway engineer. He had the cellar built to store his equipment: shovels, picks, explosives. It meant his stores were out of the way of prying eyes and itchy hands, exactly what I needed. I persuaded Gerald to move there from the Mess. The house was perfect, isolated and on the road to nowhere. Nationalist fighters are spread right across the state and a halfway house was essential. You can't transport a huge cache of weapons without causing suspicion. The flow of arms needed to be a trickle, not a torrent.'

'And you picked on Gerald to help you because he needed the money. He must be glad to have such an ally.'

'Gerald provided excellent cover, it's true, but I've been a good friend to him, though you may not believe it. He is a vain, shallow fellow, don't you find? When I first saw you, I couldn't believe his stupidity. You were certainly pretty and you had an innocent charm, but you were never going to measure up. And to sacrifice his whole career . . . Of course, I didn't know you then, and I made a bad misjudgement.'

'If he has sacrificed his career, it isn't because of me but of what you persuaded him into.'

'He didn't need persuading and you must take some of the blame. You made his situation worse. Bringing a woman to live in the house has caused endless problems. It's made moving weapons difficult, and there was always the possibility you would find out what was happening and cause a stir. As you did. That was unexpected, I admit. I hadn't bargained on your being quite so stubborn. As stubborn as I am, it appears.'

'You mean you hoped I would take fright from the accidents you arranged.' The whole shocking business was becoming clearer by the minute. How stupid she'd been in thinking that Grayson Harte was in any way implicated.

'It would have been better for all of us if you had. But you didn't. Gerald wasn't happy with the plan, but he went along with it. What else could he do? But no matter what we did, you didn't budge. Just the opposite. You became nosier than ever, and started poking into things that didn't concern you. And see where that has led.'

They were back full circle and Daisy had run out of prevarication. All she could do now was plead. 'Let me go. You must know I won't betray my own husband. You can trust me to say nothing.' When he made no response, she said in a voice that trembled only slightly, 'Surely you can't mean to harm me.'

He sat down opposite her once more and his glance was sorrowful. 'I've no wish to harm you, Daisy, not at all. I like you, I like you very much. Over the weeks we've known each other, I've felt a strong connection.'

'I've felt it too,' she said eagerly.

There was a regretful shake of his head. 'Whatever my personal feelings, though, I can't allow them to weigh with me. The cause I fight for matters most and one fact is indisputable — you know too much.'

'I can forget what I know,' she said desperately. 'Move the guns wherever you want and I'll forget I ever saw them.'

'I wish we could settle the business so. If it were up to me . . . I respect you, I admire your courage and strange to say, I *would* trust you to say nothing.'

He leaned towards her and traced the curve of her cheek with his forefinger. 'But you see, it's not up to me.' He gestured back towards the waiting men. 'My companions here *don't* trust you. And why should they? You're an Englishwoman, to them you're one of the enemy, and I can't convince them otherwise.'

She drew herself upright in the chair and tried to look at him unflinchingly, but her soul was quaking. 'So what do you intend to do with me?' She had a very good idea of the fate that awaited.

'Me? Nothing. I intend to do nothing, but naturally I cannot vouch for my comrades. I must leave you in their hands but I have asked them to be merciful.'

She swallowed hard and tried to find her voice. 'You'll let them kill me.'

'Hush, Daisy. Such ugly words. Whatever your future may be, go to it in peace.'

He rose then, throwing the chair into a corner and, without looking at her again, strode to the far end of the warehouse and out of the open door. She could no longer maintain the composure she'd forced herself to keep, and tears poured down her face. She sat, bound to the filthy chair, sobbing quietly, sobbing for a life about to be lost, for a friend already lost.

CHAPTER THIRTY-THREE

While they'd talked, the men had been listlessly kicking at the mud floor and sending odd sprays of dust into the air, but with Anish's departure they hastened into action. The man standing guard beside Daisy bent to untie her legs, then pulled her upright by the arms and out of the chair. The pain in her shoulders was unbearable, but she was beyond caring. It was her fate, it seemed, to die at the hands of strangers, unmourned and thousands of miles from home.

Her disappearance would hardly create a stir. Gerald would concoct a story that would satisfy his Colonel and anyone interested enough to ask. She could see how it could easily be done. He would pretend an urgent message had come from England that necessitated Daisy leaving immediately. A close relative, perhaps, who had fallen dangerously ill. He would say that he'd managed to arrange her travel back to England at very short notice and even now she was on a P and O liner sailing to Southampton. There would be no way of checking his story, and who would want to?

Later, he could pretend the relative had recovered a little, but that his wife had felt it her duty to remain in England. Months would pass and people would forget that Gerald had ever been married. Would he, she wondered? He might feel a passing sadness, some guilt over the nature of her death, but in the end it would suit him very well. He would be released from a wife he had never wanted.

They were at the open door, and water was falling from the sky in vertical rods. It hit the earth with an astonishing power, then danced up at least a foot high, before finally subsiding and spreading itself into huge lakes. In the near distance, she heard the roar of the river, louder and more terrifying than she'd thought possible. She could hardly believe that so short a while ago young men had swum out into its peaceful depths and launched the festival floats on their lazy way downstream. The once calm waters had become a churning, raging force.

With a man on either side of her, Daisy was pushed through the door and into deep mud, which sucked at her feet and ankles. The air was damp, thick with water, but within it bloomed a new freshness. After the musty atmosphere of the warehouse, she breathed it in with gratitude. The world was waking up, it seemed, though she would not wake with it. She felt the soft kiss of air on her face and realised that she very much wanted to live. Every one of her dreams had been destroyed, but she wanted to live.

The men were clutching her by the arms, prodding and pushing, forcing her to lurch forward through the sticky, oozing earth. It was difficult to lift one foot in front of the other and she had to concentrate hard to keep upright. Not so hard that she missed the sound being carried faintly towards her on the sodden air. Not the rain, not the river, but raised voices somewhere ahead.

The men's grip on her tightened and she could feel the tension emanating from their bodies. One of them pushed her roughly in the back and she almost fell to the ground, her legs as well as her feet soaked from mud and water. Something unforeseen was happening, and it was making her captors apprehensive. In the driving rain she could see nothing, but neither could they. Abruptly, the whole party came to a halt. The men peered uncertainly into the mantle of mist and she felt their grip relax very slightly; they stood for some minutes silent, motionless. It was almost as though she had been forgotten.

Then, in one small instant, the curtain of rain parted, and two forms materialised from out of the darkness. Two figures wrestling with each other, soaked with rain and plastered in mud. Shirts were pasted against chests, trousers hung wet and limp around flailing legs. Immediately, her jailers renewed their grasp on her arms and pushed her onwards until the small group had drawn almost abreast of the fighting men.

For the first time, she recognised one of them. It was Anish. He had not gone far, it seemed. Or he'd been prevented from going. One of the Indians lit a flame torch and held it high in the air, casting a circle of cold, white light. The flare, caught by the wind, flickered wildly but in its bright burst she saw illuminated the face of the second man. It was Gerald — Gerald, who was fighting his friend.

But why was he here? Anish had said he'd be in hiding and ridiculed him for his squeamishness. But this was hardly squeamish, for Gerald was putting up a brave fight. Could it be that he'd come looking for her, worried that the plan he'd agreed with his friend had gone adrift? More than anyone, he would know the lengths to which Anish would go. Gerald might have acquiesced in the attempts to scare her away, but was murder a step too far, even for him?

If so, he was fighting frenziedly to save her. The two men were kicking, gouging, punching each other to a standstill. It was a street brawl without rules. Every so often, one of them knocked the other to the ground, but then he would scramble to his feet and dripping with mud, fight on. It would have been almost farcical if it had not been so deadly. Two, three, four times, the men sent each other sprawling and recovered, but Anish was the larger man and she could see that he was slowly gaining the advantage.

As she watched, Gerald was once more knocked to the ground. He lay slumped on his back, but this time unable to spring back swiftly enough and, almost instantly, Anish had his hands around his throat squeezing. Slowly squeezing the life out of him. Daisy watched the tableau in horror. Her captors were agitated, fingering what she imagined were hidden weapons, wanting to intervene, but unable to separate one man from the other. They need not worry, she thought, Anish would finish the job himself. Her husband's body was already going limp.

She was overwhelmed with pity. And dread. Where Gerald went, she would follow. But he had gathered his strength into a last desperate effort and was tearing Anish's hands from his throat. One more tremendous lunge, and he managed somehow to push his opponent backwards. Anish stumbled, and lost his grip and Gerald staggered to his feet. He was barely able to speak.

'Let her go.' Through the rain, his voice came in gasps. 'Let her go.'

Anish was almost as winded. 'I can't. You know that.'

'I'll make sure she says nothing.'

Anish shook his head, and drops of water sprayed around him as though he were a dog emerging from the river. 'It won't work, Gerald. Be reasonable, man.'

'Reasonable! When you mean to kill her! Let her go!'

It was impossible, she knew. Gerald could not rescue her. He was one man against seven. Anish shrugged his shoulders, as though abdicating any further responsibility. 'I cannot. Look for yourself.'

He pointed at the small group yards from the warehouse door, and it seemed that for the first time Gerald saw her, standing mute and still, hands bound and straitjacketed, between two of her captors. He started towards them and suddenly one of the men she'd taken little notice of, was by her side. From the corner of her eye, she caught the flash of a weapon and then felt the sharp tip of a knife at her throat.

'You'd be wise to go no further. You can do nothing for her.' Anish panted out the words, but his friend wasn't listening.

From beneath a wide leather belt, he had drawn a revolver and was levelling it at Anish. Through the thunder of rain, he yelled across at the man holding the knife. 'Drop your weapon. Let her go or I'll kill Rana.' His voice was cracking, his mind evidently in chaos. He seemed at the very edge of an abyss and poised to topple over.

The man holding the knife did not move. Gerald shouted again, this time in Hindi. In response, the men drew closer to Daisy, surrounding her and blocking her view of what was happening. There was a loud explosion. A gunshot, it had to be. Then an outburst of angry voices and feet floundering through water. All but one of her captors had abandoned her.

Daisy's view was clear now and she could see through the battering rain: Anish was on the ground and lying very still. Gerald was crouched over him, his head in his hands. In a fury, her jailers surged towards him, and he turned at the sound of their approach. For a moment, he looked directly at her, and then he fled.

With the men on his heels, there was only one way to run and that was towards the river. But there could be no escape in that direction. Gerald was exhausted, his energy spent, and her captors caught up with him as he reached the riverbank. In the light of the flame torch, she saw the glint of steel, the same knife that had threatened her, and then Gerald had vanished into the churn of waters. Her heart bent beneath this new weight of sorrow. Her husband had tried to rescue her. The man who did not love her, for whom she had been only 'fun', had tried to save her life and, in doing so, had lost his own.

She was allowed no time to grieve. Once the group was certain that Gerald had gone to his death, they returned for her. Daisy had been too stunned by the sudden chain of events to make any attempt to break free. How far would she have got in any case? Her shackled arms made running almost impossible, and she had no idea where she was or where she could run to. There was no escape: she would be the third sacrifice of the night. The men dragged and pushed her through furrows of mud, through deep troughs of water, past the body of Anish and up onto the riverbank. It was clear she was to follow Gerald into the deluge.

His body, if it were ever found, would be badly battered and, along with Anish's violent death, the authorities would draw their own conclusion: the two men had quarrelled in the most deadly fashion and in the frenzy of their clash, Gerald had shot his friend and then taken his own life. There would be nothing to link either death with the men who held her.

But she was a different matter. If she were found, her death must look an accident. They would not shoot or stab her, but simply let her drown. They would unbind her and push her into the river. At festival time, there were always accidents. People got drunk, became careless. It was easy to slip in the rain, easy to lose your way and think the riverbank a safe path. Doubtless, she would be just one of several fatalities that night.

But first they would have to render her semi-conscious, she reasoned, for they would need to ensure she had no chance to save herself. Not that it was likely. How could anyone, even a strong swimmer, survive against the torrent below? But a light blow from a cudgel would do the trick and cause little suspicion.

Daisy stood on the wide, green riverbank and felt strangely at peace in a world made newly beautiful. The moon had floated free, a huge, pale disc silvering a path through an extraordinary landscape. By its light, she could see that the grass was now lush, that small flowers would begin to raise their heads above ground for the first time in months and, reigning over everything, crisp, clean air. Now, she was being dragged further along the bank to a section that towered high above the water. The men were making sure that when she fell into the maelstrom below, it would be with sufficient force to pull her under. Her erstwhile jailer seemed to be the group's chief and, when he was satisfied she was in the right place, she saw him approach, a wooden bat in his hand. Not a cudgel then, but a cricket bat.

Her mind was gradually drifting, uncoupling itself from what was happening. She found herself smiling at the incongruity of the weapon they'd chosen, found herself unsurprised that it would be just as she'd anticipated. The man raised the bat, ready to bring it down on her head in a glancing stroke. She waited for the blow to fall. But in vain. The scene had ground to a halt. She heard a click — guns? The safety catches on guns? But how could that be?

'Drop your arms immediately.' A voice echoed through the cascading rain.

Daisy knew that voice. The man at her side dropped the bat into the frothing waters below, and was grabbed from behind by a figure in uniform. She was saved, she realised. Unbelievably, she was saved. She dared to turn her head then. Her captors had been herded together some distance away, and stood in a ragged line, hands raised high in the air. Facing them was a phalanx of uniforms, a column of policemen, each with a gun pointing at a miscreant's head.

And there was Grayson Harte striding towards her, taking her gently by the arm, navigating a path from the riverbank through an expanse of mud and water towards a waiting police car, its beacon light a garish flash across the flooded land.

A large black sedan pulled up alongside and a silver-haired man emerged. He was improbably dressed in a pinstripe suit, and stepped gingerly towards them.

'Are you sure you've got them all, Harte?' His voice was low, cultured. To Daisy, he seemed a being from another world.

'I believe so, sir.' Grayson nodded towards the men flinching beneath the raised guns. 'All of the Jasirapur group, at least.'

'And the servant?'

'The police have gone with my assistant to pick up Rajiv Gupta. And the cache of arms, too.'

'Good, good,' the man muttered vaguely. He was looking across at the mud-splattered body which lay between them and the men Anish had called his henchmen. 'Pity about the lieutenant. I'd like to have seen him stand trial. Bloody traitor!'

Daisy had been standing slackly by Grayson's side, unable to stop herself from drooping, but at these words she bunched her hands together into two small fists. Anish was no traitor, she wanted to shout. This was his country. And whatever he'd done, she forgave him for it. He'd been mistaken, but he'd believed in his cause — passionately. And she loved him, as a friend, as a sister.

'I must be getting Daisy to a place of safety, sir,' Grayson said tight-lipped.

'Of course. So sorry you've had such a beastly experience, Mrs . . .'

'Mortimer,' she said defiantly.

But the man was already clambering into his sleek, black saloon. Grayson nudged her towards the waiting police car. 'You're to go to the Infirmary, Daisy. Dr Lane is waiting for you.'

The car door slammed shut, the driver hit the accelerator, and the vehicle screeched onto the rain-soaked road, tyres spinning through the mud. She twisted round in her seat and looked back. At the flashing blue lights, at the glint of police guns still levelled at the cowering men, and at Grayson busily directing each arrest. *So this is what you were doing in Jasirapur,* she said to herself.

CHAPTER THIRTY-FOUR

Daisy nestled into the deckchair's canvas fold and watched the ship creaming its way through the ocean. She had only to walk a few yards from her cabin to enjoy the freedom of the upper deck, and since few of the passengers in this select part of the ship chose to rise quite so early, she was enjoying the view undisturbed.

In contrast to her outward journey on the *Viceroy*, her accommodation spelt comfort: a first-class cabin and on the starboard side of the ship. Port outward, starboard home, POSH, that's what Grayson had said. You avoided the worst of the sun that way. It must have been even more important in the days before cabins were equipped with electric fans. Their space was small, and after a day's fierce sun, passengers must have felt they were being cooked in their bunks. No wonder they so often slept on deck, men on one side, women on the other.

Daisy thought that must have been wonderful — to lie beneath a spread of brilliant stars and watch the ship's superstructure moving gently against a clear, dark sky. It was almost enough to make her regret the newfangled fans. But she was grateful for the consideration she'd been shown: the special cabin, the friend to accompany her. In truth, she'd been too stupefied to concern herself with travel arrangements and had agreed to everything the regiment had suggested.

It had been a strange few weeks. She had stayed at the Infirmary just one night, sufficient time for Dr Lane to check her over and pronounce that, apart from cuts and bruises, she was fully fit — in body, at least. Her mind and heart were something else. There were days before she could leave for Bombay, and a matronly Moslem woman had been deputed to look after her. Amina Masri had moved without fuss into Rajiv's old quarters but spent most of her time in the house with Daisy, feeding her charge tea and titbits, patting her hand comfortingly and muttering beneath her breath at the wickedness of the world.

Grayson had visited only once, ostensibly to make sure that Amina had settled in. In their one-sided conversation, he'd talked to her of everything — the weather, his colleagues, letters from home — everything but the events of that terrible night. It had been out of respect for her fragility, she imagined, but also perhaps because his task was done and dusted. Anish was dead, and the group Grayson had been tracking so assiduously were locked away and facing justice.

She had sat and listened politely to him over the teacups, but his voice had come to her as though it were travelling through a dream. In the same fashion, she'd imbibed the Colonel's speech of regret and nodded blankly at the police chief, as he proudly declared that her captors, together with Rajiv, were now in jail and awaiting trial. She knew she must have thanked the Adjutant for his expertise in organising a swift passage home, but she had no memory of the words she'd used. Her mind was constantly telling her that none of this was happening, none of this *had* happened. And yet it had. A grand tragedy had played itself out against the setting of her small life, and she was still struggling with the aftermath. Try as she might, its echoes would not let her go.

Her time in India was ended but despite everything she'd endured, she had not wanted to leave. In the end, she'd had no choice and, almost in a trance, she'd packed her few possessions in the cardboard suitcase and waited for transport to arrive that would take her to Marwar Junction and on to Bombay.

It had been as sad a departure as it had been a homecoming, for in the end she'd been sorry to say goodbye even to the bungalow. The rains had transformed it, or rather they'd transformed its garden, and that in turn had made the house newly welcoming. Within a few days of the monsoon arriving, the land had turned green, covered in a carpet of brightly-coloured, scented flowers, which tangled themselves in and out of the long alfalfa grass. On a pathway which had once sported nothing more than dry dust, frogs and toads were in constant motion, crossing and recrossing the new lushness.

At times, the heat of the sun would suck the vapour from the ground so strongly it rose a foot high, and for several hours would hang there unmoving. Like an altar curtain, she decided, like the opaque screen she had sat behind on so many childhood Sundays. The rain encouraged snakes and cockroaches to emerge from their hiding places, brought with it mosquitoes, too, and greenfly and small black beetles. But Daisy didn't mind. The sheer freshness of the world charmed her and, whenever it stopped raining sufficiently for her to venture outside, she would sit quietly on the veranda watching the garden rebuild itself beneath her gaze.

Snippets of news gradually filtered through from the cantonment and found their way to the island she inhabited. Gerald's body had not been recovered and officially he was 'presumed dead'. It was accepted without question by his fellow officers that both he and Anish had died trying to rescue her from her assailants, and she said nothing to disabuse them. A letter had come from Jocelyn in Simla, full of warm sympathy for Daisy, and sadness and admiration for the two dead men. She was glad she wouldn't be meeting her friend face to face for, surely, she would have confessed the truth.

But everyone was happy with the story as it stood, the police too, and it seemed best to let things lie. She doubted the prisoners would complicate matters, since the tale that was being told exonerated the leader they respected and accorded him an honourable death. Why she had been captured remained a mystery to most, but there was a general presumption that it must have been for money.

Grayson's very special branch of the ICS, of course, knew differently, and though it must have stuck in their throats — particularly the throat of the pinstriped man, as Daisy thought of him — they had said nothing to contradict this view. She imagined they were playing a long game and hadn't wanted to alert other nationalist groups in Rajputana that they knew of any kind of link with the Indian Army. Their official stance was that only Indian civilians had been involved in the fracas, and that these men were being summarily dealt with.

If only it were that simple. If only she could rid herself of a guilt that was close to overwhelming. Gerald had tried to save her, had sacrificed his own life, but all she could feel for him was gratitude. There was sorrow in her heart, of course, but it was undefined, the kind of sadness people feel when they hear of the unexpected death of someone they barely knew. It was not the kind of sorrow she should feel for the loss of a husband who had died in such tragic circumstances.

Yet, when she thought of Anish, her grief was acute, and that made her feel even guiltier. She couldn't explain her feelings to herself. He'd been no more than a friend, a good friend it was true, but it must be wrong to feel his death so severely. Her friendship had been repaid in the most terrible way. Day after day, while he'd ridden with her, talked and laughed with her, Anish had been pursuing a cruel campaign of fear and confusion. His betrayal was dreadful and his willingness to sacrifice her thoroughly wicked. Yet, she couldn't stop a small part of her understanding his reasons, understanding the power of his cause and how it had pushed him into such fearful action.

Gerald was different. He'd believed only in the power of money. Money to fund a life based on vanity and illusion.

And he'd died living that illusion, his death recorded in the name of Lieutenant Gerald Mortimer. In changing his name he had made himself difficult, if not impossible, to trace. There had been no mention of Minns in the official papers, no link to those forgotten parents. She was the sole person who knew the fate of their only child, and one day she would try to find them. She had Joseph's letter safe in her suitcase. But it would be the most difficult of meetings and Daisy knew she was not yet strong enough to manage it. She must first regain peace of mind, if that were possible, and then decide what was to become of her.

Whenever she thought of the life that stretched ahead, the feelings of guilt bit harder still. She was walking to her future a free woman and the very words warmed her with shame. Gerald's death had liberated her from a barely tolerable burden. That was the unadorned truth, and it was not a pleasant thought. The marriage was no more, India was no more. Its smells and sounds and sights — the colour and shape of its plants, the grace of its people, the searing sun and the torrential rain, the cool dawn and the lovely scent of sundown — all gone. Like her marriage, gone forever.

Her thoughts had buried her deep in a lost world, and she barely noticed the man approach until a shadow fell and for a moment blotted out the brightness. A figure stood looking down at her, eyes creased against the bright light.

'I thought I might find you here.'

She'd hardly seen Grayson during the voyage. He had accompanied her to Bombay and she'd expected him to say goodbye to her at the port. But he hadn't. She'd learned then that he was coming with her, that he'd been designated her escort for the journey back to England. She'd been unsure whether to feel glad or sorry, but in the end she'd found him a tactful companion, never forcing his presence on her and for the most part leaving her to enjoy the solitude she craved.

They'd stood together in silence as the boat slipped from its berth in Bombay harbour and watched as naked youngsters dived for pennies thrown from the side of the ship. A band had been playing, and coloured streamers were being thrown by their fellow passengers to people shouting and waving from the quayside. Grayson had remained standing beside her as they slid past bright white buildings, past islands gold and amethyst in the mist of early sunlight, and finally past the great Archway of India and out into the deep blue ocean.

'Will that be your last view of India?' she'd asked, and he'd shaken his head at the uncertainty of all their futures.

'How are you this bright morning?' he was asking.

'I'm well, thank you. Much better.' Was she? Even if she weren't, she must pretend. 'I'm determined to enjoy the weather while it's still warm.'

Their first week at sea had been hot and sunny, and she'd spent hours sitting in this very deckchair, watching the changing sapphires of the ocean, marvelling at the flying fish skimming a scarcely moving sea.

'You're wise. We should both make the most of it. I've been speaking to the Captain and the weather forecast once we get into the Med isn't at all good.' He pulled a spare deckchair into line. 'Do you mind if I join you for a while?'

Daisy would have preferred to remain alone, but he'd been so very understanding that it would be churlish to refuse. It was unusual for him to seek her out in this way, and she thought there was likely to be a good reason. He fell into the chair beside her and stretched out his long limbs. For a while there was silence. It was interesting, she thought, that on the few occasions they'd sat together, neither felt the need to make conversation.

She glanced sideways at him and saw that his expression was uncertain. He was judging whether or not he should speak. 'I've just received a telegram. The trial date is set.' His tone verged on the brusque, and she could see that he hadn't wanted to tell her.

She swallowed hard but tried to sound unruffled. 'That was very swift.'

'The police are keen to wrap the whole business up. Of course, it won't wrap it up — far from it — but they're not too interested in the bigger picture, and I suppose it gives them a good feeling to have this one success under their belts.'

'Will there be many others — to wrap up? I imagine the men you caught weren't the only group operating locally.'

'Other units exist, certainly. Even in the short time I was in Jasirapur, I uncovered evidence to suggest around a dozen of them are spread across the region. The one we disrupted was small fry.'

Anish would not have liked the description, but Grayson's conclusions were an uncomfortable echo of what he himself had claimed. He'd talked of groups of fighters across Rajputana who would carry on the struggle, one after the other.

It was hard to think of him. It was impossible to think of him without recalling their last ghastly meeting. The memory was never far away, ready to pinch at her in unguarded moments. In her mind, the scene was as vivid as though painted on a canvas: the blank space of the warehouse, feet scuffing at the mud floor, rain hammering on the roof overhead and outside the constant roar of a deadly river.

With difficulty, she forced herself back to the world of sunlight. 'But your work in India has finished, I take it?'

'For the time being. I may have to return to give evidence at the trial. I don't yet know, but I'm hopeful that a signed witness statement will suffice. It's a long journey to make again.'

'Then you should have stayed in Jasirapur, at least until the trial was over. Did the regiment put pressure on you to accompany me? I wish they hadn't.'

'There was no pressure,' he reassured her. 'It's important I report in person to my employers in Whitehall, and as soon as possible. You were on your way home, and it made sense for us to travel together.'

When she said nothing, he said teasingly, 'You're making me feel you'd have preferred to travel alone.'

'I wouldn't.' And she realised with surprise that she spoke the truth. 'But I imagine the police must have wanted you to remain in India.'

'That wasn't a consideration. If I'd stayed, I would have been kicking my heels. I couldn't continue to masquerade as a District Officer. Not that I did that very effectively. But with my cover well and truly blown, it was impossible to launch any new investigation.'

'I always thought you were a strange kind of District Officer.' He smiled at her accusing tone. 'You told me you were with the ICS and that it was your first posting abroad.'

'I could hardly tell you I was a junior intelligence officer, could I? In any case, some of what I said was true. It *was* my first overseas job and I *was* seconded to the ICS. The SIS — the Secret Intelligence Service, in case you're wondering — quite often uses less devious parts of the administration to cover its tracks. Hence my role as a harmless civil servant.'

She glanced out to sea, losing herself for a moment in its gentle swell. They'd begun at last to talk of Jasirapur and she was glad. There were dangers ahead, painful territory that couldn't be avoided, but she needed to go on with this conversation. There were things she must discover, even though it might hurt.

'Were you working as an intelligence officer on the voyage out? When I met you on the *Viceroy*?'

'Pretty much. We'd been getting some alarming reports back in London. Guns were being stolen across India, but the problem was particularly bad in Rajputana. Those men on the boat, the ones who . . . the ones who caused your fall, had given us a good deal of information while they were in Wandsworth awaiting deportation. Enough for me to be sent out to discover just what was happening on the ground.'

She turned to face him, looking directly into his eyes. 'Tell me truly, Grayson. Did you always know about Anish's involvement and about Gerald's? Were you hunting them from the very beginning?'

CHAPTER THIRTY-FIVE

His gaze was candid. He was not going to fudge, not going to make things easy for her. But that was what she wanted.

'Not initially. But I came to suspect them soon after I arrived. You learn a lot hanging around the market, and it didn't take me long to discover that Anish Rana was linked in some way to an extremist group. I didn't at first connect him with any gun running. But large quantities were being stolen from the Jasirapur cantonment under the very eyes of the guards. I still didn't see how he fitted in, though. As an Indian officer I knew he wouldn't have access to the armoury. He would have needed assistance from someone. And then I saw the bungalow and saw how isolated it was. And noticed, too, that contrary to every other British family in the whole of India, Gerald employed only one servant. That started me thinking why that might be.'

'Rajiv was intensely loyal to Gerald.'

'So I imagine. I'm sure he would happily have done his bidding, whatever the task. I've no doubt that he was responsible for many of the unpleasant things that happened to you. I'm certain, for instance, that he was the one who coaxed the cobra into your bathroom.'

'And the one who locked my bedroom door and suggested there was a ghost haunting the garden.'

'Poor Daisy. You were made to suffer badly.' His hand reached across and squeezed her fingers.

'You didn't appear suspicious of the cobra,' she said a trifle indignantly. 'You made me believe it was an accident.'

'That was for your peace of mind. And it could have been an accident. Cobras will sometimes find their way into a bathroom. They try to escape from the heat, and often there are large water containers they can wind themselves around to cool off. I thought it odd, but I couldn't prove anything.'

'Like all the other things that happened. They were always odd, but they could all have been accidents. I wanted to believe they were. If ever I began to think otherwise, I told myself I must be delusional.'

'I guess that was the beauty of their plan. To make you distrust yourself, get you to think you were going crazy.'

'Did you have any clue what they were doing?'

'I had my suspicions you might find yourself in the way, but I had no idea of what you were up against. If only you'd told me . . . I kept hoping you'd decide to go to Simla and keep yourself safe. If I'd realised the kind of threats you were facing, I would have insisted.'

'They hoped I'd go, too. They certainly urged it enough but the more they urged, the more I refused.'

'Why wouldn't you go?'

'At first it was because I didn't like the company. But then suspicion took over.'

Daisy tried to remember when the first bad thought had crossed her mind and couldn't. She'd been too successful in blotting out those weeks when she'd been hunted like a small animal, weeks when she'd lived in fear of what was happening to her.

'I tried to convince myself that so many accidents were sheer bad luck, but I think some part of me knew differently and suspected I was being made a deliberate target. And that caused me to dig myself in. I felt I had to find out what was going on. I know now that by staying in Jasirapur, I laid myself open to even greater danger.'

'I hope you're not blaming yourself. What happened was the result of other people's villainy.'

'I was stupid, though.'

'You were brave.'

'No, stupid,' she insisted. 'I've never been brave.'

'Now you're talking nonsense. Your situation in that warehouse was desperate, but you showed immense courage. You didn't panic. Instead, you kept your head and kept them talking. And that gained time.'

'I think it was instinct. A simple instinct to survive. Most people would have done the same.'

'I doubt it. In any case, you'd already proved you had grit. If it's not brave to travel halfway around the world, knowing nothing of the country you're going to and not a soul who lives there, I don't know what is.'

She thought for a while. It had needed courage certainly to set off on the adventure, but her gullibility had led her along a perilous path. 'Perhaps I'm both — foolish *and* brave,' she said at last. 'I travelled thousands of miles to marry a man I didn't even know. Of course I was apprehensive, but the excitement was just too much. It drowned out common sense. I remember that on board ship, I didn't stop talking about Gerald.'

'You were elated, and why not? You were about to marry a young officer, a cavalryman in the Indian Army. He was handsome and kind. He said and did everything that was wonderful. I began to think the husband waiting for you at Bombay was a veritable deity!'

'But when you saw him, you knew differently. You knew him from the past.'

Grayson looked a trifle awkward. 'I recognised him straight away, it's true, but I couldn't work out why the boy I'd known as Jack Minns was masquerading as Gerald Mortimer. I couldn't work out either how he'd dared to marry such a sweet girl.'

'But you never mentioned his double identity.'

'How could I? He might well have changed his name legally, or he might have already confided in you. And, even if you knew nothing, would you have believed what I told you or rather what your handsome husband swore was the truth? I knew he'd discredit anything I said. He'd always disliked me at Hanbury and I wasn't going to give him the chance to call me a liar.'

'He bullied you at school, didn't he?'

Grayson nodded.

'But why?'

'Who knows? A chip on the shoulder perhaps? I came from the kind of family he wanted for himself. He knew the Hartes had been military people for generations and if they weren't soldiers, they were administrators in India, and if they weren't administrators, they were businessmen. It wasn't the kind of thing to endear me to a boy unhappy with his own upbringing.'

'I can see that,' she said slowly. 'And it's true he went to extraordinary lengths to give himself the background he craved. He changed his name, changed his history. He abandoned his family.'

'That's bad. Stupid, as well.'

'I was just as stupid not to realise he was false from the moment I met him.'

Grayson's hand again locked her fingers in his. 'How could you possibly have guessed? You were bound to accept everything he told you. Why wouldn't you — you were young and in love.'

'I still wish you'd told me what you knew about Gerald.'

'And if I had?'

'I probably wouldn't have wanted to hear it,' she sighed, 'but perhaps I wouldn't have felt quite so alone.'

'I'm sorry now that I didn't, but I never felt you trusted me. Now, I understand why that was, but at the time you seemed intent on keeping me at arms' length. When you fell on board ship, you looked so very ill, but you were adamant there was nothing wrong. I wasn't to call the ship's doctor and all you needed was rest. Then, when I saw you several days later, I remember asking you how you were, and you brushed me off, refusing to talk. It made me feel I should keep *my* distance. And when we met again in Jasirapur, I did just that — kept my distance.'

'Except you didn't. You were always popping up when I least expected it.'

'I was keeping a benevolent eye on you.'

'I found it very worrying.'

He leant forward on the deckchair as though checking he'd heard aright. 'How can you have done?'

'It made me suspicious of you. You always seemed to be where you shouldn't and then you'd appear when I didn't expect you.' She wondered whether to make a full confession and decided she would be honest. It was right to rid herself of every secret she had carried. 'At one time, I even thought you might have something to do with the accidents.'

At first, he looked dumbfounded and then aghast, but she ploughed on. 'I never told you but I went back to the temple of Nandni Mata on my own and something happened there.'

'What?'

'Someone sent a large block of stone falling in my direction. It was Anish. I can see that now. He met me on the road shortly afterwards and was careful to tell me that he'd seen *you*.'

'Which he hadn't. Is that why you ran away from me the night the monsoon broke?'

By now the deck had filled with a number of couples taking their daily exercise. Daisy looked around her and lowered her voice. 'By then, I wasn't sure who I could trust.'

'I was trying to warn you, that was all. Trying to tell you that you were heading in the wrong direction.'

'And look what happened, when I didn't heed you. But you still managed to find me.'

'It took a while. And convincing the police to turn out in force was agonisingly slow. But yes, we tracked you down, thank God, just in time.'

'I don't think I ever thanked you for saving my life, Grayson,' she said shyly.

'You don't have to.'

'I think I do. I allowed my distrust to walk me down all the wrong tracks. You see, I couldn't believe Gerald would ever allow harm to come to me, even when he was at his most horrid.'

'And he didn't. He played a crucial part in your rescue. He may have lost his fight with those men, but not before he'd managed to disrupt their whole ghastly business. Another delay that meant we reached you in time. In the end, he tried to do the right thing. You must remember that.'

'I suppose so.'

'You must,' he said firmly.

'I try to value Gerald, I really do, but it's difficult.' She glanced down at their entwined hands and attempted to put into words the confusing mix of emotions washing over her. 'I feel guilty that I can't think of him or his sacrifice as I should. I can't stop feeling wronged. Gerald never let me forget he was forced into marrying. It was the baby, you understand — and then there was no baby. And no real marriage.'

His hand tightened on hers and his voice was at its most gentle. 'He didn't know what was good for him.'

'I think he did. I've had to face the truth, though it's been hard. He never loved me, not truly. Do you know what he called the weeks we spent together in London? "A bit of fun".'

'Then he was more of an idiot than I thought.'

He stood up and pulled her to her feet so that they stood only inches from each other. His finger was beneath her chin and he lifted her sorrowful face to his. 'Believe me, Daisy, you are so much more than that.'

* * *

Several days later, they stood watching again as the ship slid its way out of harbour, this time leaving Port Said and heading into the Mediterranean. Grayson had knocked at her cabin door early that morning, and together they'd climbed to the top deck and were now looking down at the soldiers who had been assembled below for a final parade. The band played rousingly, the troops marched and wheeled within the confines of their small parade ground and, at a given signal, every man threw his *topi* high into the air and out into the ocean.

'This is where the East ends and the West begins,' Grayson remarked. 'The soldiers are marking the moment.'

Daisy craned her neck to watch the helmets bobbing away, out into the open sea. She had her own *topi* in her hand. 'Should I throw mine, too, do you think?' It was the one that Anish had given her all those months ago and she'd not yet brought herself to relinquish it.

Grayson was deliberately noncommittal. 'It might serve as a farewell ritual.'

She took a deep breath and threw the *top*i as far out as she could, watching the battered helmet until it floated from sight. It carried with it all the hopes and dreams with which she'd come to India, but it was right to consign it to forgetfulness. There could be no looking back.

Grayson's touch was light on her arm. 'I must leave you, I'm afraid. I've any number of reports to finish. It's a dismal task, but I know they'll be demanded as soon as we dock.'

That wouldn't be long, she realised. This journey, this transition from past to future, would soon be over and she would have to step ashore and begin life again. She hoped she would soon get used to the idea of England, of living once more in a bustling city, of becoming accustomed to grey skies and grey people. Right now, she had no certain idea of where she would go or what she would do.

'When we get to Southampton, will you be travelling to London?' She wasn't entirely sure why she wanted to know.

'I will. I have to report to headquarters in person. After that, I've no idea where I'll be. The general outlook is grim and I imagine things in my unit will be pretty fluid. The country has caved in and handed over the Sudetenland to Hitler, but it won't be enough. There won't be peace, no matter how much Chamberlain craves it.'

Listening to the calm slap of the Mediterranean against the ship's side, it was impossible to think that England could soon be at war again.

Grayson looked down at her, a slight smile softening his face. 'And will you be going to London, too?'

'I imagine so. I've nowhere else to go.' Her tone was listless.

'Perhaps Bridges will take you back,' he suggested.

'Perhaps they will.' He seemed satisfied with this and turned to walk towards the companionway. But before he started down the stairs, he turned again. 'Will you have dinner with me tonight?'

That took her by surprise and she found herself nodding in agreement before he disappeared from sight. As soon as he'd gone, she knew she'd been wrong to accept his invitation. She would be poor company. The thought they were now on the homeward stretch of their journey and the future was coming closer with every day, had begun to hang heavy.

Despite what she'd said to Grayson, she couldn't return to her old job, to the malicious whispers and the hard stares of girls who had rarely been friendly and often hostile. They would have plenty of ammunition now. They'd been outraged by her promotion from restaurant to perfumery, and it was clear they suspected she'd done something very bad to get there. Then she'd compounded her crime by being the first of them to find a husband, and not just any husband. She had left Bridges to marry extraordinarily well. She'd left to travel to one of the most exotic places on earth. And what had come of it? She'd been brought low and they would never let her forget the destruction of her dreams.

She couldn't return to Bridges. She could face their disdain. It wasn't that. She'd grown steely enough to do so with indifference. It was something far more fundamental. She could no longer pretend — about the orphanage, about being in service. Whatever else her ordeal in India had taught her, she'd earned the right to her own story and the right to feel proud of it. She no longer needed to fit in, no longer needed to feign what she wasn't. And the person she was belonged nowhere near Bridges.

CHAPTER THIRTY-SIX

For the first time on the voyage, they met for dinner. Grayson had made a point of inviting her to eat with him and she made an effort to look her best. Now they were in a cooler climate, her hair had regained its glossy bounce, but her cheeks were still unnaturally pale. She looked a wraith, she thought, and forced herself to use a pinch of rouge to give her face colour, then chose a frock she hoped would provide its own glow.

It was the floral silk she'd bought for her wedding. She'd decided to wear it only after much heart-searching, and even now she feared she might be tempting fate. The garment seemed to have brought her nothing but bad luck and she hadn't worn it since that unhappy evening at the Club. But instinct was telling her it was the right dress for the right time. She would wear it tonight to mark a turning point, the moment when she looked towards a brighter future. She could at least pretend it was so.

The meal was the usual ship's fare and was quickly disposed of, but after they'd eaten Grayson suggested a short stroll along the deserted Promenade Deck. It was not what she'd expected and her first reaction was to retreat back into her cabin.

'I'm a little tired,' she demurred. 'I think an early night might be a good idea.'

'Half an hour's walk is neither here nor there. And you've opted for an early night ever since we came on board. Come the evening, you're nowhere to be seen.'

That was true enough. It was part of running away from the world, Daisy supposed, of not wanting to face the future. And she shouldn't be afraid of being with Grayson. They had talked now, cleared the air. That should give her courage.

'A short walk then,' she agreed.

Soon they were strolling the length of the Promenade Deck. From the ballroom below, the strains of a quickstep reached their ears, the echoes of the music following them as they walked towards the stern of the ship. The days were still warm, and at night a phosphorescent glow lay over the smooth water, disturbed only by the narrow, silver path cut by a waning moon. When they reached the white guard rails, they stopped to watch the wake of the speeding ship. Daisy leant over, fascinated by the endless green track that pursued them, a ceaseless, silken swish of double wave as the ship creamed its way ahead.

'You can go back, you know,' Grayson said into the silence. 'Back to India.'

He had sensed her thoughts. He always surprised her in that. 'What would I go back to?'

'I'm not entirely sure, but I feel that somehow you've unfinished business there.'

She felt it, too, but the sentiment was too vague to speak of sensibly. 'If you're right about the coming war, there might not be an India to go back to.'

'There will always be an India. But a different one. An independent one. If not immediately, then certainly after the conflict we're about to plunge into.'

'Why are you so sure?' Anish had been certain that Britain would never grant independence freely.

'A war against Germany will cost a great deal of treasure — men and gold — and India will be just too expensive to hold on to. And is it right that we should?'

'No, it isn't right, and I hope India gets its wish, but peacefully.'

Above them, a fall of the brightest stars pierced the night black sky, and by their light she saw his expression. He was looking solemn. She wasn't sure he believed peace in India was possible but she hoped he was wrong.

'If ever I do go back to India, it will be far into the future. And meanwhile, I must find work.' She tried to sound light-hearted. 'But not at Bridges, I think.' An image of the Infirmary sprang into her mind: white, clean, crisp. It was an attractive picture.

'You don't have to decide immediately,' Grayson said. 'I believe the Indian Army is generous. There'll be money to keep you afloat for a few months and then a small pension.'

She gave a rueful smile. 'The Adjutant tried very hard to explain my finances, but I'm afraid I didn't understand much, and now I remember even less.'

'You'll have to decipher the paperwork when it comes. But take your time.'

They turned to walk back the way they had come, the boards smooth beneath their feet, and she matched her step to his. The buzz from the ballroom had increased and the ship's band was now swinging its way through a foxtrot.

'I don't think I need that time after all. I'm going to train as a nurse.' Her announcement was abrupt. Daisy had no idea where the words had come from but, once she'd said them, they sounded absolutely right.

'I wondered if you might. Nursing seems to suit you and with war on the horizon, there's bound to be a huge demand for trained staff.'

'I've no idea how to go about getting trained. I should find a hospital first, I suppose.'

'St Barts could be just the place.' She saw a smile crease the corners of his mouth.

'Why St Barts?'

'For one thing, it's the nearest training school to Baker Street.'

'So . . .'

'Baker Street is where I'm most likely to be based.'

She flushed slightly, but the thought didn't displease her. Grayson was an attractive man and she had liked him from the moment they'd met. In the early days, she'd had to guard herself from liking him too much. Then there had come those silly doubts and she'd kept her distance. She must still keep a little of that distance, she told herself. Her heart had taken a beating and needed time to recover.

The music was floating nearer, its strands winding their way towards them, out of open doors, up and over stairways, along decks, until the notes arrived at their feet, wrapping them close.

He paused for a moment and glanced down at her, his eyes amused. 'Enough of the future. We still have the rest of the journey to enjoy. How would you like to dance?'

'I would,' she said, almost without thinking. And then realised, wonderingly, that she'd spoken truly.

She slipped her arm in his, and together they made their way to the ballroom.

THE END

THE JOFFE BOOKS STORY

We began in 2014 when Jasper agreed to publish his mum's much-rejected romance novel and it became a bestseller.

Since then we've grown into the largest independent publisher in the UK. We're extremely proud to publish some of the very best writers in the world, including Joy Ellis, Faith Martin, Caro Ramsay, Helen Forrester, Simon Brett and Robert Goddard. Everyone at Joffe Books loves reading and we never forget that it all begins with the magic of an author telling a story.

We are proud to publish talented first-time authors, as well as established writers whose books we love introducing to a new generation of readers.

We won Trade Publisher of the Year at the Independent Publishing Awards in 2023. We have been shortlisted for Independent Publisher of the Year at the British Book Awards for the last four years, and were shortlisted for the Diversity and Inclusivity Award at the 2022 Independent Publishing Awards. In 2023 we were shortlisted for Publisher of the Year at the RNA Industry Awards.

We built this company with your help, and we love to hear from you, so please email us about absolutely anything bookish at: feedback@joffebooks.com.

If you want to receive free books every Friday and hear about all our new releases, join our mailing list: www.joffebooks.com/contact

And when you tell your friends about us, just remember: it's pronounced Joffe as in coffee or toffee!

ALSO BY MERRYN ALLINGHAM

DAISY DRISCOLL SAGA
Book 1: THE OFFICER'S WIFE

Printed in Great Britain
by Amazon

42847178R00169